Almost to Destin

FOSTER SANDERS

SPECIAL THANKS

Special thanks to Ruston Sanders, Dr. Taylor Sanders, Amanda Jackman, Margaret Rhodes, Sonjia Whitfield, Jeff Garrett, and Barney & Sally Manuel for their respective support during the course of this journey to Destin-and to Scott Jackson for his cover photograph.

FOREWORD

As a younger man, I regularly drove from Baton Rouge, Louisiana, to my farm in Amite County, Mississippi. Each trip, I particularly noticed a sign just north of the Mississippi state line. It was a small sign with an arrow pointing toward a Baptist church somewhere off in the distance to the west. I always looked down the shaded tree-lined lane as I passed by. The church was out of view from the highway, but it beckoned nonetheless. The sign had powers of its own.

While simply continuing on my way, I imagined the many life stories that had run their course within the rural congregation. I visualized happy Sunday mornings and ceremonial farewells to lost loved ones. I always wondered from where the elders came, and where their children went. I frequently thought about turning down that little country lane one day, but never did – until *Almost to Destin*. Sometimes, even the turn itself has powers of its own...

Chapter 1

In a quiet and peaceful corner of a loud and stressful world, a lovely slender woman arose and eased from her oaken bed. Like all of the mornings that came before, Leila Jane Hewitt was alone.

Leila stepped naked from her simple, cotton nightgown. Her skin was smooth, well-toned, and belied her years. She fetched a gold sundress from her closet and slipped the feathery garment on over her head. A large wall mirror caught her reflection as she eased a comb through her thick blonde-gray hair. Taking the usual morning peek at her maturing face, Leila lifted her eyebrows simultaneously with her index fingers. It gave her a slightly younger appearance. The temporary cosmetic procedure brought a smile to her well-formed lips.

Leila made her way to the large kitchen porch. Green tea was set to brew, and she began to carefully read the Atlanta Morning News on her computer. Soon, the soft purring of a familiar automobile grew louder as it came down Ebenezer Church Road. The engine was turned off and one door slammed.

"Hey, Leila!" a familiar voice shouted. Amanda never knocked. There was no real need to knock. She came to see her best friend every morning.

"Back here, ole girl, I'm on the porch," replied Leila.

"You would not believe who I've been talking to," said Amanda, still out of sight.

"I give up. Tell me," said Leila.

The kitchen floor squealed when the tall, lanky Amanda Harrison appeared from around the corner. She had a shock of freshly dyed black hair and a big smile on her face. She gave Leila a hug and plopped onto the undersized cherry rocker.

Leila picked up a big round silver bowl, grabbed a handful of peas, and started snapping. "Well?" she asked.

"Cousin Jackie, in Destin," said Amanda.

"You mean Ms. *I'm going to write a book and sell it to drunk Mel Gibson for a movie* Jackie?" asked Leila.

"That's the one!" said Amanda. "Her friends have a condo rented out in D-E-S-T-I-N for a week next month. Turns out they can't make it, so she asked me if Hank and I wanted it before they cancel."

"Well, you best be very careful," said Leila. "I was just reading an article online about how "El Nino" is causing all those sharks to be pushed to the beaches where they prey on luscious old country ladies like you. Hank does not swim, but you..."

"Hank is not going," interrupted Amanda as she picked up a handful of peas and started snapping. "YOU are!"

Leila turned away from the bowl of peas and stared at Amanda.

"Leila, honey, you have to go!" Amanda spoke with a deeper and more serious tone. "There are people there, MEN, anything can happen! Do you hear me? M-E-N! Men and lots of them! Are you listening?"

Leila hated when Amanda did this. They had explored the rural countryside together as young girls. They were inseparable since then, very different, but always very best friends. Amanda knew Leila better than anyone else. She knew exactly what was missing in Leila's life.

"Just what are we going to do? Walk up and down the beach and hope that some young lifeguard talks to us?" Leila asked.

"Maybe," said Amanda, "and then we will tell his rookie ass to get lost while we go out dancing at the famous Ocean Mist Nightclub with some fine, rich, older gentlemen!"

"It has been quite a long while since I have heard a live band," said Leila.

"Cousin Jackie is always telling me that the nightlife in Destin is full of snazzy old men from all over the South. They would be honored to meet *the most* highly eligible lady from Ebenezer Forest--and dat be you!" said Amanda, laughingly.

Leila tried not to grin, "I'm sure that a student group will be coming to visit Ebenezer Forest that weekend."

"Just cancel that appointment, honey!" Amanda said reaching for Leila's shoulder. "It is certainly all right to put yourself first every now and then. If anyone deserves to take an occasional trip to the beach, it is you, Ms. Leila Hewitt!"

Leila picked up a few peas again, looked at Amanda, and said one word at a time, "But! I-am-not-getting-in-to-the-water!"

*****

Leila Jane Hewitt was the only person from Ebenezer Church Road to ever attend college. Florida State University, only a hundred and twenty or so miles away, seemed like halfway around the world from Ebenezer Forest—but Leila wanted to be a psychologist. She wanted to understand the human mind and how its complexities were so different from God's other animals she had studied all of her life. The intellectual variety of her own thoughts, and the inexplicable quirks of the relatively few people she had actually known, fascinated Leila.

Most girls from rural Walton County finished their schooling at Walton High School. The folks that lived along Ebenezer Road also felt that the only psychology anybody ever needed came from Reverend Tom McGraw. Leila went to Florida State anyway.

Leila was greatly missed. Walton County knew her well. She had received unsought attention her entire life. As a young teenager her mother entered her into the Walton County "Ms. Azalea Pageant"—she ran away with the crown. She was stunningly beautiful! It was no contest. Her face and her figure – absolute perfection. She made the girls around her look awkward, lanky, or thick. Her physique was sleek and curvy, her lips and blue eyes entrancing. Her complexion was unblemished. But it was always her overall gracefulness that made her breathtaking. Her confidence in step, and the compassion of her heart, captivated all who came to know her.

Leila carried this same aura of natural appeal throughout college and beyond. At Florida State, she respectfully declined numerous nominations for campus and various fraternity beauty awards and similar recognitions. She chose instead to devote her time to her studies. As she did with all things that she loved, Leila excelled. She graduated with top honors in Psychology at the age of twenty one.

Florida State had been a pleasant experience for her. When it came time for Leila to move on, she was very excited to accept a graduate assistant's position in the psychology department. She stayed there only one short year.

Reverend Tom McGraw called Leila on a Thursday in late

November with the unexpected news that her mother had suffered a stroke and had passed away. Her father was incapable of looking after his own needs. He was in very poor health with emphysema. Leila was home with him before dark the very next day.

The psychology department held her position until the following June, but Leila never returned. Her life's responsibilities required a sudden return to Ebenezer Forest.

There was no mistaking the fact that Leila dearly loved Ebenezer Church Road. The majority of her time was spent in management of the family estate that her mother supervised before her untimely death. The Hewitts were by far the largest private landowners in Walton County. They dealt in cattle, some horses, but their main item of business was timber. The nearly eight thousand acres that the family owned was the site of the Florida panhandle's finest mature, hardwood forestland. Lumber sales' proceeds from an occasional thinning of this green wonderland paid Leila's expenses in college. These sales also paid the expenses of Ebenezer Church before departures of the local population resulted in worship centralization at Red Bay Church.

Leila had a vision as a young girl, and that vision became Ebenezer Forest. One of the first things she did after she took over the management of the estate was to set aside five hundred acres of hardwood bottom land. She named it Ebenezer Forest.

Species of oak, bay, magnolia, cedar, hickory, maple, wild pecan, river birch, and others thrive there together in perfect harmony. Leila identified all of the trees, and each and every single one was marked with a bronze nameplate showing its scientific and popular name. A large stream, named Hominy Creek, cuts a winding path through the middle of Ebenezer Forest. After a hard rain, it often overflows. This pumps new life into the wetland like a heart pumps blood throughout the human body.

Ebenezer Church is the only man-made intrusion into this preserved forest. It stands tall, just beyond Hominy Creek. Even though it is not still in use as an active church, Leila has maintained it in absolute pristine condition.

Over the years, thousands of visitors, ranging in age from kindergarteners to seniors, would come to Ebenezer Forest. They came to learn, and sometimes, to simply enjoy its bounty. They were greeted by the small game, turkeys, deer, and by Leila. A half or full day visit always ended at Ebenezer Church. In this sacred place, in the deep woods, Leila would always end her tours by making the connection between her Almighty Lord and His bountiful natural resources.

******

Leila received many calls about the family timber business and about the ongoing tours of Ebenezer Forest. Almost all were from men. This is how she met Jude Jackman.

Jude was a handsome, young forestry professor from Auburn University. After his third departmental field trip to Ebenezer Forest, he asked and received Leila's permission to integrate it into a specific Auburn curriculum. The course description included a twice per semester visit by forestry majors. By then he was already falling in love with Leila. The fact that Leila's family owned the largest, most fully preserved wetland-hardwood habitat in north Florida had little to do with his total infatuation with her.

Jude and Leila would follow from a distance while the students meandered through the woods of Ebenezer Forest. He would ask her about her college days and dreams. Jude would listen intently as

Leila would sometimes talk about the unfortunate series of events that had prevented her from pursuing her career in psychology. But most of the time she would invariably drift back in conversation to what had become her heart and soul—Ebenezer Forest.

Jude proposed to Leila in that same forest. They had been walking together all one spring morning when he grabbed her hand. Jude gently wrapped his arms around Leila and asked her to marry him. She certainly viewed him as someone special. But his words took Leila by complete surprise. "My father, Jude--" she said as she turned away.

"There are nurses that stay around the clock, we could work it out," Jude replied.

Turning back to face him, Leila said, "Jude, my heart is in this forest."

Leila has relived that morning a thousand times over. That was the last day she ever saw Jude Jackman. She looked for him as the Auburn buses unloaded for months afterward, but other faculty members always came to visit in his place. One of them told Leila later that Jude had left Auburn to take a new position in South Carolina.

Her life's mate became the forest. The wildlife and the trees were her children, the streams were her blood. No man was able to ever penetrate her small circle of interest. Her passion, which every woman so deeply longs to have aroused, gracefully waited, unstirred, in the forest of Ebenezer.

Chapter 2

Mark Ryan Mabry's thick black hair was whisking in the gusts of highway wind. His deep, penetrating blue eyes, protected by long lashes beneath full brows, squinted into the western afternoon sun. The dark red BMW convertible hummed smoothly along Interstate 10 in the Florida panhandle.

Mark's passenger, Jane Anderson, reached over and touched his muscular arm. "Are you trying to set a speed record from Atlanta?" she asked.

"Sorry, Jane," Mark replied. He eased off the accelerator and took the Highway 81 exit at Ponce De Leon and turned southward.

"Not much further," Mark added as he hurried toward his vacation villa in Destin.

Four and a half hours removed from any thought of his job with Mackco Advertising Agency in Atlanta's Buckhead district, Mark looked over at Jane. Her beautiful green eyes were shut. He smiled. She had been his best friend since high school.

Jane yawned and stretched her long arms. Strikingly attractive with high cheek bones, she was tall and statuesque with a lovely figure. It was a great disguise for her profession as a sex crimes investigator for the Atlanta Police Department.

Jane turned toward Mark with her eyes still closed. She eased her hands into her long chestnut hair which was dancing in the breeze. "Are we going to make it before sunset?" she asked.

"Yes, but we might have to get on the roof to see it," replied Mark.

Mark eased off the accelerator as they approached Red Bay, and sure enough, there sat the familiar deputy sheriff. Mark made this trip at least twice a month and knew the route well. It was almost as if his car was on autopilot. Jane felt the change of speed and eased upright to rejoin the moment.

A few miles down the road, Mark eased off the accelerator again as he approached a sign that read Ebenezer Church. He slowed the vehicle for a better glimpse of the familiar marker. It had an arrow on it pointing to an oak-shaded lane. Mark could see the narrow, graveled road meandering off to the East through the gentle, north Florida hills.

"I'm going to turn down it and explore this road one day," said Mark wistfully.

"Want to do it today?" questioned Jane.

"Do what?" asked Mark.

Jane, somewhat irritated, answered, "You *just* said you wanted to explore Ebenezer Church Road. Let's do it!"

"Not today," said Mark. "We are running behind. The next time I'm not in a hurry I'm going take a look. Those big, over-hanging oaks appear to form the roof of a tunnel to somewhere, don't they?" Mark turned his head for a final glance at the fading intersection and continued, "Have you ever been drawn to something – a particular place, or maybe just strangely curious about something?"

"Heck, yeah, the last time that happened to me, I almost got pregnant!" Jane said laughingly.

"And by the way," Jane continued, "you might want to reserve that little ole Ebenezer Church back there for you and Miss Brandi. You know that is what she is after." Jane raised her left hand and tapped her ring finger with her thumb.

"Jane," said Mark, "Brandi is only twenty two years old. I'm ten years older. We have never had a serious relationship, mentally or physically, other than a few kisses. I am not going to lead her on – and I do not really believe she is the right one for me."

"As discriminating as you are, Mark, your wife is probably not even born yet," quipped Jane.

"Well if she's not," Mark responded, "it would certainly be inappropriate for your committee to disapprove of the yet unborn." He loved to chide Jane about the "bitch corp", her group of friends of which she was the commander in chief.

"The corp will *always* have appropriate questions about breeding," said Jane.

"I suppose if I ever decide to get married, I must submit any final decision as to whom I would be *allowed* to marry to the honorable committee, right?" asked Mark.

"Now you're thinking straight, Marky, ole boy," said Jane as the car raced toward Destin.

"Answer this," began Mark, "will the committee please be cordial to Brandi this weekend so we can all have a pleasant time?"

"Permission granted," conceded Jane.

*****

Mark treasured the soft, white beaches of Destin and the

vigorous salty air of the gulf. He counted the days to his every visit.

No one is from Destin. That is a large part of its charm. The festive holiday mood of the once little fishing village, now gone big time, is far removed from the inner-city tension Mark encountered in Atlanta. It was just three years ago that he and Charlie McBride purchased their shared bayside villa in Sandestin Resort. Charlie McBride was already at the villa, and Mark knew the vodka bottles were in trouble.

The infamous Charlie McBride was a realtor in Atlanta. He was sprawled out on a big lawn chair and had his feet propped high on another one. He was swigging a greyhound cocktail like there was no tomorrow. His face was big, square, and red. It was getting more crimson with every glass.

"Back here, Mark," Charlie squealed when he saw the BMW pull up to the end of the drive. "C'mon over here, Jane, I want to commit a sex crime on YOU, darling. You are out of your jurisdiction!" he added.

"I'll flip your smart-assed, ole lard-butt in that lake, big boy!" Jane said laughingly.

"Charlie, have you seen or heard from Brandi or Caleb?" asked Mark as he popped the trunk open for the bags.

"Caleb cancelled," said Charlie. He rose and walked over to help Mark with the luggage. "I guess Mr. Mack needed another golf partner this weekend," he added.

"Or caddy," replied Mark.

Becky and Lisa walked out of the back door into the yard. "Hey, everybody!" said Becky.

"What's her name—uh, Miss Brandi Baker—called and left a message on the house phone that the traffic out of New Orleans is heavy, and she will be about an hour late," said Lisa.

She stepped back to hold the door open as Mark and Charlie approached. Mark threw a half-hearted nod at her for her courtesy.

"Brandi can room with me," said Jane. "I know her name-I'll take that," she said as she reached for the handle of her makeup kit that Mark had clinched between his teeth.

"I hope those gals aren't too rough on Brandi this weekend," Mark whispered to Charlie as they separated from the others into the house.

"It looks like trouble has begun before she even arrives. What's with the separate bedroom?" asked Charlie.

"We are not there yet," replied Mark. "I think she is adorable—I just don't want to lead her on."

"Give me her bridle and reins! I will lead the little filly on!" said Charlie laughingly. "I think she is hot! If she can handle the piranha outside, I'll be impressed."

"Let's just be prepared to help her out with the girls if she needs assistance," said Mark.

*****

Jane, Lisa, and Becky had moved out to the dock overlooking one of the many freshwater lakes in Sandestin Resort. They sat by the fire that Charlie had started a little earlier. Beyond the lake they could see Choctawhatchee Bay with sailboats, pleasure boats, and wave-runners enjoying the last dwindling minutes of daylight in the warm, spring evening.

Becky was thin with curly brown locks. Her pretty green eyes were the same color as the Margarita she was stirring. "Maybe, just maybe, Mark and Brandi would like to room together," she said to no one in particular.

Lisa, better nourished than Becky, always had a great big smile that was a giveaway to her never serious nature. "I'm sure Brandi would!" she said.

"If Mark would have wanted her to sleep with him, he would have spoken up," said Jane.

Jane, Becky and Lisa had been sorority sisters at the University of Georgia and all three were in the Atlanta Junior League. Becky was a researcher for a news service, and Lisa was an independent interior designer.

Every Wednesday night, without fail, the three girls met a half dozen or so of their closest friends at the Ritz-Carlton in Buckhead for their weekly pow-wow. This group commanded the biggest table in the bar area and were well known for being attractive, opinionated, and sometimes brutal--particularly on deserving males. Throughout Buckhead they were known as the "bitch corp". Very, very, few guys met their approval. But if one did measure up—he was called a "Mark".

"Mark and Brandi have known each other for less than a month, St. Patrick's Day, remember?" said Lisa. "I bet Brandi is more than ready to spend the night with Mark."

"I'm ready to spend the night with Mark, and we've never even dated," replied Becky.

"I think Mark is looking for something much more sophisticated in a woman," offered Jane.

"He is quite the proper gentleman," said Lisa. "Mark can have any girl he wants."

"Brandi is certainly not the one he wants. She's just another volunteer," said Jane.

*****

Darkness fell and the fire had settled down to its last cinders. All five friends were still huddled around the ashes when headlights flickered through the pines. A Camry pulled to the end of the driveway. The window rolled down, and a shrill voice sounded, "I'm looking for Mark Mabry's place!"

"That's us," replied Jane, loudly.

"Come on back, out here! You are just in time to do the dishes!" shouted Becky.

Brandi Baker got out of her vehicle and made her way directly to Mark.

"I've missed you so much!" Brandi said as she painted a big kiss on Mark's cheek.

Jane rolled her eyes at Charlie. He ignored her and grabbed a bag out of Brandi's hand. Mark introduced everyone.

"There's plenty of Italian spaghetti still on the stove, Brandi," said Lisa.

"You are so sweet," replied Brandi, "but I just want to relax. Come show me the villa, Mark," she added as she grabbed his hand and led him inside.

As they walked out of earshot Becky said, "Mark needs to take his little child inside and teach her how to say 'da-da'!"

"It is only 8:15 in the evening, Becky, and you are already drunk. Great!" growled Charlie.

*****

"We're finally alone," said Brandi once inside. She walked up and put her arms around Mark.

"Did you have trouble finding the villa?" asked Mark.

"Whose belongings are these?" Brandi asked pointing to

Jane's pink suitcase. "This is not your room, is it, Mark?"

"The guys and gals always have separate quarters here--house rules," replied Mark nonchalantly. Brandi looked at him with an apparent scowl, and they soon rejoined the group outside. Too tired to venture out into the Destin nightlife, they all decided to spend the evening at the villa.

*****

Saturday morning everyone shared breakfast and caught the trolley over to the Gulf front Sandestin beach. They rented six chairs and umbrellas and played volleyball with new friends until after lunch. Later, the band started playing on the poolside deck overlooking the beach.

Charlie was drinking way too much and thought he should dance to every song. The "bitch corp" had a pack of male jackals hanging around them at the bar. The girls were thoroughly enjoying the young men's attention.

Mark and Brandi went for a walk on the beach and afterwards waded out to the warm, waist-deep water. She wrapped her legs around Mark's thighs and her arms around his neck. They relaxed in the Gulf and talked as the gentle waves splashed against their bodies in the afternoon sun.

"I have been waiting to ask you something," said Brandi. "My cousin is getting married this summer, and I would love for you to come with me, Mark."

"When is it?" asked Mark.

"The third weekend in June—and the wedding is in Baton Rouge," answered Brandi.

"Darn it," Mark said disappointedly. "Brandi, I have an

important marketing project due around that time, but we'll see."

*****

Later, after freshening up at the villa, Mark and the four girls went to Baytown on the Bay in Sandestin where young professionals go to continue their revelry deep into the night. Charlie McBride was drifting somewhere in the deep recesses of his mind.

Brandi was the last to arrive Friday night and the first to depart Sunday morning. Mark walked her to her car, leaned over, and kissed her gently on the lips.

"When can I know about Baton Rouge?" she asked.

"I will let you know soon," Mark answered. "Please be careful driving home."

*****

Mark and Jane were the last to leave the villa. Jane had been very conscientious and thorough in cleaning the villa, which Mark greatly appreciated. It did seem to him that she was delaying their departure.

"I'm so tired," she finally said. "We could get some sleep and drive home fresh, early tomorrow."

"Jane, I have to be at work early in the morning. We have an important office meeting at 9 o'clock sharp, and I need to be prepared," Mark said. "I don't mind if you want to sleep all the way home."

Jane brought a pillow for the ride. But soon her head was

resting on Mark's shoulder. She later felt him ease up on the accelerator.

"Where are we?" she asked. Mark turned his head to look again down Ebenezer Church Road.

"Oh yes, I see the sign," Jane said. "You're gonna go down it one day," she sighed as she drifted to sleep.

Chapter 3

Mark worked hard all week, but his advertising project still had much work to be done. He looked forward to the familiar drive from Atlanta to Destin. It would provide him the opportunity to concentrate on the project's loose ends. He was hopeful of completely finishing the assignment over the weekend at his tranquil, Sandestin villa.

Ebenezer Church Road was on his mind when he woke up early Saturday morning. It was not only as an adventure he wanted to take, but a reminder of similar fascinations he experienced in his youth. As a young boy he took great delight in imagining the mystery of an unexplored place—or of a yet experienced event. He did not try to understand his particular fancy with Ebenezer Church Road, but realized it gave him hope for fulfillment he could only anticipate in general terms. He relished such fresh encounters. Whatever the intense expectations of his past were, they were here again- on this road. And like yesteryear, he was overcome with impatient speculation. He tried to imagine different snapshots of how the church would look. What condition was it in? What color? What surroundings?

He left Atlanta at daylight to have ample time to completely satisfy his curiosity. As he approached the familiar sign, his stomach grew tense with excitement. This filled him with a slight taste of fear—of disappointment. He hoped that this already overly magnified excursion would meet his expectations, and not end like almost all of the others.

The Ebenezer Church sign—with an arrow underneath— was clearly many times older than Mark. "Even the sign has character," Mark thought. He turned, stopped his vehicle, and took a good, long look at it.

Mark proceeded slowly down the graveled road. He wanted to prolong the adventure as long as he could—to capture and savor all of the details. He took notice of every oak tree as he passed. The early morning shadows of the oaks were bigger than the oaks themselves. One led to another, standing like soldiers in rank, guarding a secret about to be shared. A cluster of magnolias, with their brilliant white bulbs, broke through the oaks. A spattering of white dogwoods were present like younger children playing around in a yard.

He finally saw evidence of civilization. An old country store, no longer open for business, broke the scenic beauty of Ebenezer Church Road. It had two silver harmonica-like gas pumps out front and a rundown wood framed house attached on the rear side. A blue Ford pickup, at least thirty years old, was in the driveway. Mark parked and exited his vehicle. It was time to investigate.

The gate on the old picket fence guarding the living quarters had long ago been knocked down. Mark walked up the steps and knew that if anyone was home, they were aware of his presence. He was right. The door opened before he got to it. A slight, gray-headed man in his early eighties stepped out.

"You must be lost stranger," said the amiable looking codger as he hiked his britches back up to their intended place.

"No, sir," answered Mark.

"Then I hope you want to renew that mineral lease of mine that expired ten years ago," said the man.

"I'm not an oil man either, just a tourist. I'm curious about the area. My name is Mark Mabry," he said extending his hand.

"We don't see many sight-seers 'round here. I'm Jake Delaughter," replied Jake reaching out to return Mark's shake.

"I am interested in visiting Ebenezer Church," said Mark. "Is it still in existence, and how much farther down the road is it?"

Old Jake chuckled and said, "It has been closed down for over 20 years, not enough people. Ain't even a half dozen folks still left on this here road. You just go a mile further on down and it peters out at Leila Hewitt's place, Ebenezer Forest. After her parents died, Leila has lived there alone. Since both sides of the road are on her property, she put up a gate, but never shuts it. There's a big sign when you get to her property--says 'Ebenezer Forest Straight Ahead'. Anybody that wants to see the ole Ebenezer Church—or its cemetery—got to go through Ms. Leila's church gate and through her forest."

Jake started walking toward the road, indicating the visit was almost over. Mark followed as Jake kept talking, "Most of my family is buried in that cemetery at the church and they are a-waiting on me. We got room for you too, young feller!"

"Thank you for the invitation," said Mark laughingly before he thanked Jake for the information.

Mark pulled back out onto Ebenezer Road and headed for Ms. Leila's place and Ebenezer Forest.

There was a long wooded area between the store and the Hewitt's place. A couple of over-grown turn off lanes along the way indicated abandoned driveways. He eased passed the well maintained "Ebenezer Forest Straight Ahead" sign and onward through the open gate. A freshly-painted white fence and manicured pastures gave the Hewitt estate a stately and distinctive appearance.

Mark proceeded slowly and took careful note of the many mature hardwoods he passed by. The thick canopy above the aged trees blocked the sun's bright rays. It created a cool and shaded ambiance of over-powering nature and beauty.

The roof of an older colonial style home soon became visible to Mark. A full view of the sizeable white house revealed its impressive workmanship. Its detailed wooden splendor was supported by large columns. A southern style swing and four large rockers decorated an extra-wide, covered porch. The windows were adorned with wide plantation shutters.

An older model blue Oldsmobile was parked in the circular driveway. Looking just a little farther ahead, Mark could see a large archway with a sign that read Ebenezer Church. He envisioned it was where the locals used to turn on Sunday mornings to go worship. He speculated how they might have looked dressed up in white shirts and pretty dresses. Mark felt sad that it was now just a memory.

The Hewitt driveway was lined with rows of pink, red, and white roses. Mark stepped out of the BMW beneath a tremendous gray barked oak. The tree was huge and shaded the entire front yard.

Across the road was a free-standing bird pen with a few guinea fowl inside. Atop the cage, and in the trees above, were a few larger male guineas. They all watched Mark with apparent interest, but little concern.

The large blocks of stone leading up to the porch were girdled with monkey grass. There was not one sign or trace of weeds, not one wayward leaf. The yard, porch, swing, paint, and welcome sign were all immaculate.

Mark walked up the steps and across the wide porch. He lifted the door's brass knocker and tapped three times.

Through the tinted glass, Mark could vaguely see a straight hallway that went as far as the sun's morning rays would allow him to observe. Emerging from the rear of the house, he saw the silhouette of a woman walking briskly toward him.

The door opened and the full brightness of a spring morning caught the radiance of Leila Hewitt's face. The light particularly captured her blue eyes with their warmth and sparkle beyond anything Mark had ever seen. He was briefly taken aback by her smooth and stunningly beautiful face. They looked at each other for a moment until she broke the silence.

"Good morning, young man, may I help you?" asked Leila politely.

"Good Morning, ma'am. Mr. Jake at the store told me who you were, and I wanted to stop by and introduce myself. I'm Mark Mabry. I travel through this area often and became curious about Ebenezer Church and this road. I am particularly interested in its history," said Mark. He felt so awkward.

"Well, come in, Mr. Mabry," said Leila. "You caught me at a good time. I just returned from my morning walk to the church – and I always enjoy tea about this hour. Would you care for a glass?"

"Yes, and thank you very much for allowing me to visit with you without calling first," said Mark. "I gathered from what Mr. Jake told me that you would be the best historian of the community. I would like to ask you about Ebenezer Church. I've driven by the sign many times. I have become intrigued by it."

"Please have a seat on this couch. The tea is in the kitchen. It will be ready in just a minute. I will be right back," said Leila as she turned and walked toward the rear of her home.

Mark watched Leila very intently as she walked out of the room. She moved with a vibrancy and youthfulness one would normally associate with a young girl. She exuded energy and life. He couldn't help but notice that she was unusually curvaceous for an older lady. She appeared to Mark to be in her early fifties, and her ensnaring beauty shocked and stirred him at the same time.

He looked carefully around the room. It was as clean and crisp as the yard. There were several vases of fresh cut roses and their smell refreshed the room.

The furniture was old but not stiff. The quaint home filled Mark with a sense of warmth he had not felt in a long time. A particularly interesting antique clock against the wall indicated that it was thirty minutes before noon.

A picture of a much younger Leila sat atop the fireplace mantel. "What an absolutely gorgeous photo!" Mark observed. However, he thought the camera did not fully capture the spirit of the lady he had just met, or the beauty of her eyes.

He caught a reflection of himself in a large mirror hanging on the wall opposite him. Hearing footsteps, Mark swept his hair in place and sat a little taller.

"Sugar and lemon, Mr. Mabry?" asked Leila.

"Thank you, just lemon please," Mark replied.

"Not many people ask about Ebenezer Church these days," began Leila. "In its day, everyone for miles around worshipped here. I was baptized outside the church as a young girl. I never missed a wedding or a funeral except when I was away at Florida State. Most of the folks have now moved off this road. Only Jake and the Andrews family, besides me, are left. Most of the land you passed before you got to my gate is tied up in estates. The young people moved on to bigger cities for jobs or other reasons."

"You never married?" asked Mark, regretting the question as it rolled off his lips.

Leila did not answer aloud, but Mark thought he saw Leila slightly nod her head no.

Leila continued, "If you would like to see the church, just stop by early one day—any day. I've already taken the walk this morning. We used to drive back to the church, but the road is so difficult to maintain. I don't allow cars to go down it anymore."

"How far past the entrance to the church does Ebenezer Church Road continue?" asked Mark.

"It ends at the Choctawhatchee River, just another mile or so to the east," Leila answered. "One way in--one way out. Like it is to heaven," she said.

Mark sipped his tea very slowly as Leila told him all about Ebenezer Forest. Her face glowed when she talked about all of the students, and many others, who visited from different places. She talked about her favorite trees: the oaks and the sycamores. Her favorite oaks were the live oaks and the water oaks.

When Mark asked her what was her favorite undergrowth tree, she didn't hesitate. "Ironwoods," Leila answered. "They remind me of my daddy's arms before he got sick."

Mark asked her about the animals of Ebenezer Forest.

"The deer and the birds are my favorite," Leila shared. "Of course, I love them all," she added.

Leila told Mark that Ebenezer Forest had a rather fledgling web page. She was excited when Mark said he was in advertising and offered to give her some recommendations on her website as soon as he had time. Leila gave him a business card with her home page address and her phone number.

They finished their tea and Leila walked Mark to the door. She reached out and squeezed his hand. "Thank you for stopping by," she said. "I enjoyed your interest and your questions very much."

"Thank you for the tea and for telling me about Ebenezer Forest. I look forward to exploring it and visiting the church," said Mark.

He turned, walked to his car, and drove away—but with a feeling that every minute he had spent imagining this place, the road, the church, the people, all paled with the excitement he felt for what he just found. There was no disappointment this time. There was no remiss. He had stumbled into a wonderland of nature, unspoiled and clean—and into Leila, genuine and pure, and so very beautiful.

Leila stood on the porch as Mark pulled out of her driveway. Mark reminded her a little bit of Jude Jackman, particularly in the way he had looked at her. The sports car disappeared around the nearest curve, and she quickly dismissed the association.

Chapter 4

The regular Monday morning staff meeting of Mackco Advertising Agency was winding down. Albert J. Mackey stood before his group of advertising executives in a perfectly tailored suit accentuated by his sparkling and completely bald head. This weekly pep rally helped his young troops maintain the company's position as one of Atlanta's hottest and most successful agencies. Mr. Mackey, however, tended to be quite repetitive with his words of encouragement. His resonant but soft voice, if not carefully followed, could quickly lull the young professionals into a deep, but usually well-disguised, sleep.

A ritual of the staff meeting was for it to end with Mr. Mackey calling upon one of his agents for him or her to make an impromptu address utilizing the type of zeal and salesmanship he expected from his staff. It was the agents' chance to fine-tune their much used public speaking skills. Mr. Mackey's sometimes brutal critique made his weekly selection of a speaker a source of substantial fear for the very competitive group. The entire bunch knew that their status with Mackco Advertising Agency was greatly impacted by these occasional and greatly undesired "opportunities".

"Mark, you are selected today for our final words of inspiration," said Mr. Mackey.

Mark Mabry nearly swallowed the knot in his tie. He had hoped that his daydreaming had not been noticed. He did not expect to be called upon this morning. He was selected just four weeks previously.

"Yes, sir," said Mark. He slowly rose, and even more slowly walked to the side of his shorter boss. Before he began, he paused for a few seconds as he had been taught. He spoke with emotion.

"Have you ever wandered upon a truly enchanting place?"

"Have you ever been enraptured by a discovery or a setting— or a personality so different from the norm that it, or he, or she, had a compelling trancelike effect on you?"

"Isn't that the kind of product image we desire to attain for our clients?"

"Wouldn't that be a mood we would like to capture and preserve for our clients?"

"Shouldn't we attempt to portray our clients' products in such a transcended manner as to inspire not just the pocket-book of their consumers, but the imagination and fantasy of the market?"

"I leave you with two thoughts: elevation and enchantment —two most stimulating goals for creative advertisement! Thank you!"

"FABULOUS! ABSOLUTELY, FABULOUS!" barked Mr. Mackey as the room, much more than politely, clapped for Mark. "Mark," he continued, "that was short—and sweet—but very powerful! See you all next Monday!"

Caleb Hathcox walked over to Mark as the group was dispersing. He stuck out his hand and said, "I hate to admit it, Mark, but that was some damn good bullshit."

"Thank you, Caleb, but I was serious," said Mark.

"I thought old Mack had caught you by surprise," Caleb

said, missing nothing. "Where did you come up with that verbal spurt?" he asked. Caleb was by far the most competitive ad executive at Mackco—and one of the best. He was talented, ambitious, and always curious.

"Actually I visited such a place this past Saturday morning—a very special place—almost to Destin," said Mark.

"Well, wherever you grabbed it from, Albert J. Mackey really ate it up," Caleb replied.

Mark eased out of the conference room, avoiding the usual after meeting coffee break. He returned quickly to his office. He turned on his computer, waited for it to load up, and typed in the Ebenezer Forest website address that Leila Hewitt had given him. There it was. Mark devoured every heading, paragraph, and word. His impression was that it had been laid out rather nicely. Yet he proceeded to edit every paragraph. He made notes on how each could be improved, if Leila were to agree. His mind retained a clear snapshot of what he had seen on his only visit, and he imagined how his memories could be better illustrated on the website. He mentally integrated his hypothetical images into his improved text for what he felt would be an optimal presentation.

Having totally reworked the site to his mind's satisfaction, Mark looked at his watch. It was 11:30 am and time to meet Charlie McBride for lunch.

*****

Mark slipped into the booth at Doug's Deli just ahead of the noontime crowd. Charlie McBride eased past the line at the front door and began talking to Mark before he sat down.

"How was everything in Destin?" Charlie asked.

"I finally explored Ebenezer Church Road on the way to Destin – and met a fascinating lady," replied Mark.

"Were there a lot of folks down for the weekend? Were the beaches crowded?" questioned Charlie.

"Hardly anyone lives on the road except her, and she is really different," said Mark.

"OK! OK!" conceded Charlie. "How old is this babe?"

"What difference does it make?" replied Mark, obviously annoyed. "She's older. She's created her own natural environment, her own world, and she is really special," he said.

"I haven't heard you get that excited about Brandi," said Charlie. "And if you ask me, she is really special--and special looking. In fact, she is smoking hot!"

"The next time we go to Destin I would like for you to see Ebenezer Forest," said Mark. "It has tremendous potential to attract some well-deserved, national recognition and appreciation."

"You'll have to go it alone next weekend," said Charlie. "I've got that seminar in Charleston. But why don't you take Brandi to the forest? She is dying to tighten up with you."

Mark and Charlie lunched together a couple of days a week. It was an easy relationship for both. They had been friends for many years. Disagreements between them were common, but never very serious. In addition to the Destin villa, they shared many mutual friends and interests—yet they had never shared women. Generally they were never even interested in the same type. Brandi was an exception.

Mark knew, so Charlie didn't have to hide the fact, that if he wasn't in the picture, Charlie would be very interested in Brandi. Brandi was a distant interest in Mark's mind today and this would be a good opportunity to open the door.

"Look, Charlie," said Mark, "I just do not see Brandi and myself ever developing a really serious relationship. She is a beautiful girl, a good girl, and I'm thinking about pulling away from her before it gets started. If I did, it would make it a lot easier for you, if you have an interest, to maybe get something going with her."

"Are you crazy?" replied Charlie. "I'm your best friend. Brandi is absolutely nuts about you. It would be a long time after you died before she would go out with me. Besides that, I would look like a squirrel for even asking. But damn, if you feel that way about her, you should tell her now!"

Mark realized that Charlie was telling the truth on all counts. "You are right. I really need to make things clear to her. She is very sweet, and I need to handle this better," Mark said.

There was silence for a few moments. Both men were uncomfortable with what had just been spoken.

"Well, at least you are interested in this Ebenezer Forest," Charlie said, breaking the tension. "What's the old lady's name?"

"Her name is Leila Jane Hewitt," answered Mark. He smiled and said, "Charlie, you just have to see how nice a place this is, and what she has done with it."

The two men finished their lunch. They talked about their plans for the coming summer and about one of their favorite topics—the "bitch corp". When the noon hour was over, they clasped hands and parted.

*****

The week passed very slowly for Mark. His plan was to leave

at an early hour Saturday for Destin. He wanted to arrive at Ebenezer Forest before Ms. Leila took her morning walk to her church. He worried about visiting Leila again so soon after her recent invitation. She did offer that he come again at any time. But he certainly did not want to wear out any welcome he might have.

Mark pondered to what degree he should offer his many possible improvements for Leila's website. The last thing he wanted to do was to offend her.

He wondered exactly what Leila did with all of her time – and how slow were the days in her life?

He gazed out of his office window as he imagined how pleasant a job it would be to manage such a venture as Ebenezer Forest. He recalled the peace and tranquility of Leila's world. He thought of her lovely home, her exquisite yard – and – of course, Leila. He could visualize her lovely face—and her alluring, light blue eyes.

Mark gazed again and again at his watch. As each day passed, he marked it off of his calendar with a big X.

"Should I call her before Saturday to tell her I will be stopping by?" Mark repeatedly asked himself. He never made the call.

Chapter 5

Mark left Atlanta almost three hours before daylight. He was confident this would allow him ample time to arrive at Ebenezer Forest before Leila began her daily, morning walk to the church. However, the Saturday morning traffic out of the city was delayed by highway construction. He zipped past car after car on I-85 attempting to make up for the lost time. He had no idea exactly how early Leila departed, but he wanted to walk with her to the church.

He thought again about how he should go about offering Leila his ideas for her web site. He knew that she would reject any suggestion of commercialism, and that was not his intent. He wanted to simply share his expertise with her—to make the already acceptable presentation she had even better.

Mark reflected, and smiled, about his rushing to Ebenezer Forest—the fascination he had with it, and how it made him feel. At the same time, he recognized that his enchantment with the white-collar corporate world was disappearing quickly. The paperwork and phone calls aggravated him, but not as much as the workplace small talk and inter-office politics. He knew that a truly happy person should love his work. He felt that his life was cluttered and relatively meaningless, while Leila's was simple and worthwhile. He was excited about his new, special interest in the more natural world of Leila Hewitt. Internally, Mark wrestled with how he could possibly use this experience to improve his own existence. If he had his choice, he would rather contribute his time to Ebenezer Forest than work for Mackco Advertising Company.

Mark's brakes squealed as he turned much too swiftly onto Ebenezer Church Road. He slowed down, almost reverently, as he traveled beneath the oaks. His BMW seemed to be gliding through the clouds as he passed through the shadows of morning daylight. The sensation of going back in time descended upon him, along with the sweet fragrance of the morning dew. He almost didn't notice Jake Delaughter, who was carrying a tool box in one hand and waving at him with the other. Mark did not want to be rude and sounded two quick taps of his horn. He slowed his sports car down to reduce the dust that trailed him.

Mark was anticipating Leila's tree-lined estate and welcoming gate to come into view. But unexpectedly, under an oak tree in a curve in the road, a beautiful golden doe bounded onto Ebenezer Church Road. The gorgeous creature looked directly at Mark. Mark stopped his vehicle to return her gaze. The doe soon twitched her tail, and with one leap, jumped into the forest.

Mark eased his car up to the exact spot where the doe had disappeared. He believed he could barely see the deer standing motionless and camouflaged in the distance. But he was not sure. Then Mark's thoughts quickly returned to catching Leila before her morning walk. He hurried on.

When he arrived at Leila's home, Mark saw her Oldsmobile parked in the same spot. Birds and squirrels were enjoying fresh seeds that were in the feeder. The animals fluttered or scampered off as he walked up the steps. Mark rapped the door knocker loudly. Hearing no sounds from inside, it became obvious that he was too late. "Leila is already on her morning walk through Ebenezer Forest to the church," Mark thought disappointedly.

"Would she be offended if I surprised her on the lane?" Mark asked himself. "She invited me to come back at any time without calling. Would it be improper? Would it frighten her?" he pondered.

"If I don't go now, I will miss the church," Mark thought. The decision was made. He walked briskly to the gate, eased through it, and strode down the narrow lane he had dreamt about.

The sun warmed Mark as he plunged further into the plush wooded gardens. The leaves were wet and dripping. The wild and moist fragrance of Ebenezer Forest thrilled Mark as he penetrated deeper into Leila's private sanctuary. He quietly eased down the secluded lane—in and out of the intermittent shadows.

Mark soon began to notice the increasing sound of running water. He came upon a clear, trickling stream flowing towards him from the direction of the church. A sturdy wooden bridge crossed the stream. Afterwards, the lane hugged the stream closely as Mark meandered along it toward his destination.

The sunlight dancing off the top of Ebenezer Church caught Mark's attention. A huge row of ligustrums lined the side of the road as he walked even closer to the place of worship. The stream was growing larger and deeper, and it sparkled with life.

Mark felt more than a tingle of excitement as Ebenezer Church finally appeared in full glory. It was a brilliant white color with a small steeple on the fore of its roof. Two wooden doors spanned the front wall with large windows on each side.

Ebenezer Church was now only fifty yards away. He stood motionless as he admired the magnificent structure hidden in the lush and verdant forest. He could feel, as surely was felt in the hearts of the many who had worshiped here in the past, that this Godly sanctuary was something very, very special.

Mark's eyes drifted to the now swollen stream flowing from a crystalline, spring-fed pond aside the church. He could see the actual spring bubbling and rippling up from its headwater. The pond was clear and as blue as the morning sky. A baptismal dock was nestled to one side between blooming crepe myrtles.

And then the SURREAL happened!

Slowly, in this secluded and sacred place, Leila walked naked from the shadows!

Her smooth, slender and light-skinned body stood silhouetted against the green backdrop of nature. She began to ease her fully exposed figure so very elegantly into the cool, clear spring.

The steamy mist of the sparkling water enveloped Leila as she lowered herself deeper into the shallow, blissful pool.

Mark was captivated and paralyzed by Leila's gorgeous, sensuous, and so very youthful body.

He could clearly see the pure smoothness of her fully exposed skin. He could see her supple bosoms, white and full.

He could barely breathe.

Mark watched as Leila slowly and gently washed her breasts and nipples. She ran her wet fingers through her shiny hair.

He was trembling.

Leila gracefully bathed herself, then leisurely leaned back and disappeared beneath the water's surface.

Leila rose into full view again. She innocently revealed her total womanhood, her all, to nature—and to Mark.

"I can't move, or she will see me," thought Mark.

It was too late! As Leila stood up in the now thigh deep water, she shook her hair and turned toward the lane. His blue shirt startled her. She saw Mark!

Her mouth dropped and she followed it back into the water to hide her exposed body.

She was on her knees and horrified. Since the day of her birth, her father and Doctor Glending were the only men that had ever laid eyes upon her unclothed body. She raised her face out of the water and looked again toward Mark.

Mark felt so guilty—he had violated Leila's privacy. He looked straight back at her for an eternal moment. Their eyes locked into each other's. Then, Mark turned and walked away.

Leila was breathing heavily. She was in a dreamlike daze. She was feeling sensations she never experienced before, but her horror quickly passed.

She recognized Mark and was not afraid of him. She watched him disappear into the woods. She knew that he did not expect to find her, or to see her, in the way that he did.

"Have I subconsciously invited this moment by not requiring him to call before he came?" Leila soon considered.

She certainly did not want him to be painfully embarrassed. She would quickly get dressed, catch him and tell him so!

"MY GRACIOUS!" Mark thought. "I am a trespasser! I should have called! I cannot get over how unbelievably attractive she is! I cannot believe what I saw! What an unforgettable moment! I don't know if I've ever had such a sensuous experience. *I am a voyeur!* Should I leave? Should I wait for her at her house? I have to go. NO! I have to apologize."

Mark could barely remember the walk back to Leila's front porch. He sat on her steps for what seemed like a very, very long time.

*****

Leila finally appeared at the beginning of the church lane. She walked gracefully toward Mark, with her head held high.

Mark spoke first, "I am so very sorry for intruding."

"Nonsense," said Leila. "I've been skinny dipping in that spring since my baptism."

"I owe you an apology for going down the lane without calling," said Mark.

"Well, I should get a nude beach sign," Leila said as she walked past Mark and opened the screen door. "Come in, how about some fresh strawberries?" she asked.

Mark laughed as he followed her into the kitchen. Leila opened the refrigerator door, grabbed the strawberries, and walked to the table.

"Let's sit here," Leila said as she divided the strawberries and gave Mark the larger portion. They sat down and looked into each other's eyes for the second time that day.

Mark looked intently and directly at Leila as they talked. There was no denying that her face revealed accumulating years. "What stunning beauty!" he thought. Her eyes were so very alive, so deeply dreamy and enticing. They simply overwhelmed all that he saw. He could envision the unbelievable treasure beneath Leila's linen dress and was consumed with erotic recall.

*****

Something was also stirring within Leila. She knew as a woman that she and Mark had just shared an extraordinarily intimate experience.

She had never been so revealed, so exposed. She did not understand why she was so comfortable with this younger man. Did he stir longings from her past? So much time had elapsed since she had even thought of possibly, just perhaps—one day—actually being with a man.

"I need to give you a more formal tour of Ebenezer Church," offered Leila shyly. "You didn't get an opportunity to see how really nice it is inside."

*****

Mark visited for a while longer. He asked if Leila would please allow him to offer some suggestions for her Ebenezer Forest website, and she accepted. Mark told her about his and Charlie's villa in Sandestin and invited her to visit. Leila told him about her upcoming trip to Destin and the beach.

They continued to chat, eat, and laugh. At times, they just paused and looked at each other.

Their startling first encounter at Ebenezer Church was indelibly imprinted in their minds—and they both knew it.

They also both knew that this morning would always be their own very secret, and very special, memory.

Chapter 6

The next morning, Leila drove her blue Oldsmobile to Amanda's house and then followed her to Destin. The journey took thirty-five minutes, not a very long time to completely change worlds. As they crossed the US Hwy. 331 bridge over Choctawhatchee Bay, Leila could see the many high-rise hotels and condominium buildings that were springing up in the fashionable southern resort. What used to be a quiet little fishing village was now a favorite playground for all of America.

Although she lived only a short distance away, Leila rarely visited Destin. She was a freshwater, not a saltwater, woman. She preferred the shaded, mature forests to the open and flat coastal plain. Although Destin is an attractive destination for both families and party types, Leila felt out of place on both counts. She had no real family and preferred the uncomplicated country folks to the vacationing urbanites. This was particularly true to the small percentage of tourists the locals described as "lounge chair-lushes".

Leila's last overnight stay was a few years earlier. She was the featured speaker at a wildlife convention where she presented one of her slide shows entitled, "Ebenezer Forest's Wetland Habitat". Leila knew many people who lived in Destin and the surrounding area, most of whom were associated with the Emerald Coast Animal Refuge. These outdoor naturalists visited her and her forest often, usually to release a few raccoon or deer that had been nursed back to good health. Leila had never been a guest at any of their homes. The visits were always in one direction – to Ebenezer Forest.

Amanda's plan was to stay the whole week in the gulf front Miramar Tennis Resort, even though one set of tennis would have probably destroyed her troublesome knees.

Leila's plan was to go back and forth to her home to accommodate a couple of scheduled one-day tours of Ebenezer Forest. She expected that when she had all of the resort living she could appreciate, it would be easy to come up with a good reason not to return to Destin.

Cousin Jackie, Amanda's favorite, waited for her and Leila at the tennis center. "Welcome to paradise, ladies!" Jackie said as she gave Amanda a big hug. She turned and extended her hand to Leila, "It is such a pleasure and honor to see you again, Leila. Amanda sends me all of your clippings, and we hear so much about Ebenezer Forest here in Destin."

"Thank you, Jackie," responded Leila politely. "You are always such a gracious hostess."

The three friends chatted briefly and then drove around to their high-rise condo. Loaded down with luggage, they took the elevator to the fourth floor. They entered the luxurious beach-side unit, and Amanda opened the large, sliding glass doors. They walked out onto the Spanish-tiled porch overlooking the deep emerald waters of the Gulf of Mexico.

"You girls are not going to believe who walked into the Ocean Mist Club last Friday night!" said Jackie.

"I give up, who?" asked Amanda.

"Kevin Costner, HIMSELF!" exclaimed Jackie. "If he is still in town, he may well be back there tonight!"

Jackie was the eyes, ears, nose, and throat of Destin. She knew all the scoop and didn't mind sharing it with others. And in a very different and flirty way than Will Rogers ever intended, Jackie never met a man she didn't like either. She would never marry another one, but she did like them quite a bit. Her husband had been deceased for over a decade. Everybody knew Jackie. It was fairly well conceded that she was the best looking woman in Destin—for her age. She was in her seventies, but her skin looked twenty years younger and her bleached blonde hair looked unbelievably natural. Unless there was a hurricane in town, or a very exceptional male prospect, she played tennis every day.

"Leila," Jackie began, "I have two men in mind for you to meet. One is Doctor Ty Tyson, he is tall, sophisticated and gorgeous. His wife passed away fairly recently. He may not be ready to date yet, but you better get him while you can! The other man is Doctor Johnny Savage, a popular dentist. He is one of the best catches in the panhandle. I messed up by becoming his friend and not snaring him myself five years ago. He is so charming! He loves to dance, in fact we all call him Jumping Johnny! So dear, you can take your pick!"

"Now, Cousin Jackie, don't be putting such heavy social pressure on my friend Leila. She doesn't move nearly as fast as some of your tennis buddies," said Amanda, amusedly.

Leila just laughed and replied, "I don't move at all. I'm staying put in Ebenezer Forest!"

*****

Due to Amanda's persistence, Leila did agree to accompany her and Jackie that same evening to the Ocean Mist Club. The atmosphere of this well known, "wrinkle room", night spot was spacious and nice, but rather dimly lit. Jackie said the dark lighting was intentional because "the advanced aged clientele insist that it be this way to hide their wrinkles".

The first person Leila met was the infamous Dr. Johnny Savage. He knew a beauty when he saw one and wasted no time in asking Leila to dance. Leila politely attempted to decline, but Johnny said, "Darling, there is *no* 'no' in Destin," as he nearly dragged her to the dance floor.

Leila's mother had taken her dancing at the City Recreation Hall in Ponce De Leon as a child, and she fortunately recalled how to bend both knees and tap one foot at the same time.

As the band played "Respect", Dr. Jumpin Johnny showed Leila how he had earned his name. He honored Leila's outstanding looks by literally jumping up and down as he ceremoniously encircled her.

Back at the table, Amanda and Jackie were quite entertained watching Leila and Dr. Johnny dance. There were also a number of other onlookers enjoying the couple's rhythmic debut.

Amanda commented laughingly to Jackie, "Leila should know from her experience with wild animals that if she doesn't panic and run from Doctor Johnny, she might be able to survive the dance."

Leila admitted upon her return to the table that, "Doctor Savage is absolutely delightful and very high spirited."

Quite a large crowd, as usual, came into the establishment over the evening. Most were tourists, and a talented three-piece band kept the whole establishment in a festive mood.

One of the high points of the evening was Jackie's pointing

out of some of the more colorful Destin regulars as they spilled through the front door of the Ocean Mist Club. According to Jackie, they were usually present and accounted for every weekend if they were in town. Joe and Mary from Tuscaloosa; Maggie from South Carolina; "Cousin J.B." from New Orleans; Bonnie and Claude from Birmingham; "Fast Eddie" from Hattiesburg; Suzy Q. Spence from Memphis; "Joe, the pitcher from Cleveland State"; "Meg the Mermaid" from Baton Rouge; and Chuck "The Italian Stallion" from parts unknown, were among those noticed. Cousin Jackie kept Leila and Amanda in stitches with hilarious war stories about these and other interesting troopers.

Leila closely observed a row of mostly elderly men lined up at the bar. They stood shoulder to shoulder. The scene reminded Leila of a particular pine tree near a cypress pond back home. It was always loaded with turkey vultures.

Disappointingly, Doctor Tyson did not appear that evening, nor did Kevin Costner.

*****

Mark Mabry telephoned Leila the next morning about the work he was doing on her webpage for Ebenezer Forest. He read her some of his suggested new copy, and she agreed it would make a nice improvement. She was very happy to hear from Mark and was delighted with his interest in something so dear to her heart.

Mark asked Leila if she was enjoying Destin. She told him she had been to Baytown, Destin Commons, and to the Ocean Mist Club. He replied that he had never been to the Ocean Mist Club.

Mark had another reason for the call. "Memorial Day weekend is coming up and my friend Charlie McBride and I are hosting a party at our Sandestin villa on that Saturday for our friends and co-workers, mostly from Atlanta. We would like for you to please join us, Leila," requested Mark.

"Thank you, Mark, if you will email the directions to me, I will print them when I run home this week. Would you mind if I bring my friend Amanda with me?" asked Leila. "I wouldn't want to leave her alone for the afternoon."

"Of course not. I am excited you can make it," said Mark.

Leila smiled to herself when the conversation ended, "How unlike me. I *never* go to parties!" she thought.

*****

By midweek, Leila needed the rejuvenation of Ebenezer Forest. It was shortly after daylight and she could hear Amanda in a deep sleep as she eased out of the condominium. She was home in a short while. Her very reliable employee, Clyde Branson, had things in prefect order.

She spent ten minutes on the computer and then was off on her much enjoyed morning walk. She paced rather briskly through the forest. As she always did, Leila slowed to appreciate Ebenezer Church when it came into majestic view. She walked over to the inviting, sparkling spring. A male cardinal whistled to his mate in a nearby ironwood tree. She could smell the pleasant spring pollen in the air.

Leila pulled the straps off of her shoulders and let her dress fall to the ground. She eased out of her silken under garments and stepped slowly into the crystalline water. She loved the way it made her feel, so clean, so pure. It was the first time she had actually gotten into the spring since her encounter with Mark. In the adjacent cemetery, a squirrel chased a mate in a young pin oak.

Leila stepped a little deeper into the water and started to bathe herself. She gently doused her face. She moistened her breasts and neck. Then she slid her wet hands slowly through her hair. She was fully aware that she was repeating exactly what she had been doing before she noticed that Mark was watching her. She kept her back toward the location where Mark stood and imagined that he was there watching her again. She did not want to turn around and be disappointed.

Leila had bathed in her wonderful and secluded spa countless times before. Yet today, her thoughts were only of the last time. After all, it was the most sensual experience of her life. She was entranced—totally and completely—with her new youthful friend. She recalled every detail of his angular and handsome face. She remembered his fixed gaze at her naked body.

Excitement of any kind had been a rare visitor in Leila's life. Sexual excitement had been non-existent, but as she stood in the enchanting water, her mind was drifting. She saw a vivid, penetrating visualization of how Mark Mabry would look without his clothes.

"These dreams are taking me over," thought Leila breathing much more heavily and feeling heated sensations down below. A sudden, torrid surge set Leila's desires on fire. Her knees grew weak as she became totally entranced in the shadows of her secluded pool. Her mind was ablaze in pulsating ecstasy.

Then, the sizzling yearnings of her neglected passion erupted and vaporized Leila as she exploded into a cloud of quivering, sweet rapture.

*****

When the experience was over, Leila finally turned and looked where Mark had stood—but of course, he was not there.

Leila dressed quickly. She felt shameful for what had just happened.

In the last two visits to her beloved spring—the very spot where she was baptized—she had exposed herself to a man, and followed that with an ungodly straying of her passion to a height of completely, unfamiliar ecstasy.

Leila looked up at the modest steeple atop the church. "I need my guidance," she thought.

She walked over to the two large doors of Ebenezer Church, opened them and entered. An occasional spider web broke the monotony of the small wooden pews. She kneeled and gazed at the reverend's podium and the empty choir rows behind it. Sunlight sparkled down from the high windows onto her damp hair.

Leila shut her eyes and recalled a couple of Reverend McGraw's scornful quotes. "The Devil is a lion, while our Lord is a lamb," was the first that came to mind. "The Devil will sift you like wheat," was the next. Leila smiled, then prayed for a few minutes.

When finished, she stood up and walked out of the church she so dearly loved – and headed back to Destin.

Chapter 7

Spring was singing its last songs in Atlanta when Mark and Charlie McBride met for lunch at Gino's Sicilian Grill. Charlie, as usual, ordered the t-bone pizzaiola special and Mark ordered the tomato and mozzarella salad. The differences in taste were reflected in their waistlines.

The Memorial Day weekend had been chosen as the date for the large Destin party the two friends had been planning for over a month. Around ten Mackco Advertising Company guests had already accepted, including Albert J. Mackey and Caleb Hathcox. Of course, atop the list were Jane Anderson along with her entire "bitch corp"—led by staff sergeants Becky and Lisa. Mark's "friend" of the season, Brandi Baker, was invited as well as a number of Sandestin neighbors. Charlie had lined up Matthew Saunders, a very popular and talented one-man band, to provide the entertainment.

Mark slid a green olive atop a cut of tomato and asked, "Do we have room for a couple of more guests?"

"Sure," said Charlie. "Who?"

"Well, definitely Leila from Ebenezer Forest, and since she probably wouldn't come alone, I thought I might ask a friend of hers or two," said Mark, knowing full well that the invitation had already been extended to Leila and Amanda.

"Leila? You mean the little old lady from Ebenezer Church Road? Do you want her for a boat ornament in case we charter one?" asked Charlie sarcastically.

"No, she's just a wonderful person who I would like to have join us," replied Mark.

"We could get one of those senior buses to pick up the old ladies," said Charlie. "Should I buy a box of *Depends*?"

"Just don't make them feel uncomfortable if they do join us," requested Mark.

"What is the deal with this old lady? Exactly how old is she?" asked Charlie with serious curiosity.

"An inappropriate question," replied Mark.

"Just...please take a wild guess for my sake. 50, 60, 70?" persisted Charlie.

"Probably somewhere around fifty," answered Mark.

Charlie scowled and asked, "Why do you want to invite her and not my aunt?"

Mark dropped his eyes and took a sip of his tea. "She's a friend, Charlie, just a friend," he said.

"OK, OK," said Charlie relenting. "I'll buy some hamburger meat in case the old gals' teeth don't allow them to eat steak."

"Just keep an open mind," laughed Mark.

*****

American flags waved in the late May breeze. Destin was jammed full of revelers from throughout the South. Traffic had backed up for miles along Highway 98, as is always the case on major holiday weekends. Most of the tourists were concentrated on the beachfront. As the day lengthened, they returned to their vacation homes for traditional cookouts and celebrations like the one being held at Mark and Charlie's villa.

Two lively women exited the weathered vehicle and started toward the party. The smaller, prettier one, stopped to adjust her skirt. She looked at the crowd of mostly younger people and waited for her friend. They proceeded toward the end of the driveway, paused, and then approached the other guests. The crowd had assembled aside the inviting, fresh-water lake. Leila was looking for Mark, but could not locate him. Everyone turned and looked at the older ladies as they arrived.

Finally, Charlie McBride spoke up. "You must be Leila Hewitt," he said looking only at her.

"Yes, and this is my friend, Amanda Harrison," Leila answered loudly enough for nearly all to hear. "And who might you be?" asked Leila in a softer tone.

Charlie introduced himself and said, "Let me go tell Mark that you two have arrived." He walked toward the back porch of the villa and went inside. No one else spoke to the ladies.

Soon afterwards, the porch door swung open and Mark approached Leila and Amanda with a big smile on his face saying, "I'm so glad you could come!" as he shook both ladies' hands and introduced himself to Amanda.

"This is such a wonderful setting, thank you for including us," said Amanda.

"Let me show you two ladies around," said Mark as he took Leila's arm and led her and Amanda off towards the villa.

Becky turned to Jane and said, "I haven't seen our friend Mark this excited in a while. Who's the pretty old gal he is showing around, anyway?"

"She lives up in the country and runs a visitor's forest for students," said Jane.

"She is a very attractive older woman," expressed Lisa.

*****

An hour passed and Mark was still at Leila's side. He walked her and Amanda throughout the entire villa property. Eventually the threesome worked their way back to lounge chairs on the porch.

Mr. Mackey and his wife soon arrived at the party. Caleb Hathcox, his fiancée, and another couple accompanied the Mackeys. When Mark introduced Leila and Amanda to his boss and wife, Mr. Mackey looked at Leila's eyes and shook her hand for a long time. Mrs. Mackey grabbed her husband by his free arm and led him off the porch.

Jane, being her attentive self, walked over to Caleb when the introductions were over, pulled him aside and whispered, "What do you think of Ms. Leila?"

"She's a foxy old broad," Caleb whispered back. "I understand why Mark has been hanging around Ebenezer Forest."

"Mark is actually very interested in her forestry operation," replied Jane.

"Oh, really?" mused Caleb. "I'd wager he is much more interested in dragging his equipment through her shrubbery!"

Jane looked at Caleb, opened her mouth, and stuck her finger in it. "You nauseate me!" she said and walked away. Jane turned and glanced back at Mark and Leila as she departed.

*****

Brandi took a sip of her second beer and decided to approach Leila and Amanda. "Hello, I am Brandi Baker. I date Mark when we are both here in Destin," she said.

Becky overheard Brandi's introduction. Before Leila or Amanda could respond, Becky said, "We all date Mark."

Brandi frowned at Becky as she shook Leila's hand. Leila looked directly at Brandi and said, "He is a fine young man, Brandi. It is a pleasure to meet you."

Mark quickly spoke up, "Leila and Amanda, you haven't been to the pier—let's walk out to the lake and feed the bream before dinner. We'll be right back, Brandi."

Brandi looked at Becky and said, "Those two old gals are my mother's age."

Charlie began putting steaks on a huge, silver Texas barbeque pit. When the meat drippings hit the fire, the bellowing roar and smoke signaled dinner was near. Ladies brought potato salad, baked beans, and desserts to several tables as everyone gathered to eat.

Mark quieted the crowd and began delivering an appropriate blessing to commemorate the Memorial weekend. Leila and Amanda learned, for the first time, important information about their host when they were surprised to hear him say as a part of his prayer, "with special thanks to my father—who lost his life in combat so that all of us are better able to enjoy, in peace, the Lord's bounty on this Memorial Day weekend." When Mark finished his prayer, Jane walked over and gave him a warm hug.

At dinner, Mark sat with Amanda, Leila, and Brandi. He left the table briefly to restock the ice pitcher. It was Amanda's first opportunity, and she leaned over and whispered to Leila, "You didn't tell me Mark was so handsome, and I can't help but notice how much he is hanging around. Is that your new man-child?"

Amanda then winked at Leila. Leila looked at Amanda with a furrowed brow and rolled her eyes in a dismissing manner. They both laughed. However, it was already becoming quite apparent to everyone except Leila that she had the special attention of Mark Mabry.

When dinner started winding down, Matthew Saunders started winding up to play his keyboard. It was backed up by his pre-recorded rhythm. The party was on when the music started.

Charlie McBride, well into his pint of citrus vodka, jovially insisted that he and Mark help bridge the generation gap by asking Leila and Amanda for the first dance. Amanda was quick to accept and sashayed her way to the make-shift dance floor. Leila had to be more than politely encouraged. Every eye at the lakeside villa was upon the four varied-aged dancers.

The music was rather fast. Amanda and Charlie began to bump and glide, mostly bump. Charlie attempted to twirl her under his extended arm, but Amanda was too tall. She laughed and held her hand above Charlie's head, and he twirled.

Leila did not have to do much to look good. Her tight navy skirt and white blouse clung to her slender body—as she did to Mark. They danced fluidly and sensually as if they had done so before. Mark's eyes were intently upon Leila as she gracefully and innocently moved in perfect harmony with the music. Her sparkle and femininity was refreshing to even her harshest critics. The cheerful couple had been noticed by all.

A couple of songs later, Brandi's first offer to dance was from Charlie—but she waited for Mark's request. It followed immediately. The music was slow and Brandi held Mark closely. A number of guests were dancing while others were simply enjoying the festivities.

After a while, Mark and Brandi walked out to the pier. The

sun was dropping behind the trees on the far bank. When they returned later, Leila and Amanda approached them.

"We do not want to be the first ones to leave, we have had a wonderful time, but it has been a long day," said Leila. She leaned over and gave Mark a hug. "Thank you so much for including us," she added.

"We had so much fun. Thank you," said Amanda.

Mark, who was pleased by Leila's warmth, put his arm on her shoulder. "I'm so glad that the two of you enjoyed yourselves," he said, looking solely at Leila. "I hope to see you again, soon."

Within an hour, all were gone except Mark, Charlie, the "bitch corp", and Brandi. They had settled down on the porch. The flames still stirred on the open pit. When Brandi excused herself for a few minutes, Jane had her chance.

"Mark, what the hell is going on?" asked Jane.

Lisa, who normally didn't get agitated, quickly added, "I think you have been very rude to Brandi all afternoon!"

"I agree with that," said Charlie. "You certainly haven't treated her as your date." Charlie stared disapprovingly at Mark.

Marked frowned and looked toward the kitchen.

"Exactly how well does ole Leila know you, Maaaaark?" asked Becky in an obviously impaired drawl. Her face was red with alcohol and she took another sip of her umpteenth screwdriver. "If I didn't know you better," continued Becky, "I would think that ya had an 'Oed-i-pus complex' for that ooold lady!"

Mark shifted positions in his chair a couple of times and then stood up. "Does anyone have anything nice to say?" Mark asked. "If not, I'm going to go help clean up." He walked outside toward the deck.

"Let's not let it drop," said Jane. She quickly rose and followed Mark outside.

Jane caught up with Mark quickly, "Mark, you made a foolish spectacle of yourself! You have a lot to offer anyone, but you spent the whole afternoon following that old lady around like a tail-wagging dog!"

"You are way off base, Jane," said Mark, obviously irritated.

"No! You are way off base," said Jane. "I'm your best friend. If I won't tell you, who will? Everyone noticed it. There's no fool like a young fool!"

Mark turned away and started wiping down the outside tables. Jane stared at him for a full minute. She then made a loud grunt and stomped back inside to join the others.

*****

Back at the condominium, Amanda reached over and lowered the volume on the radio. She looked over at Leila and asked in a very serious tone, "Do you think young Mark has a puppy crush on you, Leila?"

"Gosh no," said Leila. "However, he is very handsome."

"He is young enough to be your son, Leila," said Amanda, very softly.

"Don't worry," said Leila as she leaned her head back on the recliner and closed her eyes. "That is exactly the way I think of him."

Chapter 8

The next morning, Amanda searched the Miramar Tennis Resort condo for her prescription eye glasses, but to no avail. She took the elevator down to Leila's car, yet still no glasses. "I've looked everywhere for them," said Amanda. "I believe I left the glasses at Mark's lake house. They cost so much, I have to get them back."

"Let's wait until a more respectable hour, and I will give Mark a call. It was a fun party though, wasn't it?" asked Leila.

"It was nice being around all those young people," replied Amanda. "If we were younger, and I didn't have ole Hank, we could have some fun with those boys!"

Leila raised an eyebrow and asked laughingly, "Did you really lose your glasses?"

Amanda roared and replied, "Heck, yes! I haven't been that conniving in years, honey!"

*****

Charlie guided the rented pontoon under the Destin Bridge into Choctawhatchee Bay. It was a fabulously clear day and other boats were darting everywhere in the emerald green water.

"Throw me a bottled water," shouted Jane to Mark, who was icing down the beverages he had just purchased at the marina into the cooler.

Jane, Brandi, and Lisa were sitting on the boat's bow in their very revealing two-piece bikinis. They had just left behind a group of adoring fraternity boys at the marina who had cat-called them out of sight. Still fighting monsters from last night, Becky was already dozed off atop a well-cushioned side seat. A blanket covered her face.

Ahead was "Crab Island". It was packed with boaters. Over two hundred boats had already beaten others to the popular shallow water hangout. Mark could see scores of sun bathers and swimmers of all ages wading about in the clear, emerald paradise. It was Destin and the sun was up—meaning it was time to party again.

Charlie spotted an open area where he could drop anchor. To get to the desired location, he had to carefully maneuver the pontoon boat to avoid hitting other craft. Tide currents made it difficult, but after several "back up and try it again"s, the task was eventually accomplished.

Mark opened a chilled green tea and watched as his scantily clad girlfriends dropped into the refreshing Gulf waters. It reminded him of Leila Hewitt easing herself into her freshwater spring aside Ebenezer Church.

The girls tried to coax Mark and Charlie into the water. Charlie preferred to stay near the beer cooler, while Mark chose to watch from the bow of the boat. Mark had enjoyed these boating adventures to "Crab Island" the first couple of dozen times, but as time passed, it was becoming more of a chore to perform for his guests than an event of real pleasure.

*****

Mark's cell phone rang, and he was glad to hear Leila's voice. Leila asked about Amanda's glasses and was happy to learn that they had been noticed during the morning cleanup. Mark knew exactly where they were safely secured. He kindly offered to bring them to the Miramar Tennis Resort, but Leila said she and Amanda would come over later in the day to retrieve them. Mark said he would call after 5 p.m. or as soon as the group returned to the villa. His thought of seeing Leila again later in the day was a pleasant one.

*****

Amanda's husband Hank worked all week at their small dairy. He loved his wife dearly and spent as much of his leisure time with her as she would allow. Amanda knew Hank was getting lonely with her away in Destin. When he called and offered to drive in from their country home, she could hardly refuse his visit. Leila wanted to give them an opportunity to be alone and suggested that she would pick up Amanda's glasses when Mark called.

Later that afternoon, Mark and the others finally returned from "Crab Island". Charlie and the guests began packing for their trips home. It was 5:45 p.m. when Mark walked Brandi to her car and hugged her goodbye. Twenty minutes later, Charlie walked out the back door of the villa and departed to Atlanta. Mark immediately picked up his cell phone and called Leila.

A half hour later, Mark waited until he heard Leila enter the porch and approach his back door before he opened it. Mark and Leila looked at each other just a breath longer than the circumstances would have expected.

"You look wonderful," said Mark.

"You certainly know how to make an older lady feel good," laughed Leila.

"I'm telling the truth," Mark replied.

"Let's sit on the porch," said Mark as he pulled up a cushioned seat for Leila. He grabbed a lawn chair from nearby for himself and sat beside her.

Leila asked Mark about his day, and the conversation drifted into stories about Mark's friends. Leila was actually quite curious about the young people she had just met the day before.

Mark talked about his relationship with Charlie and Jane. He asked about Amanda. Leila shared with Mark some of her and Amanda's adventures together as young girls.

Mark could smell the sweet scent of Leila's fragrance as they visited. They laughed and talked, and he found himself being drawn to her in an arousing way.

*****

The shadows of the house grew long and were beginning to reach far across the lake. The water was totally calm now, and the only activity was a few small birds looking for supper before dark.

"Would you like to watch the sunset on the lake deck?" asked Mark.

Leila could feel her chest tighten. "That would be nice," she replied. "But first, let's put Amanda's glasses in my purse before I forget them."

Mark went into the villa and brought the glasses to Leila. They walked outside and across the back yard, stepped onto the deck, and took the two chairs closest to the lake. A light mist was starting to drift above the reflecting water. Everything was warm and calm. For the first time, there was a long silence.

Leila slipped her shoes off and tucked her legs under her sundress. She straightened up a little higher in the chair and looked at Mark.

Mark watched her intently. It was her eyes, as always, that stirred him most.

Leila spoke first, "Mark, I want you to know how much I am enjoying becoming your friend."

"I want you to know," Mark said, stumbling with his own words, "how attracted I am to you." He reached over and put his hand on Leila's arm.

Leila's eyes widened. She was taken aback. "Where is this heading?" she asked herself as her mind raced.

Leila took her other hand and placed it on top of Mark's. She began to breathe heavily. Mark's hand squeezed Leila's arm as they touched each other.

They sat quietly for a few moments, the energy from each of them sparking to the other.

"You meet so many people in your life," Mark whispered as they held each other's gaze, "and maybe only one or two really touch your soul—and you touch mine."

"You touch me too, Mark, but--" said Leila, stopping abruptly as Mark quite unexpectedly reached up and stroked her face with his right hand. He looked deeply into her eyes. Leila felt magnetized.

Mark eased his hand slowly into Leila's hair. He gently and softly turned her face toward his. She did not resist. She was being overcome.

He leaned his muscular body over hers, so slowly, and then began pressing against her.

Leila felt weak and entranced.

His face neared hers. As it did, she spread her lips. She could smell the heat of his breath.

He kissed her ever so softly. The touch of his warm, wet mouth to hers left her limp, defenseless, and receptive.

She was trembling. She felt so young, so alive, so steamy!

And then—they heard the SPLASH at the same time! Both turned quickly toward the sound. Through the impending darkness they saw two fishermen in a small bateau approaching the end of the pier. A large jitterbug darted from the center of the splash as it was retrieved back toward the boat.

Mark moved his hand and fell back into his seat. Leila straightened her hair and tried to shield her face.

"Good evening, ma'am. Good evening, son," said one of the men, whose gray hair flickered in the fading light. The other man appeared to be younger than Mark.

Mark could barely make a sound, and Leila was benumbed. The fishermen casually worked their boat around the front of the dock for what seemed like an eternity.

As the two strangers disappeared into the night, Mark and Leila could barely hear the young man when he said, "What the hell was that? She was old enough to be his mother!"

Leila felt scorched. She could feel the tears coming and did not want Mark to see them. She stood and walked quickly off the dock. She felt mortified and humiliated as she made her way into the villa. In the silence of a bathroom, Leila could hold her tears back no longer. She wept.

She tried to pull herself together, but it was impossible. Her tears streamed down her cheeks as she looked into the mirror at her aging face. "What a fool I am," she thought. "Why, when a good man finally enters my life, does he have to be half my age? What an embarrassment! What a nightmare!"

Mark sat alone, his hands in his own face now. "I will give her enough time—however long it takes," he thought. "I will not let this end this way—turned into something ugly!" he decided. Minutes later, he walked into the house and approached Leila. Her face was red and she would not look at Mark.

"It is getting late and I should be getting back to the condo," Leila said.

Mark knew better than to try and change her mind, but he couldn't hold back what was in his heart, "Leila, I have no regrets at all about kissing you."

The warmth and depth Mark saw in Leila's eyes just a short while before had given way to a look of distress and shame-faced pain. He continued, "What those fishermen or others think means nothing to me. I don't know how to say this, but—" Mark stopped in mid-sentence as Leila interrupted.

"Don't say it, Mark, please," gasped Leila. "If I were younger, things could be different."

"Your life has never been about trying to find happiness in the minds of other people, I hope it is not a consideration now," said Mark feeling Leila slip away.

Leila turned and looked straight at Mark. "It is not a question of my happiness," she said. "It's not fair to you, Mark, I think you are very special and I am attracted to you, you know, but our age difference is too much."

There was silence. "Don't you think I should have a say in that?" asked Mark. He hesitated. "Look, Leila, we don't have to live this out tonight, just don't close the door. We are just getting to know each other—and as far as I am concerned, we are both...well...young."

Leila smiled at Mark's characterization.

Mark reached out and touched her hand. But Leila stood up, smiled again, and said, "Time to go."

Mark walked Leila to her car. He felt tense and drained. When she opened the driver's side door, he touched her shoulder from behind. Leila turned around and looked into Mark's eyes. She could see deep emotion all over his face.

She was breathing heavily again. She could feel her heart pounding and the tension in her lungs.

"Mark...oh, Mark...I must go," Leila said. She turned, climbed into her old car, and slowly drove away.

*****

"Did you get my glasses, baby?" asked Amanda as Leila entered the condo. "I haven't been able to read a thing," she added.

"I have them, where is Hank?" asked Leila.

"He's gone," replied Amanda, "but thanks for leaving us alone for the hugging."

"Let's go outside and look at the Gulf," said Leila. "We need to talk."

"Uh-oh," thought Amanda. Leila never needed to talk. The two friends walked out onto the large deck and could see a bright, full moon rising over the Gulf from the east. They took a seat on two large lounge chairs. Leila pulled Amanda's glasses from her purse and handed them to her.

"Is this about tonight?" asked Amanda. "Did that boy do

something to you, Leila?"

"Let me put it this way," replied Leila, "he is doing something to me. I think I am developing strong feelings for him."

Amanda was startled! "My word, Leila! Are you crazy? You told me you thought of him as a son! What in the hell happened?" she asked.

"We kissed tonight—on the dock behind his villa," Leila said in a low whisper.

"You did what? WHAT ON EARTH!" exclaimed Amanda. "Did you fornicate with him, too?"

"No. Not yet," Leila said with a hearty laugh.

"You have lost your ever-loving mind, girl! I'm gonna call a doctor and have you examined! Now listen to me, Leila, have you ever thought that he may be after your money?" asked Amanda.

Leila did not answer. She was thinking.

After a full thirty seconds, Amanda spoke in a slower, deeper voice, "Leila, I love you. This can't be happening. Remember what we used to say about that damn old fool, Mr. Stuckers? You would never be acting like this if you were thinking straight. If God wanted you two to be together, He would have made you the same age. I am begging you to come to your senses, Leila. What you are telling me is wrong!"

Leila stood up, leaned over and kissed Amanda on the forehead. She then walked to the bedroom and sprawled out in the bed, totally exhausted.

Chapter 9

Mark sat at the red light on North Peach Street and watched Jane walk out of the Atlanta Police sub-station. She recognized his car and waved her long arm at him. Mark pulled up next to the curb, and she quickly jumped inside.

"Hey, Janie," Mark said as he leaned over and planted a quick smack on her cheek.

"Hello, you handsome fellow," Jane replied. "Where are you taking me for lunch?"

"How about Pocarello's Italian Café?" Mark asked. "It's not very far away."

"Perfect," Jane responded as Mark darted through the heavy noontime traffic. They arrived at the popular restaurant before the expected lunch crowd and were seated in a cozy corner table. The waitress lit a short, fat candle and brought some fresh garlic bread in a brown wicker basket.

"How's the world of sex crimes—anything particularly interesting?" Mark asked.

"Just the standard rapes and molestations," replied Jane. "Speaking of sex crimes, what was the deal with all the attention you gave Ms. Leila at the party Saturday night?" continued Jane, as she got right to her main topic of interest.

"Not again," answered Mark with a big frown. "I thought you said your piece Saturday and I really—uh—I was hoping for a relaxing lunch."

"Well, have you talked to her since the weekend?" asked Jane.

Mark rolled his eyes and said, "What are you doing, conducting an investigation? If so, read me my rights."

"No, I am writing an article for 'Old Lady Magazine'," Jane said. "Have you talked to her since?"

Mark sat taller in his chair, and said in a suddenly more serious tone, "Leila came over to the villa Sunday after you all left, we kissed, and I really liked it. Put that in your article!"

"You've got to be kidding me, Mark! Tell me this isn't true," gasped Jane.

"Would you two lovebirds like to order wine with your lunches?" asked a waitress as she suddenly appeared with a pitcher of water and filled the two glasses on the table.

"I'll take a glass of the house pinot noir," replied Jane.

"So will I," said Mark.

Jane looked at Mark and said, "Bring him the oldest bottle that you have in your cellar."

Mark shook his head no at the waitress, who turned and smirked as she walked away.

"Tell me you are lying, Mark," Jane pressed.

Mark looked straight at Jane and said, very slowly, "Jane, you and I have been friends for a long time, and I ought to be able to tell you the truth without you being so judgmental. We kissed—I liked it—I like her. I really like her."

Jane's mouth dropped a little. Her eyes squinted and she touched her temple with her right hand. There was a long period of silence. Finally Jane spoke, "Mark, there is a real difference between a friend 'being judgmental', as they say, versus discussing 'good judgment' with someone they really care about."

"Good judgment is totally subjective," said Mark. "We are thirty two years old—neither of us has found the person that we are looking for. You don't really know Leila Hewitt, and I realize you don't understand – I am not absolutely sure I do either – I am just telling you that there is a real attraction that is hard to describe, that is all that I am saying."

"Well, let's just step back for a minute and look at this situation," said an obviously agitated Jane. "You are one of the most handsome guys on earth, you can have Brandi and anyone else you want, and you appear to be experiencing some goofball obsession. What would you think if it were me doing the same thing?"

The waitress returned with the two glasses of wine and the menus. "I'll take the lunchtime lasagna special," said Jane. Mark ordered the Italian salad. The restaurant had filled with patrons, and the inside temperature was rising.

"Here's the way I see it, Mark," Jane continued. "We are both idealists when it comes to who we date. It is true that you and I haven't been able to find someone who can pass our tests—or meet our expectations—but please don't handle it with withdrawal and some surrealistic fixation on a mother figure."

Mark snickered and said, "Those tests you are talking about sound more like what the "bitch corp" does than what I do. Your committee has all the tests. No poor guy is ever able to pass them."

"You passed them, Mark," said Jane, with a very serious expression on her face.

Mark smiled and said, "You mean I passed them until I became interested in a very special woman – who happens to be older? Where does that leave you when you get older, Ms. Jane?

Don't you think you might be being a little tough on me?"

"Maybe so," said Jane, "but every time you make a choice you eliminate a lot of others." She took a slow sip of her pinot noir and looked at her dear friend.

Mark looked back at Jane. "I appreciate your concern," he said in a lower and slower tone, "and I hope what I tell you will remain private for now. I'm really interested in Leila and I expect, as my friend, you will support me—whatever I choose."

She could tell from the look on his face that he meant it.

*****

After lunch, Jane walked through the police station into her office and picked up the phone, "Hello, Charlie, this is Jane, how about meeting me for lunch tomorrow?" He readily agreed.

When she hung up the phone, she shuffled arrest reports for a few minutes and made another call. She called Caleb Hathcox, "Would you like to meet me, Charlie, Becky, and Lisa tomorrow at Calendar's for lunch. We are all worried about Mark. Please don't say anything to him." She walked over to the window and looked at the Atlanta skyline. It was starting to rain.

Caleb Hathcox loved a little excitement among friends. When he hung up the telephone with Jane, he chuckled to himself for a moment. He had observed Jane's protective attitude toward Mark on many occasions and knew that her feelings for Mark were deeper than she would ever admit. "This will be fun," he thought. He stood up and marched directly over to Mark's office.

When Caleb arrived at Mark's door it was closed. He opened it anyway. Mark was reading at his desk. "How's your little ole lady down in Florida?" Caleb asked with a big smile.

Mark assessed the attack immediately. He slowly looked up at Caleb with feigned anguish on his face and said, "She and her friend were lost in an automobile accident on Interstate 10 last night!"

The smile on Caleb's face vanished and his eyes doubled in size as he gazed back at Mark in absolute shock.

Mark picked up a file on his desk and extended it toward Caleb, "Would you please review this file for me?"

"Did that really happen? Is she really gone?" asked Caleb.

"I am too upset to discuss it," said Mark. "Please help me with this file," he added. He then rose, walked past Caleb, and exited the room.

"Mark, did that really happen?" pleaded Caleb again as he followed Mark down the hall.

Mark never turned around. "No!" he answered as he rounded a corner and disappeared from sight.

Chapter 10

Time was never in a hurry in Ebenezer Forest, and Leila's week had moved very slowly. Even a walk from her back porch, down the long hallway, past the mirrors, to the front door seemed to take forever. She spent much of her time thinking about what had been developing between her and Mark Mabry.

"I have a biological attraction to a young man. That's all it is," she confessed to herself. She remembered Brother McGraw's preaching about sins of the flesh.

Twice during the week, Amanda had repeated her warnings to Leila concerning Mark—and Leila had listened. Very flattered by Mark's attention, Leila was in turmoil. "I've got to fight this sinful desire!" she admonished herself repeatedly.

One night, Leila woke abruptly from a deep sleep. She sat up quickly in her bed. Her nightgown was drenched with perspiration. A lustful dream full of passionate kisses with Mark had both stirred and startled her!

Leila hastily turned on her bedside light and began to read from the Book of Romans:

"For those who live according to the flesh set
their minds on the things of flesh, but those who

live according to the Spirit set their minds on the things of the Spirit. For to set the mind on the flesh is death, but to set the mind on the Spirit is life and peace."

Leila had been loyal to God's word all of her life. But now she felt a sense of drifting astray. Each morning she continued to take her usual walk to the church—yet without her traditional bath in the private spring. She did not want to risk yearning for Mark in a lascivious way. She would return to the swing on her front porch and read her books. She attempted to concentrate on the things that dominated her thoughts before she met Mark—namely her forest and her Lord.

Leila knew, like every woman always does, when she "might" again hear from the important man in her life. She fully expected Mark would call and ask her to show him the church, it was just a matter of time. Amanda had joined her on the front porch on the morning that Mark called.

"I would love for you to show me Ebenezer Church as you kindly offered," Mark said. "I have been looking so forward to it. When would be a good time for you?"

Leila did not want to admit to herself that even Mark's voice sent unfamiliar chills through her body.

"This weekend is fairly open. Is Saturday at 10:30 in the morning possible?" Leila asked. She hoped that Mark did not detect her shortness of breath.

It's perfect!" responded Mark. "I can't wait to visit it with you! See you Saturday."

"Have a safe drive," said Leila.

Leila turned and looked at Amanda. She could feel her heart racing. "Do you know a good heart doctor, I think I am having tachycardia?" she asked with a big smile on her face.

"Hush now," said Amanda. "There ain't nothing tacky about you. From our talking, I can see that you finally have this situation under control—and God is not going to let you be played for a fool."

"You are right, Amanda," said Leila. "I have my feet squarely on the ground. I know it would never work, and well, it would... uh...really just never work."

*****

Mark purchased two new lawn chairs for his Destin villa and had them in the back of a borrowed truck. He turned onto Ebenezer Church Road and recognized Jake Delaughter standing in front of his old store. Jake did not recognize the vehicle, so Mark slowed to a near stop to wave. Jake waved back friskly to let Mark know it had been a while.

At the oak tree curve, Mark got his second glimpse of the golden doe. She was feeding in the roadside clover and was spooked by Mark's approach. Mark could see her white tail raised in the air as she scampered into the forest.

Leila was sitting in a yard swing waiting for Mark. He pulled the truck up to the front of the house and walked over to her. The sundress she had chosen to wear was white and thin—it made her look more like a beautiful young bride than a lady about to take an outdoor hike.

The dress clung tightly to Leila's body, revealing her every secret. She was spreading fresh chopped corn for her family of birds and squirrels that had gathered around her swing. The animals gave Mark a rude glance and scurried away.

"Am I interrupting breakfast?" asked Mark.

"Lunch—I fed these little friends breakfast at 6 a.m. this morning," Leila said. She picked up a sparkling blue scarf she had placed on the fence.

"It looks like that scarf has been sewn from your eyes," Mark said as he stared at Leila's beauty in the morning sun. She looked back for a long second, then remembered her promises to herself.

"Thank you, Mark. I'm ready to go," Leila said.

"May I take my camera?" asked Mark.

"As long as you do not take a picture of me," said Leila.

"Let's argue about that later," replied Mark. He reached back into the truck and grabbed the camera.

Leila held the church road gate open until Mark passed. She shut it, and followed Mark into the quiet splendor of Ebenezer Forest.

Even though the sun had been up for hours, the leaves were still damp and glistening. Leila eased down the narrow lane silently, as she had done countless times before.

Mark's steps were less experienced in the forest. The rustling sound of his feet was soon muffled by the bubbling of the familiar Hominy Creek. When they approached a white sandy beach, Mark stopped to take a picture. He reached down and touched the water with his fingers. Even in the summer heat it felt frigid.

Without thinking, Mark asked, "You bathe in this cold water?" He instantly knew that he should not have revealed what he was thinking.

Leila did not answer. She bent over from the waist and picked the petal of a wild flower. "Smell this," she said. "It has one of the sweetest aromas of the forest."

They crossed the small bridge and walked between the ligustrums leading up to the church. When they arrived at the exact spot from which he had watched Leila bathe, Mark paused and took a picture of the church and spring. Leila felt just a twinge of discomfort when she noticed what he was doing. She veered safely out of the lens' view.

Mark continued walking along the creek toward the spring. Leila angled off toward the church. Mark took another picture and then caught up with Leila.

When Leila reached the steps she started speaking of her beloved church's history, "These steps were made of old railway ties that were fine cut and polished by my great uncle. The hinges were made in Boston." She pointed to them on the outside of each door.

"The doors were donated to Ebenezer Church by the Southern Judson Association when the building was constructed in 1895," Leila added. Mark walked closer to Leila. She opened the large doors of the church, and they entered.

"No pictures inside please, Mark. Reverend McGraw would never allow any to be taken here," Leila said as she took a seat on the front row without looking at Mark.

Mark could sense Leila's detachment. It was obvious that she was making every effort to keep her emotional distance. Not wanting to make her uncomfortable, Mark followed her to the front row and seated himself across the aisle.

Leila sat without speaking. After a while, she turned and took a long look at the striking, well-proportioned young man sitting in her church. She recalled how respective families always sat on different sides of the aisle at weddings. "I mustn't be too stand-offish," she thought. She looked back toward the podium.

The church was totally quiet.

"Reverend McGraw is the only minister I can really remember well as a young child," Leila began softly. "My mother told me that one Easter Sunday morning, when I was only four, we had a Reverend Lowe back then. He was ranting and raving, actually screaming the sermon. When he paused, my Mama said I shouted out, so everybody could hear me, 'MAMA, WHY IS THIS PREACHER HOLLERING SO LOUD?' Mama said the whole church broke out in laughter, and I don't even remember saying it."

She turned and looked at Mark and asked, "Did your mama ever tell you stories like that?"

Mark's eyes fell downward, "My mother left me and my father just before he was sent overseas and killed in action; I was very young. She died in a car accident later. I cannot remember her very well. All I have is a couple of pictures. I was raised by my Uncle Billy. He passed away when I was nineteen. He brought me up in the Presbyterian Church."

"I'm so sorry that you don't have more memories about your parents," said Leila.

Leila and Mark sat in silence. It was broken by the sound of a small scratching noise coming from the direction of the choir pews. There was another shuffling sound and a slight pitter-patter.

Mark turned toward Leila and said with a big grin, "You're quieter than a church mouse!" Leila burst out in laughter. They both stood up and walked out of the church into the bright sunlight.

"Come see," said Leila as she led Mark around to the backside of the church. A small cemetery was nestled at the forest's edge. A short white gate squeaked as Leila opened it. Well over a hundred memorial stones, of all ages, rose from the short grass. They were all small and unpretentious.

Leila walked over to the graves of her parents and looked

down. A full vase of Leila's freshly picked roses were perched atop each mound. Mark noticed that there remained one empty space next to where Leila's parents rested.

Mark watched Leila as she stood above her family. He began to feel an uncontrollable swelling of grief rising from his abdomen. The pain moved into his chest. He remembered standing alone above each of his parents. They were buried in different states. He felt a lump in his throat. He remembered how grieved he was when his Uncle Billy was placed into the earth in a grave like these. A tingling sensation arose in his head as he felt his face swell with moisture.

Leila turned and looked at Mark. His blues eyes were wet with tears. She could see droplets oozing gently down his cheeks. The emotion that Leila saw in Mark's face made her forget the caution of her many self-admonishments.

"Oh, Mark!" Leila cried out as she became overwhelmed with compassion.

She threw her arms around Mark, pulling him tightly against her body. She buried her face deeply into his chest and began to sob.

Mark pressed his own wet face down into Leila's hair. They held each other silently in this small and shadowed cemetery in the woods.

A full minute passed. They wiped their faces, and Leila led Mark back to the church. When they reached the spring, they stopped and Leila whispered, "I haven't cried like that since my father passed."

"It has been a very long time for me, too," Mark said softly.

Leila held Mark's arm, and they walked out of Ebenezer Forest together.

Chapter 11

Leila and Mark noticed the wind starting to bend the tops of the taller oaks as they returned to Ebenezer Church Road. Mark remembered that a very late-season weather front was to move through the panhandle around noon. They walked briskly through the gate and took the short walk westward toward Leila's home. There was a billowing black wall of sky ahead, and they knew a serious storm was coming.

Leila's phone was ringing as they approached the back porch, "I'll catch it later," Leila said. "Mark, please help me secure all of those loose items in the yard."

A powerful gust of wind howled down Ebenezer Road as heavy raindrops began to fall. The temperature dropped rapidly, causing the couple to experience immediate chill.

"Please grab those garbage cans, Mark," said Leila anxiously. She picked up a bucket and a rake, and hurried them to a small shed. "And please bring those small plants onto the porch for me," Leila again shouted as she reached above her head to pull a small hummingbird feeder out of a plum tree.

Mark could hear Leila's phone ringing again. The dark sky abruptly broke loose with huge, blinding bursts of cold rain. It started to pour in ferocious, whirling gusts. The yard and its flowers were being whipped hard and getting inundated with vicious fury. Water was soon gushing off of the porch's gable. The wind accelerated even more. The fruit trees in Leila's yard were bending to the ground. A birdhouse flew out of a small oak tree, and Leila ran it down. Driving sheets of rain were pooling in the yard. As Leila ran through a standing puddle, she lost her balance in the slippery grass. Mark was securing the doors on the shed when he saw Leila fall and slide to a harmless stop.

"Help me, please, Mark!" Leila shouted. He quickly ran over to her and lifted her drenched body from the ground so that she could get back on her feet. They laughed briefly.

Mark looked down at Leila's soaked, white dress. It was tightly fused to every curve of her body. He could easily see her copper-colored areolas. Her chilled perky nipples protruded through her thin and transparent clothing. She looked innocently up at him and saw his observation. She covered herself with her hands, turned, and hurriedly raced through the storm to the safety of her back porch.

When Mark joined her, he kicked off his wet shoes. Then, reaching down to his waist, he quickly pulled his soaked polo shirt over his head. "What a blinding downpour!" he said.

Leila glanced at Mark's half-naked body. She noticed his chiseled chest and shoulders—and his flat, rippled and hard stomach.

Mark squeezed his shirt, and water dripped heavily to the floor. "I'll get this up later," he said.

Mark saw Leila looking at him. Their eyes locked. He walked slowly towards her. Leila was trembling. "I'm so cold," she muttered.

The rain and wind were pounding the windows and roof of the porch. Mark put his arms around Leila and pulled her shivering body against his naked chest. They did not speak.

Leila could feel Mark's warmth and pulled herself even closer into his embrace. Only thin, rain-drenched cloth separated her breasts from his hot chest.

Mark leaned his face down against hers. A bolt of lightning erupted from the sky and struck a nearby tree. The flaming emotions within Leila's heart began to spread like wildfire through her body. She was breathing heavily.

Mark tilted her face toward his and kissed her gently. "I love the way you taste," he said softly. His tongue teased her lips, and then he eased it into her mouth. She sucked it gently at first - and then harder.

The wet sundress was high on Leila's hips. Mark eased his hands to the bottom seam of the garment and slowly lifted it above her bosom.

Leila was in a swoon-like trance. Mark reached around and unhooked her light bra as he tenderly kissed Leila's lips, neck, and then her lips again. The bra fell to the floor.

Mark could hear a low, erotic, purr coming from Leila's throat.

She felt vulnerable and helpless, yet at the same time explosive with passion.

Mark lifted Leila's dripping dress slowly above her head and tossed it on the couch. She was totally exposed. He reached around and placed his large, warm hands on Leila's buttocks and pressed her toward him.

"Oh, no, Mark," Leila cried softly. "Not this!"

Mark bent lower and kissed the underside of her breasts, one at a time, very slowly. He pulled her white, naked body even closer to him with his powerful arms.

"Oh...oh my...oh my," moaned Leila submissively.

The storm was at its height. The house was shaking from the powerful wind and sheets of rain. With every new gale-like blast, the porch door violently banged back and forth.

Mark took Leila's hand and led it down to the front of his pants.

She could feel his large, thick mass and did not move her hand. She gently caressed the hot pulsating object of her dreams. Then, she squeezed and explored its heat at the same time.

Leila could feel the devil catching hold of her resistance and ripping it from her weakening body.

Mark unloosened his buckle and let his trousers and underwear drop to the floor. Leila saw his enlarged manhood. She gasped. The pure shock of its size, and its intimidation, startled Leila.

Mark surprised Leila even more by dropping to his knees and burying his face into her lower body.

Leila rolled her eyes and drifted swiftly into Ebenezer Church. A lightning bolt struck again. "It was a sign from above," she knew!

A lifetime of prayer and worship stormed quickly through Leila's mind.

"This is not the way it is supposed to be!" her brain flashed. Her readings from the Bible, and the warnings of Reverend McGraw, leaped into the forefront of her consciousness. She remembered her promise to Amanda. In an instant, every fear she had about the difference in age between herself and Mark—and her commitment to God—jolted her into stark consciousness and alarm!

"No! No! Oh no! Oh, my God! NO!" she screamed. Leila pushed Mark's head from between her thighs and bolted away from him. She slipped and crashed face-first to the wooden floor. Her lip burst widely in the fall.

"NO!" she screamed again, as she crawled to her feet. She fell once more, this time out of the porch door, naked, into the pounding rain. She rose and ran toward the shed.

Mark, totally shocked by Leila's sudden breakdown, bolted up from his knees and raced to follow her. He forgot that his underwear and jeans were still around his feet.

The entanglement caused him to fall. He jumped up—still

nude—and raced down the steps to catch and calm Leila.

WHOP!

Mark never saw the piece of lumber that knocked him uncon-scious and ripped his skull apart.

Chapter 12

Clyde Branson had worked for Leila Hewitt for over twenty years. He adored her. She gave the Branson clan a large turkey each and every Thanksgiving and Christmas, and a ham on Easter. When Little Clyde got sick, Leila took him to a specialist in Tallahassee and made sure he received the treatment that he needed. Leila was part of Clyde's family.

When Clyde heard the report that there were severe thunderstorms in the area, he knew Leila would need some help. He took a few minutes to secure things at his house and grabbed his raincoat. He shouted to his wife, Penny, where he was going and rushed over to Ebenezer Forest. The storm arrived before he did.

The first thing that Clyde noticed was a strange truck in Ms. Leila's driveway. It had a few dents on the fenders and didn't look like the kind of transportation that usually carried people to her home. It was already raining hard.

When Clyde saw the Georgia license plate, he became a little more concerned. There was no one on the front porch, and he could see that there were no lights on in the main house. His worry was heightened.

Clyde exited the truck running toward the right side of the home with the intent of going into the back yard. The wind and rain were beating the rooftop and the nearby trees. A powerful lightning bolt struck nearby. As he rounded the corner he could see the porch door banging back and forth with every gust of wind.

"No! No! Oh no! Oh, my God! NO!" Clyde heard Leila scream. It froze him like a rock for a second.

Fear, anger and rage all gripped Clyde around the throat. His beloved Miss Leila was being assaulted!

Clyde's adrenalin rushed him into a totally protective mode! At his feet was a pile of building material he had stacked the week before. He picked up a three foot piece of 2 x 4 lumber and advanced toward the door. "No time to get my gun from my truck," he thought.

Clyde looked through the porch screen and was horrified to see a nude man kneeling near Ms. Leila. She screamed "No!" again!

Suddenly, the lady he loved and admired exploded, naked, out the porch door into the raging storm! She was fleeing like a wild animal running from a predator! Clyde crouched down so that the rapist could not see him approach. Moving quickly to arrive at the door at the same time as the stranger, Clyde cocked his board. He timed his swing perfectly. Just as the assailant's face appeared at the door, Clyde struck him in the forehead with all of his might.

WHOP!

The naked villain's head exploded with the blow. He collapsed to the ground, face-down and motionless.

Clyde could see blood gushing from the man's wound. Fairly confident that the criminal was alone, Clyde ran after Leila who had entered the shed. She had her face buried in her hands and was sobbing. He took off his raincoat and wrapped it around her trembling arms.

Leila looked up. Blood from her lip was trickling down her chin. Clyde was not the man Leila was expecting.

"Clyde! What are you doing here?" Leila cried out. The raincoat did not cover her below the waist. She clenched her legs and rolled her shivering body into a tight ball.

"It's OK, Ms. Leila, you are safe now," said Clyde. The shed was shaking from the powerful wind and rain that was continuing outside. Another bolt of lightning struck the earth nearby.

From the direction of Leila's house – over the noise of the violent tempest – Clyde faintly heard the scream of another woman.

"LEILA! LEILA! LEILA!" Amanda wailed in the distance.

Clyde looked out of the shed and saw Amanda step over the naked man's body and quickly enter the back kitchen porch of the house.

"I'll be right back to get ya, Miss Leila. It's Ms. Amanda, I'll get her. Don't move," Clyde said. He ran into the raging storm toward the porch.

Leila obeyed. The sudden appearance of Clyde, and his seeing her naked, had catapulted Leila into a deep withdrawal.

Clyde stepped over the motionless man and entered the porch.

Amanda heard him enter and raced back to him, "WHERE'S LEILA?" she screamed.

"Call the police, Ms. Amanda," Clyde said.

"Where's Leila?" repeated Amanda frantically. She had recognized Mark when she stepped over his naked body. "Did he rape her? Is she alive? WHERE'S LEILA?" Amanda demanded even louder.

"Calm down, Ms. Amanda, she's safe now," said Clyde. He

saw Leila's cell phone on a table. He picked it up and dialed 911. The porch door blew open from a gust of wind as the storm continued to rage around them.

"Send the police and an ambulance to Miss Leila Hewitt's place on Ebenezer Church Road. There's been a rape and..." started Clyde.

"RAAAAPPEEE!" screamed Amanda. "WHERE'S LEILA?"

"Hush now – please!" said Clyde trying to calm Amanda down.

"It's another lady here, ma'am. Please hurry," said Clyde. Click.

Clyde grabbed an umbrella from its indoor bucket and one of the blankets on Leila's nearby couch. He held the umbrella over Amanda's head as they exited the porch and sidestepped Mark's body.

"Is he dead?" asked Amanda.

"I hope so," answered Clyde, as he and Amanda hurried to the shed.

The rain began to subside as they sloshed across the inundated yard toward the shed. Upon entering the dimly lit shelter, Amanda fell to her knees and wrapped her long arms around Leila.

"Oh, baby!" Amanda cried. "What has that dirty bastard done to you?"

Leila had a blank stare and did not answer. Her face was pallid except for the heavy blood on her lip and chin. Her mouth hung open, and she was uncontrollably shaking.

Amanda and Clyde helped Leila to her feet, wrapping the blanket around her head and face. Leila had to lean on Amanda for support. Clyde intentionally held the umbrella in a low position in front of Leila's face as they left the shelter. He did not want her to see Mark's body. He thought it best to proceed at an angle toward the front of the house, rather than have Leila step over Mark, who was lying near the back porch. Halfway to their destination, one of the storm's final bursts of energy blew the umbrella away from Leila's head. The blanket that had covered her face flopped aside, and she got her first full unexpected view of Mark's body – still naked and motionless in the wet grass.

"NOOOO! Leila screamed at the top of her lungs. "NO! GOD OH! GOD NO! NO!"

Leila flung the blanket from around her shoulders. Clyde's raincoat fell from her body as she ran sobbing, and nude, toward Mark.

"OH, MY GOD!" she cried out.

When Leila saw the blood pooled around Mark's head, she shrieked louder in horror, "OH NO! HE'S DEAD!"

Clyde pried Leila's hand away from Mark's lifeless arm. With her arm now free, Leila reached out to Mark's face and whipped it fully around toward her. The sight of his gaping wound shocked Leila into further emotional collapse. Leila tried to hold on to Mark as Clyde and Amanda wrestled her away from his unclothed backside. They were soon able to subdue her enough to get her into the house and into her bed.

When the rain eventually subsided, nothing at all seemed to move in Ebenezer Forest.

Chapter 13

An emergency medical ambulance and three Walton County deputy sheriff's cars raced down Highway 81. The loud and ear-piercing sound of sirens was a huge alarm signal for the normally quiet countryside. Every person within miles knew that something very ominous had occurred.

Jake Delaughter could hear the screaming vehicles as they approached Ebenezer Church Road. When they turned in his direction, he hurried out to the roadside. He could hear the rubber tires screeching around the graveled curves before they came into sight. The three lawmen's cars were the first to race past the old store. Jake got a quick look at the grim-faced deputies and suspected there was crime involved. The ambulance was right behind them.

"Ambulances mean real trouble on Ebenezer Church Road, they are usually followed by hearses," Jake thought when he saw the long white vehicle speed by. He was very disturbed. "I've got to get down there. Something terrible must have happened!" he told himself as he hurried to his truck.

*****

Upon arriving at their destination, four junior deputies and Colonel Max Barnett scrambled out of their patrol vehicles. The sirens had been quieted, but the lights above their cars remained flashing. Clyde Branson motioned the men over to the side yard. They could see the nude man near the back porch—Mark was still in a face down position in the wet grass.

"See if he is dead, Tommy," Colonel Barnett growled. Deputy Tommy Tucker was Barnett's right hand man.

The Colonel was huge, with bear-like hands and a bald head. "Slomosky, get them knees moving and grab my camera out of the car. Take some pictures before the medics move this guy," the Colonel ordered to the deputy.

The ambulance backed deep into the front yard, its siren still blaring full blast. Two medics were directed by another deputy to take a stretcher around to Mark's body. They waited for pictures to be taken and then flipped Mark over, exposing the deep wound in his forehead. One of the medics put a stetho-scope to Mark's chest and announced, "He's still alive, but his pulse is very weak."

"Put him on the stretcher, then hold up here until I tell you where to take him," ordered Barnett as he turned toward Clyde.

"What happened here, Clyde?" The Colonel knew Clyde's entire family and also that Clyde was a very reliable man.

"I came to help Ms. Leila in the storm," Clyde began. "I heard her screaming in the back. I came around and this man was raping her on the porch! He hit her, and she ran out toward that shed." He pointed to the out building.

"When he chased her through the door," Clyde said, "I hit him with that board." He pointed down at the piece of lumber, still stained with Mark's blood. Clyde was excited and breathing heavily.

"Where is Ms. Leila?" asked the Colonel.

"Inside with Ms. Amanda," replied Clyde. "She came by after it happened."

"Do you know this man, Clyde?" asked the Colonel as he looked at Mark in the stretcher.

"I've never seen him before around these parts, Colonel Max," replied Clyde.

Jake Delaughter pulled his old truck past Leila's house so he could watch the scene from a distance. Several other onlookers that lived on the main highway had followed the commotion down Ebenezer Church Road.

"Tommy, tell all those people over there, except Jake, to go home. It's over. Let Jake hang around if he wants to," instructed Colonel Barnett.

Barnett then spoke to the two medics, "Take this guy to the Good Health Regional Hospital on Hwy 331 and tell admissions he is under arrest. They are to keep him locked up in the security section, if he is not D.O.A."

Barnett turned and looked at the young, tall deputy who had been shadowing him. "OK, Owen, here's your chance. Follow the ambulance to the hospital and don't let this man out of your sight! He is dangerous, don't screw this up! By the time your shift ends tonight I will have you a replacement. You get going!" Barnett ordered as he waved his arm to hurry Owen on his way.

Deputy Tommy Tucker was watching the onlookers leave the area as they had been ordered. The Colonel shouted over, "Tommy, go run that Georgia license plate real quick!"

Barnett looked over to another officer and said, "Sit down with Clyde and rough up a full written report—I'll check it later."

Colonel Barnett entered the back porch and saw Leila's

white dress on the couch and her bra rumpled on the floor. A chair had been knocked over. He observed a man's trousers, underwear, and wet shirt. He bent down and pressed on the pockets of the pants without moving them. He felt no wallet. "Hey, Slomosky," the Colonel ordered, "come inside and photograph this crime scene real good."

Barnett continued toward the long hall that ran through the middle of the house. "Colonel Barnett here," he announced loudly. "Ms. Amanda, where are you?"

"Hello, Max," Amanda said softly as she walked from Leila's bedroom and shut the door behind herself. Her family dairy delivered milk to the Barnett home every morning.

"How's Ms. Leila? I need to see her," said the Colonel.

"She is in shock. The bastard beat her and raped her," Amanda whispered. She opened the bedroom door, and Colonel Barnett followed her to Leila's bed.

The drapes of the bedroom were closed, and the room was dimly lit. The Colonel could see that Leila's lip was busted and had swollen to twice its normal size. Leila's eyes were shut, but she opened them and looked at Amanda and Colonel Barnett as they approached her bed.

Barnett's dark blue sheriff's uniform painfully provoked Leila's emotions once again. Her eyes squinted almost shut as her mouth opened widely. Her sudden deep whine pierced the room and it quickly turned to a loud sob. Leila rolled her body away from her visitors as she wept.

Amanda grabbed the Colonel's arm and he followed her back into the hall.

"I'm going to call an ambulance for Miss Leila," said Colonel Barnett, speaking louder now.

"That is not necessary, I'll take care of her," Amanda said.

"It is necessary!" said Colonel Barnett firmly. "You ride with her. I'm sending her to Sacred Lady Hospital in South Walton for forensic examination. I'll get a statement from her when she is in better condition." He turned and walked out of the front door without further discussion.

"The truck belongs to Richard Paul Baker if it is not stolen," said Deputy Tommy Tucker as the Colonel approached. "His papers are in the truck. He lives in Atlanta. I'm having his record run now."

"Call Gillespie Wrecker Service and have them pick up the truck. Pull Baker's Georgia driver's license, check the photo, and make sure the thug outside is Baker," barked Barnett. He added, "Then notify Baker's family and tell them he is under arrest."

Colonel Barnett pulled out his cell phone and ordered the ambulance for Leila. He then ordered Deputy Tucker to, "Wait for Miss Leila's ambulance, follow it to the hospital, and order a rape kit for her. Call me before you leave the hospital and make damn sure Ms. Leila gets in that ambulance!"

The rest of the deputies were rounded up and told to stay with Deputy Tommy Tucker until he left with Leila Hewitt.

Home invasions and rapes are rare in Walton County, and Colonel Max Barnett knew the media would soon be looking for all of the sordid details of this case. He sped back to his office to prepare for the press conference.

Chapter 14

Before Colonel Barnett arrived back at his office in DeFuniak Springs, he got a call on his cell phone from a beat reporter for the Destin News. "There will be a press conference at my office at 4 p.m. this afternoon," he advised this close friend. "This will be big! I'll call you back in an hour to give you a head start on the story!"

A few minutes later, the Colonel pulled to the rear of the Sheriff's compound. He entered through a back door and walked straight to the desk of Sheriff Clark's secretary. The pretty redhead was listening to music on the radio and fixing her makeup, "Lana, call the boss at his ranch and tell him Ms. Leila Hewitt out at Ebenezer Forest was raped, and we arrested the guy that did it. Tell him everything is under control and that there is a press conference at four, if he feels like getting dressed. Call Channels 5 and 7, and give them the press conference alert – tell them it's a rape, and that it'll be worth it for them to send their crew over. Then, e-mail notice of the conference to all the other usual folks on our list."

"Oh, good," said Lana with a big smile, "we haven't had a big press conference in two months. I've got to do something with my hair!"

Another female assistant from the next room said, "Deputy Tucker on the line for you, Colonel." Barnett picked up a nearby phone and hit the flashing button.

"What ya got, Tommy?" asked the Colonel.

"I ran down an address and phone number for Richard Baker," said Tucker. "I called the number. Richard Baker answered! He loaned his truck to a Mark Mabry, M-A-B-R-Y. Get this: Mabry is an ad executive from Atlanta. I checked Mabry's photo I.D., and we have the right man. I am waiting on a full background check on him now."

"The minute you get the rundown on Mabry call me. What's going on with Ms. Leila?" asked Barnett.

"An emergency room doctor just saw her. He gave her a sedative to knock her out," replied Tucker. "She has been assigned a room, and your buddy Doctor Ty Tyson is on the way over here now to conduct the rape examination."

******

Mark Mabry was lying motionless in a special, high security treatment room at Good Health Regional Hospital. A CT scan showed he had scattered subarachnoid bleeding in the frontal lobe. A neurologist was driving in from Pensacola for further evaluation. He was intubated and attached to a breathing machine and other equipment to monitor his condition.

The young emergency room physician on duty cleansed the deep gash in Mark's forehead and then performed a lengthy debridement procedure. He cut away the destroyed tissue and removed the dirt and splinters from the wound. It was necessary to clip away some of the shattered bone fragment from Mark's cracked skull. The doctor knew from the size and depth of the injury that a plastic surgeon would be better trained to address this particular task, but that was not possible on a Saturday in DeFuniak Springs. He stretched and pulled the wound the best he could and temporarily stapled it together. "Specialists will have to help this man later, if he lives," the doctor thought.

*****

When the doctor finished his work, he turned the patient over to a nurse's aide. She was very pretty with thick brown hair and brown eyes. She pushed Mark and the ventilating equipment into another part of the same room and uncovered his body.

Deputy Owen Cooper was the youngest and newest deputy employed by the Walton County Sheriff's office. He stood outside the treatment room, looking through the plexiglass barrier of the special security section—designed for criminals. He had watched Mark being treated by the doctor, and now he watched the aide as she started water running in a nearby sink.

The aide took the washcloth and ran it over Mark's entire naked body, carefully removing the grass, dirt, and blood. She then slowly cleaned and rinsed every inch from Mark's toes to his dark wavy hair.

Deputy Cooper watched as the aide finished her task. She took a very long, deep look at the disfigured face of her handsome, unconscious patient. He noticed tears as they ran down her cheeks.

*****

Doctor Ty Tyson entered Sacred Lady Hospital and was met in the lobby by Deputy Tommy Tucker. The doctor was sixty-ish and tall, 6 feet 4 inches to be exact. He had thick, solid gray hair and was immaculately dressed. His perfectly smooth complexion was accentuated with dark, attractive eyes.

"Good afternoon, Deputy Tucker, it is certainly a pleasure to see you again," the doctor said in his usual very formal manner.

"Hello, Doc," grunted Tucker. They chatted briefly about the case as they rode the elevator to the second floor.

A female assistant joined them at the nurse's station and they continued to Leila's room. Amanda was seated on a hallway couch. She took a good long look at the handsome physician as the group approached her. Deputy Tucker had already mentioned Doctor Tyson's name to Amanda. She recalled that this was the same man who had been suggested by Cousin Jackie as a possible dating prospect that Leila might find interesting.

The doctor did not even look at Amanda as he and his assistant whisked into the room and closed the door. Deputy Tucker waited outside in the hall.

Leila was asleep in the hospital bed. She was wearing a green gown that she was provided when she arrived at the hospital. Doctor Tyson picked up the chart from its hook and read it. He noticed her age was 56, and took another look at Leila. "My gosh," he thought, "what a lovely and youthful looking specimen."

Doctor Tyson lifted Leila's gown. He opened the rape kit and pulled out a pair of magnifying spectacles—and a pair of large rubber gloves. He put them on.

Leila lay motionless and totally exposed. The doctor began a slow visual examination of her nude body. He started at her head and noted her cut and bruised lip.

When Doctor Tyson turned his attention to Leila's lower torso, he gently opened her legs and pulled a medical illuminator from his pocket. He bent over and took a very close look. After pulling two shiny rubber-tipped speculums from the kit, he held them like chopsticks and opened her womanhood. He raised his eyebrows and moved even closer. After pushing the two plastic instruments just a little deeper, he inserted his gloved right index finger for barely a second. Then he just shook his head, pulled off his gloves, closed the kit, washed his hands, and walked out of the room.

In the hallway, Doctor Tyson pulled Deputy Tucker aside and whispered, "She was *not* raped – that pretty, ole gal is a virgin!"

*****

Later in DeFuniak Springs, Colonel Max Barnett walked outside the Sheriff's office and stood in front of the cameras from three local television stations. Also present were reporters from Fort Walton, Destin, Panama City, Pensacola and Tallahassee. He read his prepared remarks and gave a copy to the press.

"This morning at approximately 11 a.m. a local woman was a victim of a brutal battery and sexual assault in Walton County. Her name will not be released. We ask all press that her anonymity be protected.

Thanks to the acts of a heroic neighbor, a man is under arrest and our office is in the process of completing the necessary paperwork so that the State Attorney's Office may soon charge him with multiple felonies.

The arrested man's name is Mark Ryan Mabry, age 32. His last known address is in Atlanta, Georgia. The allegations against this man are that he committed an extremely violent, sexual assault against a Walton County woman who is now hospitalized with multiple injuries.

The Walton County Sheriff's Office would like to inform our residents that this appears to be an isolated criminal attack and the arrest of this accused eliminates any further public danger. Our office's formal arrest report on this matter will be released tomorrow at noon. Thank you all."

Chapter 15

At 7:25 p.m. Eastern time in Atlanta, Charlie McBride received a phone call from a Sandestin neighbor. The lead story on Panama City Eyewitness News television was that "Mark Mabry from Atlanta" was under arrest for sexual assault and home invasion! Charlie immediately dialed Mark's cell phone and got no response. His next call was to Jane Anderson.

"This can't be true! There has to be a mistake!" said Jane in an alarmed voice. "Let me make some calls right now, Charlie, I'll call you back as soon as I have some information," she added.

Within an hour, Charlie received a call back from Jane.

"Charlie," Jane said panicky, "I just got off the phone with a Deputy Tommy Tucker from Walton County. It is Mark! The deputy told me he is in the hospital in critical condition!"

"WHAT!" gasped Charlie.

"The supposed rape victim is that damn old woman, Leila!" responded Jane, her voice shaking. She gave Charlie the name and location of the hospital.

Jane was supposed to go on duty that night, but informed Charlie she was going to call her Captain and take an emergency two-day leave. She also told Charlie she had worked the previous night and was going to catch some much-needed sleep. She would leave for Destin very early the following morning.

"I am leaving to see Mark, now!" Charlie told Jane. "I'll be at the villa later—you have a key—call me when you get close." He hung up the phone, quickly packed and started his drive to Good Health Regional Hospital in DeFuniak Springs.

*****

At dawn Sunday morning, Leila opened her eyes and looked around her hospital room. She could see Amanda asleep on a nearby cot. She started to reach up and touch her swollen lip, but every muscle in her body ached. She was drained and exhausted. Leila had never previously taken a sedative, and was now under the influence of a very powerful one. She closed her eyes again and drifted in and out of sleep.

A short while later, she heard Amanda turn on the television. The morning news was a repeat of the prior night's edition. When she heard the name "Mark Mabry" she bolted forward in the bed.

"Mark did not attack me!" she screamed. "Where is he? Is he all right?"

"Shush now, Leila, Clyde saved you from him. He was preying on you!" said Amanda.

"He didn't try to hurt me at all, Amanda!" said Leila as she started to sob.

Amanda walked over and wrapped a blanket around Leila's shoulders. "You poor baby," Amanda said. "He beat you up. I had a bad feeling about that boy," she added.

"No, No!" cried Leila, shaking her head.

*****

The Good Health Regional Hospital receptionist informed Charlie that Mark was under arrest and could not receive visitors. Charlie did learn that Mark had shown some improvement over the past several hours and had been taken off of the critical list. It was too early in the morning to call anyone, so he headed to the villa to await Jane.

Charlie stopped at a convenience store for coffee, and the local Sunday paper was already in the rack. He picked up a copy and saw the following headline on the front page:

"ATLANTA MAN ARRESTED FOR HOME INVASION AND SEXUAL ASSAULT"

Charlie knew that Mark had been smitten by Leila. "There's no way in hell Mark would have done something like this. He never lost control of himself—ever!" Charlie thought. He drove to his villa and climbed into bed, but could not sleep.

The phone started ringing shortly after daylight. Becky, Lisa, Caleb Hathcox, and a number of other friends called Charlie to discuss Mark's arrest and his medical condition. They were all in total disbelief. At 8:42 a.m. Albert J. Mackey called.

The news of Mark's arrest had been picked up and carried by all national news services. In Atlanta, the "Constitution" ran the story on the front page of Section B.

"Charles, this is Albert J. Mackey," Mark's boss said in a very officious tone. Mackey first asked about Mark's medical condition. He previously talked to Caleb Hathcox and was aware that Mark had suffered a serious injury.

When informed that Mark was doing better, Mr. Mackey

said "Charlie, I hate to ask you to do this for me because Mackco will support Mark as much as we can. At your very first opportunity, please tell him I have no other choice. I am sending him a letter, to his address here in Atlanta, suspending his employment until this matter is resolved. Tell Mark that I send him my best wishes—but this is something that the company has to do."

"Mr. Mackey," Charlie said, "Mark is seriously hurt and is going to need insurance badly. Can you please help him on this?"

"OK, Charlie, I will call my lawyer and get his advice as to what can be done for Mark. I'll word the letter the best I can," said Mr. Mackey grimly. "As far as the general public will know, Mark is laid off for now!" The phone went dead.

The next phone call Charlie received was from Jane. She told Charlie that she had left a message for the man she needed to talk to, a Colonel Max Barnett with the Walton County Sheriff's Office. A sheriff's department secretary had returned her call and said that Barnett had agreed to meet her after church around 2p.m. at his office in DeFuniak Springs.

Charlie informed Jane that visitors were not allowed to visit Mark. Jane said she was going to kill some time and drive down to Ebenezer Church Road, then back northward to her meeting with Colonel Max Barnett.

*****

At 9 a.m. Sunday morning, Leila was discharged from Sacred Lady Hospital. Policy required that she be transported to the front door exit in a wheelchair. An attendant came to Leila's room with the chair, and Leila was seated for the elevator ride to the ground floor. Amanda told Leila she would go wait out front until her husband Hank arrived, then she would walk back in to get her.

As soon as Amanda exited the revolving doors, Leila instructed the attendant to wheel her over to the reception area. She picked up a house phone, got an outside line, and called the Walton County Sheriff's Office. She asked to speak to Colonel Max Barnett. He was out of the office and would be tied up for some time. The operator wrote down Leila's home phone number and said she would have the Colonel call Leila as soon as he called in for his messages. Leila said she would be at her home number in about forty-five minutes. She ended her conversation by telling the operator that it was absolutely urgent that she speak to Colonel Barnett.

On the ride back to Ebenezer Forest, Amanda received a phone call from Reverend McGraw. There are no secrets in Walton County. He had heard that Leila was the victim of a sexual assault. Without as much as a word to Leila, Amanda told the Reverend that they were headed back to Leila's home – and that his prayer and comfort would be greatly appreciated. The Reverend said he would come by to visit Leila in the afternoon.

"Hank, I cannot leave Leila alone," Amanda said to her husband as they pulled into Leila's driveway. Her car was parked where she left it the day before. "I'll be home when I can, honey," Amanda said. Hank kissed his wife, hugged Leila, and left.

Leila was accustomed to being alone. She loved Amanda and usually appreciated her dear friend's company. Today, she preferred privacy to do what she knew needed to be done. Still drained from all that had occurred, she chose not to argue Amanda's decision to stay over.

Leila entered her home and walked into the living room. She took a seat on her flowered couch. It was in short reach of her house phone, and Leila was not going to move until it rang. Her thoughts were now solely on Mark's two immediate problems: the charges against him and the extent of his injury

"I have to undo this injustice now!" she thought. She shut her eyes and prayed for the health of her young friend.

*****

Later in the day, Colonel Barnett walked through the front door of the Sheriff's Office. Jane Anderson, the sex crimes investigator from the Atlanta Police Department, was introduced to him by the receptionist. Jane handed the Colonel her business card. Barnett read the card quickly. "Please follow me back to my office, Ms. Anderson," he said politely.

As they passed, the receptionist whispered, "I have an important message for you, Colonel Barnett." She handed him a yellow slip of paper. The Colonel entered his office and took his chair. He glanced at the paper. It read "Ms. Leila Hewitt wants you to call her at her following home phone number as soon as possible—it is very important." He laid the piece of paper down on his desk.

The Colonel looked up at Jane, smiled and said, "What can I do for you, Ms. Anderson?"

Jane began with general background information about Mark. She presented a very different profile of Mark than that of a typical sexual predator. She started by telling Colonel Barnett that Leila and Amanda had previously visited Mark's villa in Sandestin. Jane said that Leila had been back to visit Mark alone, and that she knew for a fact that Leila and Mark had kissed and possibly more. Jane added she had personal knowledge that there had been some prior "petting" and other sexual contact between Mark Mabry and Leila Hewitt, the full extent of which she did not know. She added that she was certain that Amanda Harrison was privy to this same information.

A deep furrow appeared in the Colonel's brow. His eyes squinted. A lump formed in his throat as he realized that he had been negligent in establishing the full extent of the relationship between Leila Hewitt and Mark Mabry.

Barnett recalled that Clyde told him that Amanda came upon the scene of the crime after it had happened. It never occurred to him that Amanda also possessed much more knowledge than she had volunteered. He wondered if his face was as red as it felt to him. He realized other essential questions should have been asked as well.

Colonel Barnett finally spoke, "Our office established last night that there was actually no penetration, Ms. Anderson. One thing is for sure, your friend Mark Mabry did rough up his victim, and there was certainly an aggravated attempt." He looked nervously down at the yellow piece of paper and then back at Jane.

"I know the victim myself, and I would like permission, as a matter of professional courtesy, to talk with her—with you present if you wish," said Jane.

The colonel looked down at the yellow slip of paper again. "This message is from the victim," he said. "Let's just see what's on her mind." He picked up his phone and dialed the number.

Jane could only hear Colonel Barnett's side of the conversation.

"Hello, Ms. Hewitt, Colonel Max Barnett here."

Pause.

"He has regained consciousness and has suffered a severe

concussion and a fractured skull."

Pause.

"If you want to talk to me in person rather than on the phone, I will drive out in a few minutes," offered Colonel Barnett.

Pause.

"There is a lady here, an Atlanta police officer, who says she knows you. She has asked permission to speak to you. Her name is Jane Anderson. Do you mind if she is present when you and I talk?"

Pause

"We'll be there shortly," said Colonel Barnett.

Chapter 16

Leila opened the screen door and walked outside to her front porch to wait for Colonel Barnett and Jane Anderson. Amanda had been talking on her cell phone in the rear of the house and was unaware visitors were on their way.

"Would you like some green tea, honey?" asked Amanda as she joined Leila on the porch.

"No thank you," said Leila. "Amanda, I have been so upset about Mark's injury. I have to tell you." She leaned her head downward into the palm of her hand. "It is completely my fault that Mark is hurt. I am so embarrassed," she said with her voice quivering.

"Now, baby," said Amanda, "don't get all worked up again. And don't blame yourself for this, Mark was trying to force himself on you."

Leila looked up at her friend and said, "It was my fault. The storm came, and we were both all wet and--" Leila paused. Tears started to roll down her cheeks.

"Look at your lip, Leila!" interrupted Amanda in a raised voice. "My heavens, Leila, can't you see that boy had no business being over here trying to get in your pants? Can't you see that, baby?" She reached over and put her hand on Leila's shoulder.

Leila and Amanda could hear the soft purr of an automobile engine as it approached on Ebenezer Lane. A familiar light tan station wagon turned into Leila's circular driveway. Reverend McGraw turned off the engine and exited the vehicle.

Leila was not expecting his visit. The Reverend had his black, hard-bound Bible in one hand and flowers in the other. He was wearing a bright, white suit. He ascended the porch steps with a very concerned look on his plump and reddish face.

"Praise the Lord, you are all right, Leila. Hello, Amanda," began the preacher as he walked over to Leila and gave her a long hug. Amanda stood up and kissed the Reverend on his cheek.

"Take my seat, Brother McGraw, while I fetch you a glass of tea," said Amanda as she hurried to the kitchen. The Reverend looked at Leila's swollen lip and observed the fresh tears still drying on her cheeks.

"We will wait and pray with Amanda," said the Reverend.

Amanda returned to the porch with a pitcher of tea and placed it on a table next to the Reverend.

After he was served, the Reverend said, "Let's bow our heads and pray." He spoke slowly.

"Our heavenly Father, our power and strength comes because we are filled with the Holy Spirit, which gives us the ability to receive the offense of others and respond as Christ responded to those who offended Him.

Father, we know that the sinful attack that has happened upon our beloved sister, Leila, rests solely upon her attacker. We pray that our sister feels no shame or stigma, her heart never turned towards the crime committed upon her body. She remains pure in Your eyes. We pray that she can feel the love and compassion and the understanding that each and every one of us in our congregation has for her victimization.

Your word tells us there are no shameful skeletons in being a victim of violent abuse, and that devotion to Your Holy Gospel is spiritual in nature, as is our eternal commitment to You. In Christ's name we pray, Amen."

Upon hearing these words, Leila lowered her head and gave way to tears.

*****

The emotion of the moment was abruptly distracted by the clearly marked Sheriff's vehicle pulling in behind Reverend McGraw's station wagon. Colonel Barnett was dressed in full uniform. He waited for Jane Anderson to walk around beside him, and the two law officers walked up the front porch steps together.

It was evident to the visitors that Leila had been crying. Her face was flushed and her eyes were bloodshot. Fresh tears on her cheeks glistened in the Sunday afternoon sunlight.

The necessary introductions were completed and Reverend McGraw said, "Well good folks, it looks like I need to be running along."

"No, please don't," said Leila in a voice strong enough to

indicate that she sincerely wanted the Reverend to stay.

"Would you all like to move inside?" asked Amanda.

"No," said Leila quickly and politely. She had something to say and she was not going to delay it a minute longer.

"Colonel Barnett, Jane," Leila started with a new found strength in her voice, "I want to tell you—face-to-face—that Mark did not try to rape me at all!"

"Leila, you are still confused from—" started Amanda.

"AMANDA! Please, be quiet and don't interrupt! PLEASE!" Leila said loudly as her face scowled and tears began to fall again.

"Mark *did not* attempt to force me or hurt me in any way," Leila continued softly, now crying. "I hurt my lip when I slipped on the wet floor!" Leila paused to catch her breath. She continued in almost a whisper, "Clyde heard me saying no, but my heart was saying yes."

Leila turned and looked directly at Reverend McGraw. His mouth had fallen open and he stared back at Leila.

"I have sinned!" confessed Leila. Her face was writhing with emotion and she was now openly sobbing.

"I wanted Mark as much as he wanted me. My flesh was weak! Mark is hurt because of me, and he needs your prayers, Reverend McGraw," said Leila as she buried her face into her hands and wept some more.

"Dear God, please forgive me," Leila pled.

Across the porch, Jane Anderson's face was red with an anger she could no longer restrain.

"There was a crime committed yesterday! It was a crime against Mark Mabry!" Jane exploded.

Jane's face was bright red. "WHY DID YOU LET THIS HAPPEN?!" Jane shouted. She paused for a second, then added, "Leila, you have DESTROYED Mark Mabry!"

Chapter 17

Bats take more time to get out of Hades than it took Reverend McGraw Sunday afternoon to pick up his Bible and make an uncomfortable exit from Ebenezer Forest. He wanted to share God's grace with Leila in her turmoil, but he was wise enough to know this was not the time.

Jane Anderson had spit truth from her lips, and her words tore Leila apart. Excruciating blows of regret and guilt punched Leila into deeper remorse. Leila continued to softly cry as her visitors prepared to leave.

Even Amanda realized that Mark Mabry was paying an onerous price for his attraction to her dear friend. Amanda took Leila by her arm and led her into the house. They walked slowly down the dark hall toward Leila's bed, where she would spend most of her time for the next few days.

Colonel Barnett said nothing to Jane as they left the porch and returned to their vehicle. He didn't have to. He knew that Jane was fully aware that shoddy procedures had contributed to irreversible damage of Mark's reputation. There was important corrective work to be done, and he was resolved to take care of it.

As the two officers drove down the shady lane back toward the highway, Jane recalled Mark's fascination with Ebenezer Church

Road. "What an off the beaten path to absolutely nowhere but hell!" she thought.

*****

Upon returning to the Walton County Sheriff's Office, Jane followed Colonel Barnett through the building to his post. She watched as he quickly made a computer entry overturning the arrest status of Mark Mabry. He picked up his telephone, called Good Health Regional Hospital, and instructed them to move Mark to a private room. Barnett then asked to speak to the guard on duty and ordered him to return to the Sheriff's Office.

Colonel Barnett looked up at Jane and said sheepishly, "Would you like to stick around and review the press release I intend to transmit as soon as I can put one together?"

"Yes, thank you," said Jane. "If you don't mind, I will walk across the street to the café and get a bite to eat. I am famished."

"It should be ready in about thirty minutes," replied the Colonel.

Jane pulled her cell phone from her purse and called Charlie McBride with the good news.

"Thank God!" said Charlie. "I am going to leave right now to visit Mark in the hospital."

"Please call Albert Mackey," requested Jane. "I will meet you at the hospital as soon as I can."

Jane spoke to Lisa and Becky during her meal and asked them to call the rest of the "bitch corp"—and everyone else that matters—to tell them Mark had been totally exonerated.

When she was finished eating, Jane returned to the Sheriff's Office. The Colonel came out 10 minutes later and handed her

118

the following press release:

Charges Dropped

All potential criminal charges holding Mark
Ryan Mabry, age 32, of Atlanta, Georgia, are
now deemed to be without probable cause by the
Walton County Sheriff's office. Mabry has been
held on allegations including rape and home
invasion. Investigation of this matter has revealed
that prior indications from complaining witnesses
are not substantiated. Mabry remains hospitalized
for injuries received in an altercation which will
not involve any criminal culpability on his behalf.
No other details are expected to be forthcoming.

*****

Jane hurried down U.S. Highway 331 to visit Mark in the
hospital. No one had been able to see him since his admittance.
"No one" meant her and Charlie. No other persons had rallied
to his side over this ordeal. The two of them were his only family.
The thought of this reality greatly saddened Jane.

As Jane took the elevator up to Mark's floor, it occurred to
her that Brandi had not been called since his arrest. "The news
story was probably not front page news in her home town," she
thought. She decided to call her later.

When Jane opened the door to Mark's room, Charlie was
standing on the side of his bed. The white bandage around
Mark's head was the size of a motorcycle helmet. His face was

extremely swollen and bluish in color. Both eyes were black.

Mark made no initial response to Jane's entry. He was motionless. Jane walked over, leaned down, and kissed Mark on the cheek. A very slight upward turn of Mark's lips revealed his obvious pleasure at the sight of Jane.

"Oh, Mark! I have been so worried! I am so thankful you are going to be all right," Jane said as she clutched his arm tightly.

"He is still extremely groggy, Jane," said Charlie. Mark tried to say something but mumbled an unintelligible sound.

Charlie and Jane talked softly to Mark. They could see his eyes watching them, but there was no real response. He was unable to speak.

After a short while, an older nurse came in and said she was there to give Mark antibiotics and a sedative. The nurse said it was necessary for visitors to leave so that Mark's bandages could be changed. Jane told Mark she did not have to be at work until Wednesday and that she would return to sit with him for most of the next two days. She hoped that Mark understood her words.

Outside Mark's room, Charlie told Jane that a hospital administrator asked him about Mark's insurance. Mark's wallet was still missing. Charlie said he had not been able to re-contact Mr. Mackey again, but he would explore the insurance matter with him as soon as possible.

The two friends made their way down to the hospital cafeteria for coffee. They sat in a private booth and discussed Mark's dire situation.

"Charlie, Mark's injury appears to be very serious," said Jane. "I pray that he can make a full recovery," Jane added.

Charlie lowered his eyes and then looked up at Jane. "I hate to have to tell you this, Jane, but I picked up Mark's chart and read it. It indicated he has an abnormal CT scan," said Charlie, most dejectedly.

Jane's face grimaced in shock and her mouth opened widely. She gasped, and dropped her face as she gave way to tears. "That crazy old bitch!" she muttered.

Chapter 18

The occasional cool breezes of early June soon gave way to the long, parched days of mid-summer in the South. Reverend McGraw was a regular visitor to Ebenezer Forest. With his and Amanda's support, Leila slowly returned to almost where she was before young Mark Mabry entered her life.

Leila could not remove what had happened from her consciousness. But she gradually acquiesced to what her pastor and her best friend continued to preach to her. They said, basically, that any feelings she felt for the much younger man "were not in accordance with life's normal plan" and certainly "not in God's usual vision".

Leila kept occupied with the many vacation-time visitors that came to her secluded retreat. Yet lingering chagrin cast a long shadow over her beloved forest. Every showing to her guests induced conflicted memories of Mark Ryan Mabry, her almost lover.

*****

Less than a week after the storm, Mark Mabry was transferred to Doctor's General Hospital in Atlanta. Upon arrival, he underwent a neurosurgical procedure to evacuate the hematoma that had been enlarging between the inside of his skull and his brain. After the surgery, his condition was expected to greatly improve. He was removed from his ventilator and was astonishingly able to eat just two days after surgery. He was then moved from ICU to regular in-patient quarters for weeks of physical therapy.

A month later, Mark was wheeled out of the hospital with a completely hairless head and a still heavily-bandaged forehead. He was confined to his home to await the extensive plastic surgery needed to reduce his gaping, stapled wound to, hopefully, just an unsightly scar.

Mark passed the days away by reading the works of Will Durant. The history of philosophy was much more interesting to him than his stalled advertising career. This diversion kept his mind from his traumatic injury. He learned long ago, the hard way, what many of history's philosophers concluded—that things in life were never just black or white, but rather many shades in between.

There was no remorse in Mark's heart for the attraction he had for Leila. He fought all negativity related to what happened on that fateful Saturday. The thought of Leila's beautiful eyes, and the torrid recall of her innocent passion, would not allow him to color any part of his memories as either dark or sinful.

"There is a reason for all things," Mark thought as he languished with his injuries and interrupted dreams.

*****

Brandi contacted Mark shortly after his corrective plastic surgery. It was a total surprise. An older sister of hers was a stewardess based in Atlanta. While visiting her sister, Brandi called and asked Mark if she could come over to see him. Mark had mixed emotions about welcoming anyone, but he did not feel like he could refuse her offer.

When she arrived, Brandi was extremely surprised by the extent of Mark's injury. His face was still very swollen and his forehead was well wrapped. The strong pain medication he was taking slowed Mark to a level that left him ill at ease.

Brandi rarely looked directly at Mark, and conversation between the two was forced at best. There was no talk of how things had occurred in Ebenezer Forest. She apparently had some vague idea.

It was almost certain, as Brandi departed, that she would never return.

*****

Mark also suspected that his one-time budding rapport with Leila Hewitt was probably now unsalvageable. This left him dispirited, but not without thin hope. He became more pessimistic as time passed.

Dealing with a serious injury is always difficult. It becomes more onerous when a person is alone – it can depress even the strongest of people. Mark had been fending for himself for over three weeks when Mary Kate Nelson, an ex-girlfriend, showed up unexpectedly at his door. Mary Kate had dated Mark for over a year.

Upon her arrival at Mark's home, Mary Kate explained her appearance, "I came over to find out for myself how you really are doing." Mark had been fairly close to Mary Kate in the past, close enough for him to accept her curiosity.

"All of our old mutual friends want to know what really happened," said Mary Kate. "Everyone wants to know the facts and the extent of your injuries," she added.

Mark reluctantly gave Mary Kate a somewhat abbreviated account of how he was injured, without naming any names. He also gave a minimized description of his injury. Mark wanted to be nice to Mary Kate, but narration of his "incident" made him very uncomfortable.

Mark was pleased when the conversation finally moved forward. Mary Kate insisted on Mark allowing her to give his home a much-needed cleansing, as she used to do when they were dating. At first Mark declined the offer, but Mary Kate said that the contribution would be her *get well* gift to him. Mark appreciated her kindness and accepted it. Mary Kate did an excellent job of cleaning Mark's house, and the task took several hours.

Mark enjoyed the company—it took his mind off of his injury. He and Mary Kate recalled many of the lighter moments of their prior relationship. She brought him up to date on many old friends as the evening unfolded. Mark asked if Mary Kate would like to stay over, rather than take the long drive back to her house. They ordered pizza and watched television. Mark was very appreciative of her helpful visit.

As it grew very late in the evening, Mary Kate fell asleep on the couch. Mark turned off the television and went to his bedroom.

A few minutes later, his door opened and Mary Kate entered the room. She slipped under the covers and wrapped her arms around Mark.

They slept together that night.

*****

The very next morning UPS delivered a package to Mark's front door. It was about the size and shape of a mail order book. Mark signed the receipt, shut the door and looked down at the return address:

L. Hewitt
62 Ebenezer Church Road
Red Bay, Florida 32455

Mark removed the brown wrapping and tore open the box. Inside the package was his wallet. It had been missing since the day of the storm. Also, inside was a letter written in longhand on thin white paper.

Dear Mark,

I recently found your wallet under the glider couch on my back porch and got your address off of your driver's license. I am so sorry I did not get to see you and apologize in person before your return to Atlanta.

I feel solely responsible for the injury you received. Clyde Branson is a good man and only heard my screams, which even today I cannot remember. He thought he was protecting me from real danger. I know you would never hurt me.

I also feel responsible for the news reports that falsely portrayed you. This was all caused by a situation that I should have never let develop. I was flattered by your attention; however, I should have been more faithful to my Lord and convictions. I apologize for all my weaknesses.

I hope you can find it in your heart to forgive me. I equally hope you can find a young woman to love. There are no youth in my family and it is one of my biggest regrets. Your whole life is still ahead of you. This is not true for me.

Again, please forgive me. I pray for your full recovery. Best wishes in the future.

Sincerely, Leila Hewitt

Chapter 19

"Nothing will cure a woman better than time and another man," said Cousin Jackie to Amanda as they lounged poolside at the Sandestin Hilton. "Doctor Ty Tyson has asked me about Leila three times. That handsome devil already has a hook in one lip," she added.

"OK, here's the plan," said Amanda leaning forward. "Leila is coming with me to Destin this Friday night. I will bring her to the Ocean Mist Club without even telling her a thing. Can you have 'Doc' there around 9 o'clock that evening?" she asked.

"I don't know what Leila did to him in that hospital room, but like my daddy used to say, you can always tell when a bird dog is pointing. Doctor Tyson will be there at nine!" said Jackie.

"Well pass the Buuttteerr, please!" laughed Amanda.

*****

Jackie is not only a regular customer of the Ocean Mist Club, but also a close friend of the owner. She called and reserved her usual table in the most strategic location for a view of the entire club. When Leila and Amanda appeared at the door, Jackie quickly got their attention and motioned them over. Doctor Ty Tyson was already present.

The Ocean Mist Club is not a place that the younger generation usually frequent. When Leila appeared at the door Friday night in a light blue sleeveless dress, every man of every age took notice. Her thick blond hair was casually pulled to one side in a pony-tail. Compared to the other restaurant guests, she looked youthful and stunning.

Doctor Ty Tyson stood up and pulled the chair out next to him. He proceeded to guide Leila into the seat he had designated for her. He wore a very well pressed, dark suit with a solid red tie. Jackie made the formal introductions.

Leila had absolutely no idea that Doctor Tyson had examined her while she was sedated at Sacred Lady Hospital, or that he would be joining them for the evening. When Jackie introduced her to Ty, he grasped Leila's hand firmly into his and said in a deep and deliberate voice, "You are even more stunningly beautiful than the first time I saw you."

Leila, with a quizzical look, replied simply, "Thank you." She took quick notice of how handsome and distinguished this gentleman appeared. With the doctor's shock of gray hair and heavy dark eyebrows, he was most imposing.

Leila recalled that Jackie had mentioned his name on a prior occasion—and she also remembered that his wife had passed away in the not too distant past. She was particularly pleased that he appeared to be approximately her age.

As the foursome ordered their beverages and appetizers, Doctor Tyson directed all of his attention and conversation toward Leila. He was familiar with her Ebenezer Forest project, having read much about it in the Destin newspaper.

"He has such a deep and very romantic voice," Leila noticed.

Leila slowly sipped her water and observed the doctor inch closer and closer to her. Jackie and Amanda excused themselves to talk with some friends they recognized across the room. They were gone until dinner arrived. Leila had accurately concluded by then that her introduction to Dr. Tyson was not mere happenstance. She smiled to herself and realized that she did not mind the ploy. After all, he was very attractive.

After dinner, the house band played one of their favorite love songs, "St. James Infirmary". Ty asked Leila to dance, and she followed him to the dance floor. He held her tightly against him as they gently moved to the slow music. Leila's face reached only to Ty's chest and she could feel the strong muscles of his long, lean body.

"He is so much taller than Mark," Leila noticed. As the word *infirmary* was sung occasionally in the tune, she thought of Mark again—and felt guilty. Ty pulled her even closer to him. Leila shut her eyes and moved with the music.

Later that evening Ty asked if Leila would like to accompany him to his condominium to "see the beautiful view of the gulf from my balcony—and to share one of the favorites from my wine collection." Leila politely declined. "I am loyal to my spring water and need a good night's rest," she explained.

She did agree to Ty picking her up at ten the next morning for a sail on Destin Harbor and lunch afterwards.

*****

Amanda and Leila were staying in Jackie's guest suite in nearby Gulf Pines. When they returned home for the evening, Jackie asked, "What do you think of Doctor Tyson, Leila? Don't you find him to be a real Southern gentleman?"

"He is not an Ebenezer Forest type of person," replied Leila. "He's not going to feel at home there, and I certainly don't want to hang out in Destin."

"Oh, I beg to differ. The way he was acting tonight, he'll come to your forest. He might even buy a jeep!" said Jackie.

"When I saw him walking down the hallway to visit you in the hospital, I wished it was me he was going to examine," said Amanda.

"WHAT!" exclaimed Leila. "What do you mean, *examine* me? Did that man EXAMINE ME? Why didn't you tell me this, Amanda?!" shouted Leila.

"Honey, you were knocked slap out on medication," Amanda said. "When Doctor Tyson and some female assistant checked your privates, he was doing his medical job, honey. He is a *professional*, a darn good one and a darn good looking one!" Amanda added.

"I can't believe you never told me he was the doctor that examined me, especially since you two set me up for this meeting tonight!" said Leila with a big grimace on her face. "And I am going to be on a boat with him tomorrow—alone!"

Chapter 20

Destin is the jewel of the fishing villages remaining in Florida. Like the others, it is fighting a difficult battle to retain that identity. To the south of Destin is the Gulf of Mexico, and to the north is Choctawhatchee Bay. Sandwiched in between the larger bodies of water is the beautiful saltwater treasure, Destin Harbor. The town was built around the harbor. Still today, dozens of charter boats, full of ambitious fishermen, leave before daylight and return in the late afternoon with their daily catch. Less privileged tourists and locals line the docks to view the snapper, mackerel, cobia, and many other varieties of fish that are strung along the piers in proud display.

Over the years, unscrupulous developers have gradually squeezed the fishermen from their wharves, replacing them with jet-ski businesses, barrooms, and architectural monstrosities. Long, multicraft boat slips protrude into the harbor at various spots.

Leila and Ty strolled down one of the new long walkways and climbed aboard a very impressive sailboat. Ty put the bag of ice he was carrying into a mahogany trimmed cooler. Rather than eating after the outing, Ty had picked up a catered gourmet lunch. It included a six pack of Leila's preferred spring water.

After starting a small gas motor, Ty backed the sloop out of its slip and continued to back halfway across the harbor. He stopped the boat and dropped its anchor.

"Would you like to go below and slip into your swimsuit?" Ty asked.

"I am so sorry, Ty, I didn't realize I needed one," said Leila. She wore blue shorts and a white blouse.

"You don't need one for me—but if you swim naked, your beautiful body may attract a crowd," said Ty. The comment and its implications made Leila feel uncomfortable and she tried to ignore it.

"All I have in this bag is a big hat, sunscreen, and a shawl," Leila replied.

"I need to cool off," said Ty as he dropped his trousers to the deck board exposing a skimpy, red bathing suit. He pulled his shirt over his head without unbuttoning it. The thick gray hair on his chest funneled downward into his swimwear. He stepped his lean, muscular body atop the side of the boat and made a very nice dive into the inviting emerald water.

Ty splashed around for a few minutes, then swam over to a small ladder and climbed into the boat. Leila watched as he shook the water off his shoulders and quite unashamedly adjusted himself.

"Please, come sit by me and warm me up," said Ty as he collapsed into a built-in double seat on the bow.

"Would you like my shawl?" Leila asked.

"Well, if you won't sit on me, please come sit by me," Ty said laughingly.

Not wanting to be rude, Leila obliged and took a deck seat much nearer to her host.

Ty rolled on his side to face Leila. His hair was wet and

mussed. "I think you are one of the most luscious and alluring women I have ever met," he said in a very serious, low tone.

"Well, let me guess," replied Leila with a smile, "the next thing you are going to tell me is that my eyes look like blueberries."

"And I have just the whipped cream for them," replied Ty quickly.

Leila's face flushed as she popped to her feet. This type of crude repartee was uncharted water for her. She walked to the rear of the boat. Ty followed quickly.

"I am sorry, Leila, I did not mean to offend you. It was in poor taste and was very disrespectful humor," said Ty very apologetically.

A horn blew on a nearby passing motorboat, and Leila looked up to see a half dozen people waving at Ty. The doctor put his hand on Leila's shoulder and whispered, "Please forgive me."

*****

Ty was very respectful for the rest of the outing. There was pleasant conversation as he served Leila an exquisite lunch. Afterwards, he lifted the anchor and they motored out of the harbor into Destin Pass. He turned north under the Destin Bridge. After passing the many boaters gathered at Crab Island, Ty put out the sail for a very relaxing cruise under the canvas. The dolphins and sea gulls were welcome companions for the trip.

The breeze and current gently moved the boat across the open water. Leila, with the aid of the refreshing aroma of the sea, was able to gradually drift away from her recent disturbing memories. Her handsome captain stirred her warmly into thoughts of possible sunnier days ahead.

Back at the dock, Leila watched as Ty meticulously hosed down his craft. He kept his boat, like himself, in exceptional shape. He knew all of the other yachtsmen and their families. He introduced Leila to more of them than Leila could later remember.

Leila noticed how much respect everyone seemed to have for Doctor Ty Tyson. The brief, uncomfortable comments of the morning were distant memories as Ty drove Leila back to Jackie's home in Gulf Pines.

Amanda and Jackie were lounging on the back patio with a couple of neighborhood ladies when Leila and Ty turned into the driveway. Ty put his arm around Leila, and she tilted her face to receive his soft kiss on her cheek.

"I am so drawn to you, Leila. May I call you for dinner soon?" Ty asked as he looked into Leila's eyes. She gave him her phone number.

Ty reached his large hand around the back of Leila's head and pulled her lips into his. Leila felt weak and did not resist. For a second, her mind flashed back to her porch and the storm. Her chest became tight and she could not breathe. Ty drew back and looked into Leila's eyes, which were very widely open.

"I could never get enough of you," Ty said.

"I'm not used to this," Leila said as she leaned her head onto Ty's shoulder.

"It is something we will definitely have to practice," Ty replied. They both smiled, and Ty kissed Leila on the forehead.

Leila hugged his shoulders and hurried to rejoin her friends.

Chapter 21

Deep within Ebenezer Forest, Leila stepped naked into her church-side spring. It was the first time since the fateful storm that she was able to bare and relax the way she had done for so many years. The sun was shining, and the woods were full of life. The squirrels were chasing each other, and the birds were singing. Leila could smell the fragrance of the summer flowers and taste the fresh aroma of the nearby trees.

Leila had come to accept responsibility for Mark's injury and prayed for him on this morning as she bathed. She thought of Mark as she ran the refreshing water over her face and through her hair. She even looked over to where he had been standing on his first unannounced trip back to Ebenezer Church.

Her feelings for Mark were still there. "But the obstacles are real and insurmountable," she thought. "I have been too weak – from now on I will be strong," she promised herself.

With Reverend McGraw's help and guidance, Leila had sought God's forgiveness for her transgression. "God has forgiven me. I know this in my heart," she thought.

Leila lowered her body completely under the water and stretched her arms. Still under water, she slicked her hair back and ran her fingers through its thickness. She let her face emerge first and slowly stood up. She felt clean and pure. "God is not finished with me," she knew.

Leila had a feeling of new commitment to her Lord as she stepped out of the spring. She realized she had been missing "her personal baptismal immersions", as she liked to think of them.

On the walk back to her home, she thought about her boating excursion with Doctor Ty Tyson. "I have spent most of my years alone in these woods and I don't want to die that way," she admitted to herself. "Ty has spent his life helping other people. He stood by his wife until she passed away, and perhaps I need to see where this goes."

Leila knew that there would be difficulties balancing her love for Ebenezer Forest with an acceptance of, or a commitment to, any man.

"Doctor Ty Tyson is a good, respectable person – and he is my age," she thought. She smiled as she remembered his long, sumptuous body diving into the warm, salty harbor.

*****

After the walk back, Leila shut the gate at the end of the lane and turned toward her house. She could see an unfamiliar car parked in the drive and a female sitting on the front porch steps. As she got closer, she recognized the tall, younger woman. It was Jane Anderson.

Leila felt her flesh tighten as a sudden surge of fear grabbed her body. When close enough to speak, she asked in a concerned and excited voice, "Has Mark taken a turn for the worse?"

"Quite the opposite," replied Jane as she stood up and stepped down from the porch so as to not tower over Leila. "His doctor says he will have no permanent brain damage, just a nasty scar on his forehead until he can get more extensive plastic surgery – which is in the works," she added.

"Thank God!" said Leila. "I have been very concerned about Mark's injuries."

"The other reason I stopped by was to apologize to you, Leila," began Jane. "I was so upset that Sunday afternoon when I came here with Colonel Barnett. I lost control of myself. I have had several talks with Mark, and I realize that it was just a strange and tragic series of events that somehow just occurred."

Leila could not hold back her emotions. "I would never intentionally have done anything to hurt Mark," she said as she began to tear up. "I am so fond of him. I should have never screamed like I did – Clyde thought that he was protecting me," she added.

Leila wiped the tears from her cheek and took a deep breath. "Mark would have never harmed me. What happened to him is still just a bad dream," she said. She looked down at the ground.

Jane put her arms around Leila and hugged her. "I did not want to upset you again, I came to apologize," she whispered. "We all love Mark, and I know you never wanted all of this to happen, Leila. Please forgive me for being so harsh."

"Please come in," offered Leila as she raised her head. "I am so glad you came by to visit."

Jane followed her inside, and they talked for a while. Jane could feel the warmth and genuineness of Leila. Jane knew Mark better than anyone else. She realized that looks alone had not attracted him to this special lady with an uncommonly good heart.

"I am on my way to Mark and Charlie's villa," said Jane. "I have two weeks of unused vacation time. I am going to be there alone for one week, and then my mother is going to come down for a while. I would love for her to meet you. Would you please join us one day for lunch?" Jane asked.

"I would love to," replied Leila. "Please call."

The ladies exchanged phone numbers, and Leila watched as Jane circled her vehicle to the west and disappeared down Ebenezer Church Road. She re-entered her home and walked down the long hall toward the back porch. When she arrived at the glider couch, she looked down at the exact spot where Mark had pulled her wet dress off over her head. She remembered their deep, wet kisses and the way he had looked at her.

"RRRing...rrrring" sounded the hallway phone. She was still remembering Mark when she answered the phone.

"Hello, Leila, this is Ty Tyson," he said in his now familiar, deep and raspy voice.

Leila agreed to meet Ty for dinner at 7 o'clock the following evening at Café 30-A. It is a very popular restaurant on the scenic route 30-A that hugs the coastline between Destin and Panama City Beach.

She hung up her phone and walked down the dark hall. Relaxing into a chair, Leila leaned her head back on a soft pillow and shut her eyes. She could not prevent drifting into an unwelcome review of her recent past, it had become common-place.

"My life is so quickly changing," Leila thought...however, she was unsure if it was for the better.

Chapter 22

Leila was excited about her dinner at Café 30-A Restaurant with Doctor Ty Tyson. The popular spot is well known for its ambience and great food. She selected a fashionable white dress with blue stripes and a little blue bow on one sleeve. She looked adorable.

Highway 30-A is a little less distance from Ebenezer Forest than is Destin. Grayton Beach, Watercolor, Seaside, and Rosemary Beach are a few of the charming settlements along the route that allure thousands of affluent visitors each summer. The inland lakes, jogging and bike paths, and wooden bridges add to the area's charm. However, the scenic gulf coast is Highway 30-A's main attraction.

Leila timed the drive perfectly and walked through the front door of the restaurant at 7 o'clock sharp. She looked around as best she could and then asked the hostess. Her date had not yet arrived.

She selected an elegant booth in the corner of a high ceilinged section of the main dining area. The hostess lit a pleasant smelling candle and brought Leila a wine list and a menu. When the hostess returned, Leila ordered her usual bottled water.

After about twenty minutes, a somewhat svelte lady with

a broad smile approached the table and introduced herself to Leila.

"Hello, my name is Harriet Crommelin. I am the owner. Everyone calls me Harriet." she said, most cordially.

Leila stuck out her hand and told Harriet her name.

"May I treat you to a glass of wine on the house?" Harriet offered with a very delightful southern accent. "Doctor Tyson called, he is running late. He is one of our regulars, and we would like to make you very comfortable until he arrives."

Leila respectfully declined the gracious offer.

Five minutes later the hostess returned to Leila's table and announced, "Doctor Tyson called again and asked that you please excuse his tardiness. He said to tell you that he will be here just as soon as he can."

The hostess started to walk away, but turned back to add, "Doctor Ty dines with us quite often. He is so sweet."

Another five minutes passed. A waitress walked up to Leila's table and placed a reddish glass of wine in front of the empty seat next to her. "Doctor Tyson always starts with his favorite pinot noir," she said as she smiled at Leila.

Ten minutes later, Doctor Tyson entered the restaurant and stopped for a brief talk with Harriet. He disappeared into the restaurant's office and came out holding a large bouquet of long-stemmed red roses.

The Doctor hurriedly made his way over to Leila. He leaned over, kissed her on the cheek, and handed the flowers to her.

"Here—to the very fairest flower of them all," Doctor Tyson said, almost ceremoniously.

Leila was delighted. She blushed as other couples in the room looked on with approval. "Thank you so much, Ty," Leila said deeply touched. The waitress quickly brought a vase with water to the table and arranged the flowers across from Leila.

Ty walked around to an empty seat next to Leila. He draped his long left arm around her shoulder, putting his other hand on her right knee. This made Leila feel a little uncomfortable, but she gave no indication.

"This is one of the loveliest dresses I have ever seen," Ty said feeling it with his fingers. "And dearest, tonight, your eyes do look like blueberries," he said with a big grin.

Leila smiled back. "He is very charming," she thought.

Ty drank the waiting glass of pinot noir rather quickly—and another one—even before his Greek salad arrived. A third glass arrived with his dinner, which was a seafood pasta dish. Leila ordered an Italian salad with a calamari appetizer as her main course.

There had been very little opportunity to have a serious conversation the previous weekend with Ty captaining his sailboat. In the relaxed quietness of the cozy restaurant, the two chatted with ease. At one point during dinner, Leila asked how long Ty had been married. She was surprised when he answered, "six years".

Not one to ask a lot of questions, Leila did ask one more—if Ty had ever wanted children.

"I have three," he replied. "They are grown and live in St. Louis."

Ty did not offer much additional information to whatever Leila asked over the evening, yet he had plenty of questions for her. He wanted to know everything about her—from her youth to her recent past.

Later, as Leila guided a spoonful of spumoni toward her mouth, Ty asked a question that stopped Leila cold, "Do you know how much I want to make love to you tonight?" He moved his hand to Leila's leg again and looked longingly into her eyes.

Leila's mouth opened slightly at the directness of the question. It caught her totally off guard. She paused and was silent for a full thirty seconds. She looked up at him with her pretty blue eyes and raised her left hand in the air. With her thumb, she flicked her ring finger about five times.

"No sex before marriage," she said in a flirty, silly little voice. She put her hand on Ty's hand that was still atop her leg.

"For me, that would be after marriage," replied Ty, dryly.

"No, I am very serious," Leila said as she looked directly into Ty's eyes. "My religious convictions mean everything to me."

"I own a rental condo over on the beach, just a few blocks away. It is empty this week, let's go over there after dinner and spend the night—no sex," said Ty, seemingly half teasing.

"I don't think that would be a very good idea," replied Leila. "I don't want to put myself in that position. I think you are a very attractive and interesting man, but I want to marry before I share that kind of intimacy," she added, most seriously.

Ty said he understood and respected Leila for her beliefs. He ordered one more pinot noir and told Leila that he had several patients over the years that preferred death over sex. They both laughed, he more than Leila.

Afterwards, Ty held Leila's hand as he accompanied her to the parking lot. Upon opening her car door, he hugged Leila tightly. She could taste the wine on his lips when he tenderly kissed her goodnight.

They gazed at each other one last time under the moonlight and then drove back to their respective worlds.

Chapter 23

Ms. Leila Hewitt
62 Ebenezer Church Road
Red Bay, Florida 32455

Dear Leila,

Thank you for your kind and thoughtful
letter. I have just recently been taken off of
my medication. I really haven't felt like myself
enough to reply until now. However, I am
starting to feel much better.

Leila, I do not blame my injury, nor the news
stories that followed, on you. I do not feel that
you owe me an apology, but if it makes you feel
better, please know that I accept it, just as I do
everything about you.

Only you and I know the real emotion of
what happened. The last thing I ever wanted was
for you to be unfaithful to your Lord or your
convictions. I was weak, not you. Please forgive
me.

My main regret is the separation from contact with each other that has resulted. I want you to know that my feelings for you have always been real. There is a difference between love and lust, and my passion to be with you has never been about lust.

I pray, even though you ended your letter to me with "best wishes in my life ahead", that the road to Ebenezer Forest will remain open to me for a visit.

Yours truly,
Mark Mabry

Mark read the letter several times. It said what he wanted it to say. He folded it into an envelope, opened his front door, and walked it to his mailbox.

Back inside, he picked up an Atlanta Braves baseball cap hanging on a hat rack. At a nearby mirror he stopped and took a long look at his un-bandaged, ghastly wound. He gently put the cap on his head. It came down just far enough on his forehead to cover his injury and stop the questions he had been getting each time he left his home. He heard a car horn beep outside and hurried out to meet Charlie for lunch.

Mark was not driving, nor had he returned to work. Charlie had only an hour for lunch, so they were pressed for time. A local sandwich shop fit the schedule perfectly.

"Let me see the scar. Is it getting any better?" asked Charlie as the two friends talked during lunch.

"It could be worse," replied Mark.

"When do you think you will be able to get back to work?" asked Charlie.

"I really don't have any idea when that will be," replied Mark. "Even though my arrest was totally vacated and expunged from the records, Mr. Mackey has been very distant to me, in fact, basically unavailable," said Mark.

"Well, I wonder why he would be upset with one of his young guns getting hit in the head with a two by four, after trying to have sex with an old lady – who incidentally, preferred to run off screaming," Charlie replied with a wink.

"You know how to make a friend feel really wonderful," replied Mark with a polite smile. "You well know that I have not been happy with my job at Mackco," he added.

"So you want to be a 32 year old burnout?" questioned a now serious Charlie.

"What's the difference between that and being a realtor of any age in today's market?" asked Mark. Charlie laughed and shrugged his shoulders.

"Jane will be at the villa for a little longer," declared Mark, changing the subject.

"I am going to Destin myself next weekend, are you up to going with me?" asked Charlie.

"I won't know until I see my doctor this week and find out when he is going to do the skin transplant. Whenever I do go, I want to stop and visit with Leila. We have never had a chance to really talk since this all happened," said Mark.

Charlie put his sandwich down on his plate and stared at Mark. "Mark, you need to get that ole gal out of your mind. Hasn't she caused you enough trouble already?" he asked.

Mark frowned and didn't reply. He took a drink of tea and pushed the rest of his french fries toward Charlie. Charlie looked down and picked up a couple of fries.

"I talked to Jane last night. She stopped by to see Leila and said they had a very cordial visit," said Charlie.

"Really, that is great!" replied Mark with a very pleased smile. "She is such a wonderful person, Charlie. I hope you will have the opportunity to know her better."

"Apparently Jane was impressed by Leila to some degree," said Charlie, "but every single one of your friends say that you were not thinking straight about having a relationship with her, even before the blow to your head. Mark, to be honest with you, I think you need to reconsider even a friendship with Leila—for the good of you both."

"I appreciate you sharing your thoughts with me, Charlie, I really do," said Mark seriously as he looked directly at his friend, "but you have heard me say this before—happiness should never be sought in the minds of other people."

Charlie made a little nod of his head toward two pretty, young ladies who entered the restaurant and said, "Take a look, Mark, just take a look at those young hotties—now that is what I'm talking about!"

Chapter 24

The mailman got out of his vehicle, walked up on the porch, and handed Leila her mail. She handed him a bag of dewberries and said, "These are for Sally's pies." The mailman and his family were members of Leila's new church.

"Thank you, Ms. Leila, and God bless," said the postman as he continued on his way.

When Leila flipped through the letters, she noticed an Atlanta return address on one of them. She knew it was from Mark. She quickly opened it, but read it very slowly. She read his sentence about "love and lust" several times. She laid the letter down on the table aside her chair, then picked it up and read the entire letter again. Tears formed in her eyes as she thought of the handsome young man and about what happened to him on that stormy day. "He would never be unwelcome on Ebenezer Church Road," she thought. She folded the letter from Mark and put it away in her bedroom dresser.

Leila took her morning walk to the church, planning on working in her garden later. But the letter brought back feelings that she had been trying to forget. She decided to focus on something else. When Leila returned to her home, she picked up a copy of "Christian Family Journal". She was skimming through it when the phone rang.

"Hello, my fair lady," said Doctor Ty Tyson in a very cheerful voice.

"Hello, Ty," replied Leila. "It is nice to hear from you," she added sincerely.

"I am over here in Tallahassee serving on a medical review panel this morning. I wanted to see if it would be OK if I stopped by to see you on my way back to Destin? I think I am becoming addicted to you," Ty said. Leila laughed.

"That would be very nice. What time will you be arriving here?" she asked.

"The meeting will break up around four o'clock, so I should be there, certainly before six," Ty said.

"Would you like for me to prepare an authentic, country supper for you?" asked Leila.

"I could not think of a better way to spend an enchanting evening," answered Ty.

Leila provided Ty the easy directions to Ebenezer Church Road. When the conversation was over, Leila was extremely excited about her new plans for the day. She rarely had guests over for dinner and never a single, handsome man. "There is cooking to be done—and a house to tidy up—and a dress to pick out—and my hair," she thought with a broad smile.

*****

At 5 p.m. the smell of pork roast floated through Leila's sparkling southern home. Creamed sweet potatoes and fresh collard greens were simmering on low burning flames. The iced tea was made, with lemon added. It was waiting to be poured over the ice that Leila had already crushed. And to top off the evening's feast, strawberries for the shortcake dessert were being chilled in the freezer. They would taste crunchy under the whipped cream.

Leila chose one of her favorite dresses, off-white colored with ruffles at the shoulders. It fit very snugly above her waist and then flared stylishly to her knees. She took a nice, long bath— leaving her feeling clean and refreshed.

Leila smiled to herself thinking about how her recent involvements with first Mark, and now Ty, had given her new and stirring anticipations.

She watched her clock in the kitchen as the hands moved ever so slowly toward 6 o'clock. When she finally heard Ty's car making its way down Ebenezer Church Road, she took a last quick look at herself in the mirror and met him at the front door with a smile.

Ty arrived wearing a very well-tailored black suit that accentuated his elegant gray hair. Leila looked up at his dark, sparkling eyes beneath those thick, bushy eyebrows. "My goodness," she thought.

Ty leaned down and kissed Leila, long and softly on her cheek. She felt her knees weaken. Ty then leaned over and raised Leila upward to meet his moist lips. His aggression took Leila by surprise – but she did not resist. The deep, sensuous heat of his mouth lingered when she finally pulled away.

"I don't know what smells better, the food or you," Ty said in his deep romantic voice. Leila blushed, leading him by the hand to the living room. Ty made himself at home on the couch.

"The only other thing more I wish I had for you this evening Ty, is a bottle of the wine you like—the 'pi-not no-ir'—did I pronounce it right?" Leila asked quizzically.

"Tonight, you will be my wine," said Ty, as he pulled off his jacket and draped it across the back of the couch. He reached over and took Leila by her arm, trying to kiss her again.

"Hold on, big boy, let me get you some tea," Leila said politely as she side-stepped the kiss.

Ty had settled down into a comfortable leaned-back position when Leila returned. Leila took a seat across the room and related more of the history of Ebenezer Forest and its church. Ty took notice of Leila's college-aged photo on the fireplace mantel. "You have been stunningly beautiful all of your life," he said.

"The beauty of a person's heart is all that really matters," replied Leila.

"I can tell you have an exceptionally beautiful heart," answered Ty. "Do you ever share it with anyone?"

"I try to share my heart with everyone," answered Leila. Off in the distance they could hear the rumblings of an approaching late afternoon thunderstorm.

"Are you hungry and ready for supper?" Leila asked.

"Very much so," replied Ty.

"Just relax while I bring the food to the dining room. I will call you in a few minutes," said Leila.

Leila had every aspect of the meal expertly planned. In the kitchen, she placed the serving dishes on a double-leveled rolling cart. She then added a decorative vase with some fresh picked flowers. The elegant presentation was then rolled into the dining room.

The centerboard from her formal dining room table had been removed so that the two place settings were within an arms reach of each other. After lighting two tall candles, Leila filled the drinking glasses with ice and sweet tea. She walked over to the switch and dimmed the lights down to a very cozy and romantic level. Totally satisfied that everything was picture perfect, she walked back to the living room and announced that dinner was served.

Ty walked into the dining room. Stopping to look at the magnificent setting, he said, "What a wonderful table you have prepared for such a special evening."

Leila served their plates and before eating said this short prayer:

"Bless us, O' dear Lord, and help us always remember those who are not as fortunate as us. Thank You for this wonderful meal that we are about to receive and keep us always mindful of Your Commandments. Amen!"

As supper began, Leila asked Ty about his medical review meeting in Tallahassee. He discussed it briefly, but insisted on encouraging Leila to talk about her beloved Ebenezer Forest. He seemed truly interested in the most important thing in Leila's life.

They continued with very relaxed conversation as they leisurely enjoyed the cozy and fanciful meal. Ty complimented Leila repeatedly on her cooking skills. "What a delightful evening," Leila thought.

When both were finished eating, Leila excused herself to get the dessert. Outside, an ominous thunderstorm had moved above Ebenezer Church Road and it began to rain.

When Leila returned, Ty raised his glass and made a "toast of tea" saying, "For the absolutely wonderful and romantic meal that you have prepared, my dear." She served the strawberry shortcake, and when they finished eating, Ty made yet another "toast of tea"— this time for the "beautiful lady from the forest". They sipped their beverages for a few minutes more while the storm intensified over Ebenezer Church Road.

******

Leila suddenly had a very light-headed sensation. She set her glass down on the table and put her hand to her forehead.

"Ty, I am starting to get a dizzy, queasy feeling," she said. He did not answer. He got up from his chair and walked around behind her. He slowly massaged Leila's shoulders and temples.

"You are just getting a little vertiginous, Leila," Ty said softly as he continued gently rubbing her. She was not familiar with the word and had no idea what he meant.

Leila's body was becoming more and more limp and uncontrollable. Her eyes began to water.

"I am floating – feeling nauseous, uh – spinning," Leila said desperately as her eyes began to flutter.

"Help me, Ty!" Leila cried.

"I have you, baby," replied Ty as he picked Leila up like a young child and carried her into her bedroom. Leila's head flailed back and forth as she mumbled incoherently.

Ty laid Leila out on her bed and began removing her shoes. He unbuttoned her dress and deftly pulled it off of her arms and legs. He slowly removed her bra and then eased her panties down her helpless thighs.

Leila was confused and now barely coherent. She cried out with slurred words "WHHAT? ooooh...WHHAT? TY! Help! TY! WHHAT? Ty...Noo."

Leila was totally aghast as she saw Ty removing his clothes

and climbing, so heavily, on top of her. She felt the excruciating pain of his ravaging thrusts as her mind went blank—and the room grew totally black.....

Chapter 25

Leila was lying flat on her back. A loud, banging noise awakened her. She tried to lift her arms, but they were heavy. She could not raise them. Her head was spinning. She tried to sit up, but she was helpless. She had no coordination. Confused and disoriented, Leila fell back into the bed and slept.

A good while later, Leila heard a beating on the glass window just a few feet from her head.

"LEILA! LEILA! Are you in there?" a woman was shouting loudly. "LEILA! LEILA!"

A small metallic tray was atop Leila's bedside table. She could just barely reach it. She grabbed it and slung it at the window – and missed. The tray struck the wooden casing of the window and made an audible THUMP.

"I hear you, Leila!" Amanda screamed. She picked up a garden stone and quickly smashed the glass. She then proceeded to beat a hole just above the window latch.

Amanda hurriedly removed several jagged edges of glass and flipped the window's latch open. She raised the window, swatted the blinds out of her way and pulled herself up into the opening. In a few seconds, she was wiggling her large frame through the window into the bedroom. She turned on the overhead light and rushed over to Leila.

"What's wrong, honey? What's the matter, baby? Why haven't you been answering the phone?" Amanda asked frantically.

Leila did not answer.

"Tell me what is wrong, Leila," insisted Amanda as she hugged her mute friend.

Amanda raised Leila to a sitting position. She was nude. The blanket that had been covering her fell down to her lap.

"Why did you break my window?" Leila asked in a whisper as she pulled the blanket back up to hide her body. Amanda noticed that Leila's eyes were totally bloodshot.

"I have been calling you all morning, honey," said Amanda. "I came by once before noon and thought maybe you might have taken a ride with someone, but I decided to come back. Leila, please tell me what is wrong with you."

"What time is it?" asked Leila, very slowly.

"It is five o'clock in the afternoon," replied Amanda. "Have you been drinking, Leila?"

"Five o'clock! How can that be? I don't remember how..." said Leila in a slurring voice. "You know I don't drink alcohol, Amanda. Where did the day go?" she asked.

"Honey, you look like the living hell—tell me what happened," pressed Amanda.

"I feel real sore all over," replied Leila weakly.

"OK, honey—I'm serious. What the hell has been going on here, Leila?" Amanda demanded in a firm voice.

"I cooked supper for Ty last night and...and I remember us having some toasts...and then I...uh...then, I can't remember exactly," said Leila still drawling her words.

"My word, LEILA! TOASTS! YOU GOT DRUNK!" exclaimed Amanda. "What all happened?"

"I can't remember how it happened after supper...I just can't," said Leila.

"How what happened, baby?" asked Amanda in a concerned voice.

"Look at your dress and brassiere laying on the floor and your panties over there," continued Amanda as she pointed to the rocker. "It is pretty obvious what happened, Leila. But it is all OK, darling. It was bound to happen sometime."

"I can't really remember how he--" said Leila, stopping suddenly. "Please hand me my robe, Amanda. I feel so dizzy," Leila requested as she sat up straight.

Amanda got the robe out of the closet and handed it to Leila. She grabbed Leila by the arm to try and get her to stand up to put on the robe.

Leila tried to rise, but did not make it.

"Ow, Ow, my dear God. It hurts so much," Leila moaned as she coupled over. Her face contorted with pain.

Leila reached down and grabbed her pubic area with both hands. "Amanda, my poonie is so sore!" Leila cried out again.

"You hush now, baby. You hush – that's just the way it is," said Amanda in a low voice.

Amanda walked Leila into the living room. "You just sit here —don't move—let me go out to the kitchen and heat you up some vegetable soup," offered Amanda. "I will be right back in just a couple of minutes with some nourishment for you," she added as she left the room.

Leila was drowsy, but more awake when Amanda returned. She consumed the soup very quickly and asked for some water —she was extremely thirsty. When she finished eating, Leila asked Amanda to help her back to her bed. She fell asleep very quickly.

Amanda called her husband, Hank, and told him, "Honey, I won't be home tonight. Leila is under the weather and I'm going to spend the night over here with her."

Chapter 26

As soon as the first beams of the next morning's sunlight shot through her shattered bedroom window, Leila awoke with wide eyes. She was in great despair. "I do not drink," she thought. She reached down and touched herself. She was still extremely sore. She walked into her bathroom and washed her face with cold water. She then turned on her shower and stood beneath it for a full ten minutes. She had to cleanse herself of her assailant's filth!

Wild thoughts were running through her head. "Ty Tyson violated me, and I cannot clearly remember it! My body has been totally messed up for a day and a half! I still have a severe headache! I have not heard from that demon! OH NO!" she thought as she began to fully realize the extent of what had occurred.

Leila walked into the living room and over to the couch where Amanda was sleeping. She shook her, and Amanda opened her eyes and sat upright.

"Are you feeling better, darling?" Amanda asked.

Leila pulled a chair up in front of the couch and sat down. Her eyebrows were furrowed. She looked frazzled and mad.

"Amanda, I was raped!" Leila said emphatically.

Amanda adjusted the blouse she had slept in and blinked her

eyes widely a couple of times. "Honey, I know what you did was out of character, but you were not raped. You just got caught up in the moment," Amanda said almost apologetically.

"Ty gave me some kind of drug that knocked me out," said Leila in a softer voice.

"And you took it?" asked Amanda. "Why?"

"NO! I DID NOT TAKE IT! He must have put something in my tea!" said Leila with a tone of exasperation.

"Leila, yesterday you told me you were drinking, making toasts and all," said Amanda.

"Toasts with tea! Amanda, SWEET TEA! You know I do not ever drink alcohol, *ever!*" insisted Leila.

"Leila, you have regrets. I slept with two guys before I met Hank, and I have regrets too – big regrets. I know exactly how you feel," said Amanda in an understanding voice.

"Amanda, Ty Tyson slipped me some kind of pill that knocked me out, and he raped me. Do you hear me? HE RAPED ME!" said Leila emphatically as she began to cry.

"Leila, I love you with all my heart," said Amanda as she wrapped her arms around her friend, "but no one is going to believe you, baby. You didn't even tell me that yesterday."

Leila raised her head and wiped the tears from her cheeks. She thought for a few seconds and said very slowly, "Amanda, I made a commitment to our Lord before – and reaffirmed it to Him after what happened with Mark – that I would never have intercourse before marriage. I even told Ty that last week. Ty drugged me and then raped me – and I am not going to let him get away with it, so help me God!"

Leila stood up, walked over to the telephone, and picked up the telephone book beneath it.

"What on earth are you doing, Leila? Don't do that, please

don't call anyone. Let's talk about this!" pleaded Amanda as Leila thumbed through the directory.

Leila picked up the phone and dialed a number. When someone answered Leila said, "May I speak to Colonel Max Barnett, please?"

After a long pause Leila said, "Hello, Colonel Barnett, this is Leila Hewitt."

"I would like to file an official charge against someone for rape."

"Me, I am the victim – and I am still too weak to drive."

"No sir, I'm ok...now."

"Could you, or someone else, come out and take my report?"

"Thank you, Colonel!"

Click.

Chapter 27

Leila hung up the phone with Colonel Barnett and walked around the corner to the dining room. She was pleased to see that Amanda had not cleaned up the room. Every serving container, plate, and glass was in the exact same place where she had originally placed them upon the dinner table. The fork she had used was on the floor. The uneaten remainder of the pork roast was still next to the mostly full pitcher of tea. The glass she had been drinking from was not on the table!

Leila hurried back to the kitchen, and there was her glass – in the sink. It had been rinsed out and turned upside down in the drain. "That explains what he did!" she exclaimed aloud.

Leila walked back into the dining room. Amanda was still sitting in the same place on the couch with her face buried into her hands.

"Are you going to support me when they get here, or are you going to tell them I was intoxicated?" asked Leila.

Amanda raised her head and looked up at Leila. She had tears running down her cheeks. "Of course I am going to support you, Leila," Amanda said, "but I am afraid that no one will believe you. Doctor Ty Tyson is a respected man, and a lot of time has passed since night before last..."

"Just tell them the whole truth – everything you have seen," said Leila.

"Do I tell the officers about the toasts?" asked Amanda.

"Tell them everything," replied Leila.

About thirty minutes passed before Leila and Amanda heard the sheriff's vehicle making its way down Ebenezer Road. This time there were no sirens.

Both women had washed their faces, dressed and straightened up the living room. When two men walked up on the front porch, Leila opened the door. She and Amanda greeted Colonel Max Barnett and another familiar face.

"Leila and Amanda, this is my chief deputy, Tommy Tucker," informed the Colonel.

"Yes, I remember Deputy Tucker from my ambulance ride to Sacred Lady Hospital," Leila replied. "Please come inside, gentlemen."

Deputy Tucker acknowledged Leila and Amanda as the four of them took a seat in the living room.

Colonel Barnett opened his report book and pulled out a ballpoint pen. He looked over at Leila and said, "Now, please tell me what happened, Miss Leila."

"Night before last, I had a man over for dinner," began Leila. She was talking very slowly and was having difficulty expressing herself. Tears began to roll out of her eyes.

"Everything was fine," Leila continued. "The dinner table is still set exactly the way it was night before last. I want you to see it. I went to the kitchen after dinner to fix the dessert and... uh...he put something in my tea." Leila's face was anguished and she felt a swelling in her chest and neck. Her emotions began to release. She started to cry softly.

"Whatever it was," Leila continued, "it made me real dizzy

at first – and then knocked me unconscious." She began to cry harder.

"Then, he took me to my bedroom and raped me!" Leila blurted out as she began to sob loudly. Amanda leaned over and put her arms around Leila.

"It's going be all right, baby," Amanda said softly.

The Colonel let Leila cry for a minute. "OK, Miss Leila, who was the man that did all of this to you?" he asked.

"Doctor Ty Tyson," replied Leila.

Deputy Tommy Tucker's mouth dropped. Colonel Max Barnett lowered his head and raised one finger to his brow. Leila and Amanda both witnessed their reactions.

"I had to break into the house to wake her up yesterday afternoon. I saw what he did to her," said Amanda.

"Leila, have you been seeing or dating Doctor Tyson prior to all of this?" Colonel Barnett asked, remembering his prior experience.

"Sort of," replied Leila.

"How many times?" asked the Colonel.

"About, four times," Leila answered after a few moments.

Colonel Barnett pulled out his report pad and began to write. After a minute or so he said, "This is what I want to do today. I want to get a complete written statement from both of you, but out of the presence of each other. Amanda, would you please step outside on the porch until we call you."

"Yes, Max," said Amanda. She hugged Leila and quickly exited through the front door.

Colonel Barnett and Deputy Tucker stayed inside the house with Leila almost an hour. They started at the beginning of Leila's first meeting with Ty and had her relate, in writing, her entire history with him up to, and through, the night of the alleged rape. They also had Leila briefly write what had transpired since then.

The officers viewed Leila's bedroom and saw the broken window. They next observed the dining room, particularly the dinner table. Following Leila into the kitchen, they duly noted her rinsed-out glass in the sink. They took no pictures.

The deputies asked Leila to read her statement when it was completed. Afterwards, she signed it.

The Colonel asked that Leila and Amanda exchange places and repeated the entire process with Amanda. Amanda was asked to write down every bit of information she knew about Leila and Ty Tyson. The Colonel specifically asked her to include in the report what she had seen when she first entered Leila's bedroom.

The Colonel also asked Amanda to write down her recollection of every exact statement Leila had made to her about the alleged rape. Amanda hesitated before she included the "toasts" that Leila had mentioned. Then she thought, "Leila has surely informed them of that."

Amanda also recalled that Leila instructed her to tell the lawmen *everything*, and she did.

When finished, the officers asked Amanda to read and sign her statement.

Colonel Barnett called Leila back inside. He wanted to have a few private words with Deputy Tucker, and they walked out on the porch.

In a few minutes, they re-entered the house and the Colonel said, "Because of the fact that so much time has passed, and this being a dating situation, I am going to pass all of this information on to Sheriff Clark personally, and maybe the State Attorney. I will give you a call in the morning, Miss Leila."

The two officers thanked Leila and Amanda, then returned to their unit.

*****

As they departed, Deputy Tommy Tucker asked, "What's the boss going to think about this one? Isn't this getting a little too close to home?"

"I didn't hear a strong enough set of facts to even bother the boss with such crap," replied the Colonel as he opened his lighter and lit a cigar. "I'll handle this tomorrow."

Chapter 28

Amanda returned to her home soon after the deputies departed. Leila was left alone with only the memories of her assault.

Leila's mind raced dejectedly in her unfamiliar state of despair. Still feeling spoiled and unclean, she immediately took yet another shower. It did not help. She tried to sleep again, but could only toss and turn. She could not bar the feelings of dirt and violation from her mind. She, in her own assessment, had somehow invited or allowed the attack. She simply had to rid her body of every molecule of filth that Ty Tyson might have left.

As the night passed, Leila could not enjoy even a minute of sleep. She fought the concept of revenge over and over in her thoughts. "There is a difference between revenge and justice," she concluded. "I will get justice," she vowed.

Leila showered again before daylight—this time standing under the showerhead for an even longer time. She slowly turned in a circle to meticulously cleanse every exposed molecule that he may have touched.

Finally convinced that she had washed herself as much as possible, Leila walked outside to the darkness of her front porch to wait for the sun to appear. When daylight finally arrived, she didn't move. She waited for a call from Colonel Max Barnett.

At 9:06 a.m., Leila's phone finally rang. "Good morning, Leila, this is Colonel Barnett," he said.

"Thank you, Colonel, the same to you," Leila replied.

"Leila, I know you are very upset about this matter, but there are procedures that we have to follow as officers of the law. The Sheriff didn't feel that the facts you gave warranted action without further review. The encouraging news is that he has instructed me to discuss this matter with the State Attorney when he returns from his vacation in about two weeks. There is a chance that the State Attorney may want to have a grand jury look at your statement, so the file will remain open."

There was a long moment of silence.

"Colonel Barnett, I was raped. Are you going to arrest Ty Tyson?" asked Leila, her voice shaking.

"Not at this time, Leila, that is all that I am saying. But I am going to personally see to it that the State Attorney will review your and Amanda's statement. He will be the one to make the final decision," said the Colonel.

"Is there anything I can do?" asked Leila.

"I'll let you know if I need more from you, Leila. Have a nice day," said the Colonel. Click.

*****

Leila buried her face in her hands. She did not cry – yet there was emotion swelling inside her of tremendous magnitude.

"Why should I be surprised about Colonel Barnett's call? I saw the look on his and Deputy Tucker's face when I said Ty

Tyson's name," she recalled.

Leila remembered reading from the Book of Psalms, "Refrain from anger and forsake wrath". With her stomach boiling with frustration, she had but one road to travel.

She returned into the house and picked up her Bible. It was her best friend. She knew where she needed to go. She went out the front door and onto Ebenezer Church Road.

When Leila arrived at the gate to Ebenezer Church, it squeaked when she swung it open. Briskly, she strode to her lifelong place of strength and worship in the woods.

Even the initial appearance of her beloved church gave Leila more energy and hope. Her pace quickened like a desert nomad with first sight of an oasis. She opened its two majestic doors and walked toward her reserved seat on the front row.

Rather than take the seat, Leila kneeled down in front of it. She looked up at God's image on the inside front wall of Ebenezer Church. Still somewhat out of breath, she lowered her head and prayed to Him for guidance. After more prayer, and a relatively short wait, the Lord answered.

He told Leila what to do! She received His full message. She needed the help of her "personal contacts" book. The person she needed to talk to was still in Destin.

She quickly rose to her feet, exited her sanctuary, and retraced her steps to her home. The contact book was on a table in her living room. She thumbed through it hurriedly and picked up her phone. After two rings, Jane Anderson answered.

"Jane, this is Leila Hewitt, I need your help—I've been raped!" Leila cried as she exploded the news to her newfound friend. "Could you please meet me—let me tell you what has happened—and give me some advice?" she asked desperately.

"Calm down now, Miss Leila—I can tell that you are upset. I

am at the beach now. If you could be at Mark's villa after lunch, say, one o'clock this afternoon, I will do what I can to help," Jane replied.

Leila thanked Jane and hung up. The meeting was less than two hours away, and it was an approximately forty minute drive. She picked up a pad and quickly made notes so that she would not forget any detail when she talked to Jane.

Afterwards, Leila bowed her head and prayed. She prayed that Jane, with her experience as a sex crimes investigator with the Atlanta police department, could help bring Ty Tyson to justice.

She opened her Bible to Proverbs 20:22 and read, "Do not say 'I will repay evil', wait for the Lord and He will deliver you."

*****

Leila reached Sandestin with time to spare. She circled her car through its shaded streets until time for her appointment.

Jane gave her a warm hug and welcomed her inside. Leila vowed to herself to control her emotions. She failed miserably.

Leila told Jane her complete experience with Doctor Ty Tyson, the best she could, from the beginning. Her first emotional breakdown began when she told Jane about her recollection of making "toasts of tea". A few moments later, Leila began to gasp for breath and totally weep after saying, "Jane, I can't remember very well what happened after that!"

Jane asked Leila to recall, as specifically as possible, how many times she left the dining room before and during the meal. She also asked Leila to describe, as much as possible, each and every detail she could recall before her memory left her. They were rather few.

What most caught Jane's attention was Leila's initial recollection of what she had experienced as she came out of her impaired state of mind.

Jane stopped Leila briefly to pull a yellow legal pad out of her briefcase. She made a time line starting with the exact date and hour of Ty Tyson's arrival at Leila's home.

Jane noted the approximate time of the first sounds that Leila remembered hearing as she regained awareness, followed by the exact time of Amanda's entry through the bedroom window. She continued the timeline, moment by moment, up to the minute of her conversation with Leila.

Jane questioned Leila in great detail about what physical symptoms she recalled – at what specific times on the timeline. She wanted to know *exactly* what Leila had experienced.

Leila was then pressed harder by Jane to describe every sensation she could recall concerning her head and brain, thinking processes, breath, heart rate, stomach, extremities and feminine area.

When Jane was finished asking questions, she looked at her watch. It was 2:30 p.m.

Jane walked over to a telephone directory and flipped it open to the yellow pages. When someone answered, Jane said, "Good afternoon, my name is Jane Anderson. I am an officer with the Atlanta Police Department. I want to see if it is possible to bring someone over to your lab in a few minutes so that we may submit a urine sample for analysis—time is of the essence!"

After waiting a short while for a confirmation, Jane said, "Good, I am coming from Sandestin, can you tell me exactly how to get to your lab?"

Jane wrote down the information and turned and looked at

Leila. "We have to go give a urine sample NOW," said Jane. "We are at the outer time limits of still being able to detect the type of drug that I suspect may be involved."

"What do you suspect I was given?" asked Leila.

"Let's just wait and see," said Jane. "The total loss of memory... if it is what I think it is, we need to get going. We are right at 72 hours!"

"Can I do it in a jar now – to save even more time?" asked Leila innocently.

Jane laughed, "No! If a drug is still in your system, the lab will have to certify that it came from you at a certain time. Let's hurry."

Chapter 29

Two days later, Leila received the much awaited report from Jane Anderson.

"Leila," Jane asked, "to your knowledge, have you at any time in the past been prescribed, or taken any type of drug that is a member of the benzodiazepine family?"

"No, Jane, I am not familiar with that name. I haven't taken any type of prescription drug. I can't remember a single occasion in the last ten years, none. I can only remember a tetanus shot many years ago," said Leila.

"Have you ordered any drugs from overseas, or has anyone given you any kind of medicine that you took, particularly sleeping pills – or sedatives – in the last few weeks?" asked Jane.

"No indeed—I would never take anything like that," Leila replied.

"The formal lab report was just received," Jane said. "Analysis indicates a definitive presence of residual traces of benzodiazepine, the exact form of which is believed to be Rohypnol. Limited trace quantity precluded further testing."

"What is it?" asked Leila quizzically.

"Rohypnol," said Jane, "is primarily used as a preoperative sedative and is a hypnotic drug, a sleeping medication NOT marketed for use in the United States. In Atlanta we call it a 'roofie'. We see it quite frequently. It is also called on the streets a 'roachie' or a Mexican valium."

"My Gracious!" said Leila, obviously distraught.

"This is exactly what I thought it might be when I heard your account," said Jane. "One of the unique characteristics of Rohypnol is the loss of memory suffered by a victim after ingestion. Roofies are all over Atlanta, and I am very familiar with the symptoms. Your experience is right down the line," Jane added.

"Well, at least we know what he did to me now," said Leila in a somber voice.

"I have already typed the statement that I took from you. I will attach this lab report to it and pay a visit to Colonel Max Barnett," said Jane. "I will give you a call after I have had the opportunity to meet with him."

"Thank you so much, Jane, you are a God send," said Leila, most appreciatively.

*****

The Walton County Sheriff's receptionist brought Jane a cup of coffee as she waited almost a half-hour for Colonel Barnett to see her. Finally, she was allowed to proceed back to his office. He was reading the local paper.

"Good day, Ms. Anderson, what brings you up to the big metropolis of DeFuniak Springs this morning?" the Colonel asked, extending his massive palm.

"Colonel, I am here to speak with you today on behalf of Ms. Leila Hewitt. I want to officially present some additional evidence on her behalf," Jane replied.

The Colonel's face made a slight, but very noticeable, scowl and his eyes widened. "Well, this is quite a surprise. The last time I saw the two of you together, you were at her throat," he said sarcastically.

"We have mended our fences. She called me after her assault a few days ago," Jane replied.

"What do you have?" asked the Colonel anxiously.

"First of all, I know that you conducted separate interviews with Ms. Hewitt and her friend Amanda," said Jane. "As you are aware, I am a detective in the Sex Crimes Division of the Atlanta Police Department, and we see these types of cases weekly – by the dozen. I took the liberty of getting my normal statement from Ms. Hewitt. I want to give you a copy of that statement, just in the event that I may have picked up a little something extra that may be helpful to your investigation."

Jane handed the Colonel the complete bundle of paperwork she had carried into his office. He started flipping through it, reading parts of it as he went. About halfway through, he stopped.

"Thank you, Miss Anderson. I have been in law enforcement for almost thirty years and have some experience myself," the Colonel said as he looked at Jane with furrowed eyebrows. "I do appreciate your kind assistance. This matter is going to be worked through our normal channels. I will supplement our file with what you have presented. Is there anything else?" he asked with a tone of finality.

"Yes, sir, there is," said Jane, not ready to leave just yet. "The last two pages are from Mid-Bay Laboratory. You will note that the urine analysis obtained from the victim detected Rohypnol within the requisite post-assault time allowance. The symptoms experienced by Ms. Hewitt were exactly those indicated as typical characteristics of the drug found."

Colonel Barnett was silent as he read the detailed analysis. A full minute passed. Then he looked up at Jane with a hard glare and said, "The presence of 'residual traces' always present a big problem for this type of case."

Jane did not bat an eye. "It presents a big problem for Doctor Ty Tyson," she said firmly.

Colonel Barnett's face turned even redder than it normally was. He looked back down at the lab report and collected his thoughts. After a few seconds he looked back up at Jane and said, "The State Attorney will be back from vacation in about a week. When he returns, your complete file, including this lab report, will be added to our office's presentation to him. We will not be taking any further action until we get an opportunity to get some direction from him."

Jane started not to say anything, but couldn't hold back, "In our jurisdiction this is a strong case, Colonel."

"You are not in your jurisdiction, Ms. Anderson. You, of all people, know that Ms. Hewitt has issues. But look, I appreciate what you have brought us this morning, and we are going to take a hard look at it," said the Colonel as he stood up indicating the meeting was over. Jane bit her lip, thanked the Colonel, and left.

When he was certain that Jane had exited the building, Colonel Barnett picked up his phone and called his boss, Sheriff Wayne Clark. When the sheriff answered, Colonel Barnett said, "Sheriff, do you mind if I ride out to your ranch? We have a real problem." There was a pause. "I am on my way," Barnett said.

Jane headed south down U.S. 331 toward Sandestin. She knew where the prosecution of Doctor Ty Tyson was surely headed—and she didn't like it one bit.

Chapter 30

Jane was more than a little experienced dealing with the politics of law enforcement. Atlanta is a tough town, and she worked in one of its boiler rooms. With the appearance of a junior leaguer and the tenacity of a junk yard dog, it was best not to provoke her—and Jane had been provoked by Colonel Max Barnett.

Back at the Sandestin villa, Jane hurried to a phone book and made a note of Doctor Ty Tyson's office and home addresses. She grabbed a Destin city map and decided to do a drive-by of both locations. She proceeded to his private medical office first. It was in a strip center on Airport Road. A swimming pool supply store was on one side of Tyson's office, and a real estate office was on the other. The sign in front of his office indicated that Doctor Tyson was a general practitioner.

Jane then drove to the doctor's residence that was located on Indian Trail Drive—a very upscale residential street that runs along Choctawhatchee Bay. The doctor's large home was located on the water.

The house next door to the home of Dr. Tyson was for sale. Jane wrote down the real estate agent's phone number for later use. It was getting late, so she decided to pay a visit to the real estate business that she had previously noticed adjacent to Doctor Tyson's office.

"Hello, I am Jane Taylor," Jane said as she introduced herself by her first two names to a rather portly real estate agent who was alone in the office.

"You stopped by just in the nick of time, I was about to lock up the doors and close shop for the day," said Dick Lafleur, who proceeded to introduce himself.

"Would you rather I come back tomorrow?" asked Jane.

"Oh, no!" replied Dick with a big smile. "Attractive young buyers like you are always welcome around here. Am I going to sell you a house today – or a condo?"

"We have a little coffee shop just up the road," said Jane. "How about we go up there, and you tell me a little bit about Destin. I'm buying."

"I've never had an offer from a prettier girl," replied Dick. "I'll meet you there," he said.

Within minutes, they were seated, served, and drinking coffee. Jane told Dick Lafleur that she worked in the medical field, was relocating, and looking for a job. "Do you think there are any job openings in the doctor's office next door to your office?" she asked.

"Well, there is a pretty high turnover in Doctor Tyson's office. He only hires beautiful women to work for him, so there is a good chance 'old doc' would be very much interested in your application," Dick said with a wry smile.

"Why a big turnover?" Jane asked.

"Honestly," Dick said with a more serious expression, "Doctor Tyson has a reputation of being a real womanizer, and it might not be the ideal place to work unless you like rich, lecherous widowers."

"Do you know the names of any of the women who have left his employment?" Jane asked.

"Are you sure you work in the medical field? – Well, actually I don't care," said Dick obviously growing suspicious of Jane's special interest in Doctor Tyson.

Dick took another sip from his cappuccino and continued, "If you want to know all about Doctor Tyson you might talk to Heather Hays, who is now working for Doctor Mitchell on Mountain Drive. She is somewhat of a friend of mine – and can tell you plenty about that creep."

Before Jane left her new friend, she told Dick she might want him to show her a house, or two, in the next couple of days. It had been time well spent for Jane.

*****

The next morning Jane tried to locate a home phone number for Heather Hays, but to no avail. She drove to Doctor Mitchell's office and ran the license plate numbers on the employees' vehicles parked in the rear of the building. A red Mazda convertible came back as owned by Heather A. Hays. Jane then called the doctor's office and asked the receptionist what time their office closed. Jane went to the beach.

At a quarter to five, Jane returned to Doctor Mitchell's office and watched the red Mazda pull out of the parking lot shortly after 5 o'clock. She followed the vehicle to a local grocery store, then to a small duplex on Calhoun Drive. She waited about 15 minutes and knocked on the door.

A small, pretty lady with dark hair peeked through the crack of the chain-locked opening.

"Are you Heather Hays?" asked Jane.

"Yes I am, why?" replied Heather curtly.

"My name is Jane Anderson, I am with the Atlanta Police Department working a local case. Do you mind if I have a few words with you?"

"About what?" asked Heather, obviously alarmed.

Jane didn't usually divulge information through a cracked door, she never knew if other people were within earshot. However, she kept talking, "I would like to get some background information on one of your former employers and would appreciate just a little of your time."

"I have been instructed not to discuss anything with anyone," Heather said emphatically.

Heather's comment took Jane by surprise. "Instructed by whom?" she asked instinctively.

"I have been instructed not to discuss anything with anybody," said Heather firmly.

"Look, please take this," Jane said, handing Heather her business card.

"If you change your mind, or need any help, please give me a call. Sorry for the intrusion," said Jane.

Jane walked back to her vehicle. "She was instructed, not warned – sounds like either a lawyer or the law," she thought. Either way, Jane knew something was in the works.

Chapter 31

Mark Mabry sat up very slowly on the side of his bed. He was still experiencing a little dizziness if he moved too quickly. It had only been two days since his skin transplant surgery. His eyes were dark charcoal colored, almost black. When he looked at his own heavily bandaged forehead, he thought to himself and smiled, "I look like a raccoon with a turban."

He walked slowly through his house and out onto the front porch. The daily edition of the "Atlanta Constitution" was in its usual place on the steps. He had to be careful bending over to pick up the paper, or else he would lose his balance. He walked back into his living room and started flipping through the paper. When he reached the business section, a prominent article caught his attention.

"MACKCO ADVERTISING COMPANY SOLD TO NEW YORK FIRM," was the headline! The story was an absolute shock! Albert J. Mackey was retiring, and Caleb Hathcox was appointed Acting President during the transition of management. The story made it clear that a new president would be selected soon from among the acquiring company's existing officers. The story also stated that national accounts would be transferred to a New York location. In the future, a smaller work force would be maintained in Atlanta.

Mark laid the paper on a nearby table. It was painfully clear why Mr. Mackey had not been returning his calls. He thought for a few minutes, then picked up his cell phone and dialed Charlie McBride.

After a brief greeting, Mark began to inform Charlie of the Mackco developments.

"Yeah, Mark, I read that article two hours ago and figured you could possibly become a casualty. There will probably be quite a few," Charlie said grimly.

"Well, Charlie, I have been thinking about changing careers, here is my opportunity. I want you to list my house as soon as possible," replied Mark.

"Don't overreact, Mark, you are one of Mackco's sharpest and most productive employees. You haven't received the pink slip yet, have you?" asked Charlie.

"I know it is coming," replied Mark.

"Maybe not," said Charlie.

"How soon can you get my house entered on MLS?" Mark asked.

"Where are you going to live, Mark? Aren't you moving a little fast?" questioned Charlie.

"I'm not happy in a white shirt, or even in the corporate world, Charlie," said Mark. "I've got a little money in the bank and equity in this house. I am going to move to Destin and figure it out. Things always happen for the best!"

"OK, Mark, if that is what you want to do, I will be over right after noon with a listing agreement and a salad for you from the Greek Kitchen," said Charlie.

"No anchovies, please," replied Mark.

*****

The letter of termination from Mackco arrived before the salad. A check representing three month's severance pay was included in the letter. The money helped soften the news. There was also an assurance of a good personal recommendation from Mr. Mackey, if one was ever needed.

Charlie showed up with lunch, but it did not help Mark's light-headedness. He fell asleep within minutes after Charlie departed with the executed listing agreement. About four hours later, the phone rang. It was Mary Kate Nelson.

"Mark, I am so glad you answered the phone," said Mary Kate, very disconsolately. "My father had a stroke, and I am in the Atlanta airport about to catch a plane to New York City. My mother has been ill for some time. I don't know if I will be coming back."

"Mary Kate, I am so sorry to hear that," Mark replied with sincere dejection. "I hope your father will be all right."

"It does not sound very encouraging," replied Mary Kate. Mark could tell that she was holding back her emotions.

"Please stay in touch with me and let me know how things are going," requested Mark.

"I hope you will stay in touch with me," said Mary Kate softly. "You know how much I care for you. Would you consider visiting me in New York when you are feeling better?"

Mark did not want to share with Mary Kate that he had just lost his employment and that money was now a real concern. "You know I will stay in touch. You have been very nice to me since my injury, you know that my prayers are with you. I am so sorry to hear about your father," Mark said sincerely.

Mark and Mary Kate said their goodbyes. He did not know if they would ever speak again.

*****

Mark rested motionless in his shadowed bedroom. The events of the last month raced through his wrapped and still throbbing head.

"In difficult times, adversity can bring opportunity," he thought.

His mind drifted to that special place that still dominated his imagination and dreams – Ebenezer Forest. "I'd wager its trees grow stronger after a hurricane," he mused.

"It will be that way for me," Mark resolved, drifting back into a deep, deep sleep.

Chapter 32

Jane Anderson placed an early morning telephone call to real estate agent Andrea Anders. Andrea was the listing agent on the Indian Trail residence next door to Doctor Ty Tyson. Jane advised Andrea which house she wanted to view and asked that the showing be after 5 o'clock in the afternoon. Jane speculated that the owners would likely have returned from work by that hour. She requested that the realtor not ask the owners to leave their home for the appointment saying, "I always have more questions than realtors can normally answer." Jane also requested to meet the realtor a half-hour early "to learn a little more about Destin".

Andrea Anders was a very snappily-dressed, married lady in her late forties. She was waiting at the designated diner on Main Street when Jane arrived. After the greetings, Jane asked Andrea some general questions about Destin. Andrea was very upbeat and talkative. Jane could quickly tell that she was not the type of person to hold much back. She wasted little time proceeding directly to her real topic of interest.

"Are the sellers of the Indian Trail property moving out of town?" Jane asked.

"They are primarily scaling down," replied Andrea. Jane

wanted to know what "primarily" meant but did not ask.

"Tell me about the neighbors. They are always very important to me," requested Jane.

"On the west side are the Brunsons, they are elderly and retired; they attend my church. On the east side is Doctor Tyson, a fairly recent widower," replied Andrea.

"Doctor Ty Tyson, oh no! Do you know him?" baited Jane.

Andrea lowered her eyes somewhat sheepishly.

"Is he as bad a womanizer as they say?" pressed Jane before Andrea could answer her prior question.

"Is Doctor Tyson being a neighbor a deal killer about wanting to see this house?" Andrea asked Jane softly.

"I don't know, I have heard so much," said Jane. "Please tell me what you know to be true about him."

Andrea looked up at Jane with furrowed eyebrows, "Jane, I am not a gossip. Since you apparently have already heard a lot about Doctor Tyson, I will tell you what I know. After I tell you this, if you still want to see the house, please do not bring this topic up with my clients, the Rountrees. Mrs. Rountree was very close to Doctor Tyson's wife, Mary Beth. According to Mrs. Rountree, Mary Beth and Doctor Tyson were having serious marital problems, and she appeared to be in good health. But she died suddenly." Andrea took a long sip of her coffee.

"Since then," Andrea continued, "and it hasn't been that terribly long ago, there have been a lot of parties at the Tyson house. The Rountrees made several late night complaints to the local police. Doctor Tyson is friends with a bunch of local politicians, some of whom were even partying with him next door. Of course, the complaints have gone absolutely nowhere."

"Is that the real reason why the Rountrees have their house up for sale?" asked Jane.

"To be totally honest, yes," replied Andrea.

"Look, Andrea, you have been very up front with me, and I appreciate it very much," said Jane. "I don't think that, under the circumstances, I want to infringe on the Rountrees any more than I already have. It sounds like they are rightfully upset. I do not want to waste any more of their good time. I would appreciate if you not tell them the reason for my cancellation. It will only compound the discomfort they already have with this situation."

Andrea understood and made the cancellation call to the Rountree residence.

Jane then asked Andrea, "Is there any more to this that you would please share with me?"

"No, but our company does have a very nice listing on the far end of Indian Trail that you might be interested in," replied Andrea.

"Andrea, you have been candid with me, and I need to be the same with you," Jane said very earnestly. "The truth is that I am a detective from Atlanta working as a volunteer on a serious sexual assault case that occurred in this area. I have a very good reason for calling you about your listing, but it is not to purchase the Rountree's house. I owe you an apology for this intrusion. Please believe me when I tell you that it is for a very good purpose."

"I think I am getting the picture," said a wide-eyed Andrea.

"I do want to ask you two more things," said Jane. "First, do you have any more information about Doctor Ty Tyson that might be in any way helpful to me?" she asked.

Andrea paused for a long moment. "Nothing that I can share," she said.

"What does that mean?" Jane questioned quickly.

"That is all that I am going to say, all I can say," replied

Andrea firmly.

"OK, I understand," replied Jane. "The other thing that I would like to say to you is this—I am only going to be around Destin full time for a few more days. If you should run into me anywhere, or with anyone – even Dr. Tyson – would you please not reveal what I have told you about my volunteer work?" Jane asked.

"Well, I cannot say that I am happy about you calling me for this listing," replied Andrea. "I do appreciate you telling me your real purpose and not disturbing the Rountrees this afternoon. I won't say anything to them or anyone else."

The two ladies exchanged cards and parted company. Jane had learned some additional information from Andrea, but nothing that was totally unexpected or shocking.

With only a few days left in Destin, it was time for Jane Anderson to take her efforts to a new level.

Chapter 33

Jake Delaughter was working in his front yard when he saw Leila's car coming down Ebenezer Road toward the highway. He walked over to his gate as an invitation for her to stop. Leila obliged and opened her passenger window.

"All I ever see headed towards your place lately are sheriffs' cars, Ms. Leila. Is everything OK down there?" Jake asked. He had read the local newspaper article some time back reporting that all charges against Mark Mabry had been dropped. He had also noticed the recent other official visit.

"Everything's fine, Jake," Leila replied unconvincingly. "There will be a lot more traffic this afternoon. I am expecting a large group of forestry students from Troy State shortly after lunch."

"You know if you ever need anything, all you have to do is call," Jake offered for the countless time over the years.

"Thank you for worrying about me, Jake. I am going to have you down for chicken and dumplings again soon, I promise," said Leila as she pulled away from her lifelong neighbor. "He must think my life is falling apart," she thought as she turned north at the intersection.

The emotional aftermath Leila was experiencing since being violated had been shared, like almost everything else in her life, with her best friend, Amanda. With Leila's approval, Amanda had fully informed Reverend McGraw of the situation. He scheduled a private support session for Leila on this particular morning at her new church in Red Bay. Of course, Amanda would be there as well. This meeting was not an unwelcome exercise for Leila. The springtime excitements of her life had all turned to hellfire, and she needed her church now more than ever.

Amanda was waiting in the parking lot. Leila joined her and they walked into the church. Reverend McGraw was waiting at his office door and gave them both a big hug. When they were seated, the reverend recited The Lord's Prayer.

After the traditional prayer, the Reverend looked up at Leila and offered his thoughts, "Sister Leila, I know that you have been going through some hard times in your life recently, and these are the times that our blessed Lord is especially here for you. God's greatest vision for all of us is that we remain virgins until we marry. But if sexual intercourse has been forced on you with violence and against your will, you shall remain pure, guiltless and shameless in the eyes of the Lord. Only your physical virginity has been stolen. You will remain a virgin in the eyes of God and His church, this church, until you willingly share your body within the bounds of holy matrimony!"

He paused and looked directly into Leila's moist eyes. She felt he wanted her to say something.

"Reverend McGraw," Leila answered slowly, "it was totally against my will. I was raped." Leila paused, "There is something else we need to talk about. I haven't had a chance to really talk to you since that day on my porch, when I admitted I had sinned by lusting for Mark Mabry. There was no intercourse then. But those sinful thoughts...look what happened! Mark has been scarred for life! I would have never been exposed to the man that raped me!" Leila started to cry.

"I feel so soiled," continued Leila. "I DO feel guilty!" Tears rolled down Leila's cheeks. Amanda reached over and gently placed her hand on Leila's shoulder.

Reverend McGraw let Leila cry for a while and then started afresh, "In the Mabry instance, Leila, you had a sexual attraction that I would classify as an episode of immorality. You were able to stop before it became a sin against your body—in spite of your admittance to lust. But Leila, there is a big difference between lust and a sin against your body." Reverend McGraw paused and continued, "The Bible says that all other sins a man commits are outside his body, but he who sins sexually, sins against his own body. This is a strong admonition, but mere lusting is not an actual sexual sin against your body." The Reverend cleared his throat.

"In the second instance, the rape," the Reverend proceeded, "there was a sin committed against your body, Leila, but it was not committed by you. Even though you have committed and confessed to a lesser degree of immorality in the first instance, you are still a virgin in God's eyes – any way we look at it!" The Reverend leaned back in his chair with an air of pride in his eloquent pronouncement.

Leila felt somewhat lighter inside about her complicated circumstance. She wiped the last drying tears from her cheeks.

Then to the dismay of her minister and Amanda, Leila changed the subject. "Let me ask you this, Reverend McGraw," inquired Leila as she leaned forward. "What does the Bible say about relationships between people with significant age difference?"

Upon hearing Leila's question, Amanda missed a breath and

felt her knuckles tighten.

The Reverend's brow wrinkled. The preacher thought quickly while he slowly cleared his throat, twice. Finally, he resorted to the truth, "There is nothing in the Bible that I know of that prohibits relationships based on age. In ancient times, a 12 year old person was considered an adult. It was not uncommon for 12 year old women to wed 40 year old men. I know that many people in our own church would consider such a relationship to be immoral. But there is really nothing in the Bible that would support such a conclusion. As long as two people are of lawful age, married, and true to each other, there is no apparent sin in the house of the Lord."

"My whole life," Leila said softly, her mind obviously jumping around, "I have believed there could be no more precious gift than to be able to present myself as a virgin to my husband on our wedding night – committed to him, and him only, forever." There was silence in the room.

"That is still possible, Leila, in the eyes of our Lord," said Reverend McGraw, softly.

"Leila, please remember this," the reverend said, "you will always achieve atonement from our Lord, Jesus Christ, for any sins that you may have committed in the past, through prayer and repledged commitment. Let us pray to Him."

"Dear Lord," the reverend prayed aloud,
"Please help us remember that love is patient and
love is kind. It does not envy. It does not boast. It
is not proud. It is not rude. It is not self-seeking.
It is not easily angered. It keeps no record of
wrongs. Love does not delight in evil, but rejoices
with the truth. It always protects, always trusts,

always hopes. And it always perseveres. Just like You, our Lord, love never fails. Amen!"

When the prayer was over, Leila and Amanda hugged the reverend again and walked outside together. Amanda was quite upset about the age difference question Leila had just asked, but decided to save her concerns for another time.

"Thank you so much, Amanda. Brother McGraw's words have been a true comfort," said Leila. She kissed Amanda on her cheek and drove off to welcome the afternoon visitors to Ebenezer Forest.

Chapter 34

Jane Anderson was positioned in a strategic location to see all of the vehicles parked near Doctor Ty Tyson's medical clinic. At 5:30 p.m. there were only two cars remaining in the rear of the strip center. The tall, well-dressed physician, with his shock of gray hair, walked out of his office and crawled into the freshly-polished Mercedes 550-SL. He proceeded down Airport Road, taking a right turn onto Miracle Strip Parkway. About three miles down the road, he turned left into the Bar Harbor Restaurant, Bar and Marina parking lot.

The waterfront establishment, located on the north side of Destin Harbor, was a popular after-work watering hole for locals. Jane waited about five minutes after Doctor Tyson entered the building to exit her vehicle and follow him inside.

This would be the last investigative ploy she had time for before she needed to return to work in Atlanta. It was a role she was familiar with, and she had set the trap beautifully. She chose a very low cut and sexy black dress.

It was the same dress that Jane's fellow officers in her sex crimes unit called the *black anaconda*. It showed every vivacious curve of Jane's long and comely figure. The guys in her unit would tease Jane by saying that when she wore the *black anaconda,* it attracted her villainous prey like flypaper – where they would soon meet their crushing destruction. Jane knew that this highly educated doctor was heads and shoulders above the street criminals that she normally targeted. She was highly motivated and badly wanted this predator in a very different way than he was about to want her. It was time for Jane to meet the "not-so-good" doctor!

A doorman welcomed Jane. She noticed a room full of mostly men in the lounge off to her right. Every head turned to see Jane's knockout presentation as she eased toward the bar. Two fishermen stepped aside to let her make an order.

Jane immediately spotted Doctor Tyson sitting with two other gentlemen in a water-view corner. She caught the doctor's eye, but avoided looking in his direction again. When she received her drink, Jane walked over to the huge glass window overlooking Destin Harbor. She stopped about three feet from the doctor's table. A quick glance revealed that Jane did not recognize the other two men seated with him.

Jane pretended to be looking at the fishing fleet docked outside and the numerous boats enjoying the late afternoon in the harbor. The three men at the table of her interest had definitely taken major notice of her, but were engaged in a serious and very whispered discussion.

Jane decided to return to the bar. The only empty stool was at the end farthest from the front door. There were about twenty people between Jane and the doorman.

Jane got her first glimpse of a very large man whose huge frame blocked the entry portal. As he moved into the barroom, she got a much better look. It was Colonel Max Barnett! "Dammit!" she thought, knowing her afternoon jig was up.

The Colonel knew where he was headed and never looked

at Jane. He took the remaining empty chair at the table with Doctor Tyson. Fortunately, his back was toward Jane.

There was a double doorway into an adjacent dining room directly behind where Jane was seated. She immediately paid the bartender for her drink and left the bar through the doorway. At the far end of the dining room was the kitchen. Jane walked right into and through the kitchen amidst all of the kitchen help. She took a side door back out to the front parking lot. She was breathing heavy and had unfamiliar butterflies in her stomach as she made her way back to her car.

"It would have been much worse if Colonel Barnett had noticed me," thought Jane. She was totally frustrated. "Heather Hays knew something and wouldn't talk. Andrea Anders knew something and wouldn't talk, and now this," she reflected.

Jane had a good view of the front door and decided she would at least wait until the meeting inside broke up. Depending on what happened next, she would determine then if she was done for the evening. Jane felt foolish as she sat in her tight *black anaconda* dress—with herself the only person being squeezed.

A few minutes passed. A short middle-aged fellow, with the appearance of a tourist, exited the restaurant. He walked about ten feet away from the front entrance and stopped. Jane had not noticed him previously. He made at least two calls on his cell phone and then waited a short while longer. He appeared to take an incoming call and engage in a brief discussion. He looked across the parking lot towards Jane's car and started walking in her direction.

Jane looked down toward her lap to give the approaching man the appearance that she was reading. She could hear his footsteps as he neared her, but Jane did not look up. She expected the man to walk past her vehicle, but shockingly, he rapped on Jane's window with his knuckles. Jane started to reach for the 38 revolver under her seat, but instead looked up at the stranger.

"Put your window further down, Ms. Anderson," said the man as he pulled a badge out of his back pocket. "My name is Donald Baxter, FBI agent out of Pensacola."

Jane rolled down her window and took a close look at the badge.

"I just talked to my boss," Baxter began, "and he asked that I come over and get you out of here. He said to tell you that we are fully aware of your efforts. He also instructed me to ask you to please totally back off this matter for the time being. We have your contact information, and the boss said he will fully brief you in due time."

"Who's the boss?" asked Jane.

"He did not instruct me to tell you that," replied Baxter. He pulled a business card out of his shirt pocket. "You can call this number if you want to confirm my credentials. Do you want me to write my badge number on it?"

"I can remember it," replied Jane.

"The boss also asked, as usual, that you not share the information you have just received with anyone other than your superior, you know the program," said Baxter.

"Roger," replied Jane rolling her eyes.

"Thanks for understanding and your cooperation. We already have a lot of time on this case," said Baxter.

"You are welcome," replied Jane.

"And hey, Ms. Anderson," Baxter continued with a big grin as he turned to walk away, "nice dress!"

Jane was both agitated and relieved. She started her car to leave, and at that moment, saw Colonel Max Barnett walk out of the restaurant. She was pleased to know he was right in the line of fire of a federal investigation.

Chapter 35

The summer was the busy season for Ebenezer Forest. Church youth groups, scout troops, day camps, and forestry and wildlife majors visited in steady numbers. They came to enjoy and study the Choctawhatchee hardwood bottomland when it was most plush and vibrant.

The deer, black bear, butterflies, birds, and snakes—and of course the magnificent trees—were all among the favorite attractions. The excitement and enthusiasm of the young people, as they spilled out of their cars and buses, always gave Leila renewed fullness of heart. She was becoming reacquainted with the sweet aromas of the forest that had nurtured her all of her life; it was making her feel energetic and alive again.

Leila watched from her front porch as a group of elementary students and a few parents disappeared in single file down the wooded trail toward Ebenezer Church. Jane Anderson had called to briefly say that she would stop by for a visit on her way back to Atlanta. She arrived right on time.

Leila hugged Jane and shared the iced tea that was always ready whenever she expected visitors. There had been no real communication between the two ladies since Jane phoned Leila after presenting the lab results to Colonel Barnett.

"Leila, I have done some modest snooping around about Doctor Tyson," Jane began. "What I have mainly learned is that he does not have a very good reputation when it comes to women."

"I was a complete fool," said Leila quite matter of factly.

"I wouldn't put it that way, Leila," replied Jane. "I have reason to believe that your experience was probably not an isolated assault committed by Doctor Tyson."

Leila had been praying to avoid being overcome with vengeance and chose to remain silent.

"I do not feel very optimistic about what the official Walton County response to your complaint will be. I have some reliable information that there is – or might be," said Jane stumbling, "some indication that this matter is far from over."

Leila's eyes squinted with puzzlement.

"I am not free to tell you everything I have found out, but there are some encouraging developments," stated Jane emphatically.

"I certainly do not want what Ty Tyson did to me to be repeated with other women," Leila replied firmly.

"In the event that no charges are accepted on your case, you do have other options," said Jane. "You could retain a lawyer and file a motion to have the Walton County Sheriff's Office, and the Walton County State Attorney's Office, recused from the prosecution of your case. You also have the right to file a civil suit against Doctor Tyson. I believe that would be a good option. If you choose to file a lawsuit, you can likely have your name sealed because of the nature of this case."

"I think Ty Tyson is a very evil man, Jane," said Leila earnestly. "Do you think that I am in any sort of danger?"

Jane had not given that possibility much thought, but as the question sunk in, it did raise some concern. "Do you own a gun, Leila?" Jane asked.

"I do have a single-barrel 410 shotgun for poisonous snakes, rabid foxes, or other sick animals," she replied.

"I don't see a yard dog around here or a security system, is that right?" asked Jane with a tone of concern.

"All I really have as a watchdog is Mr. Jake up at the corner, but he is a good one," replied Leila.

"Well, nothing is likely to happen, but you should be as careful as possible," said Jane. "Please stay on alert until this whole ordeal is over. You just never know," added Jane.

"Jane, I want to ask you about Mark, how is he doing?" inquired Leila. "I have been praying for him every day and night."

Jane took a long sip of her tea and said, "A lot has happened recently. I talked to Charlie this morning, and Mark is still recovering from a skin transplant on his forehead. We won't know if more surgeries are needed for a while. Unfortunately, the company he worked for was sold, and he lost his job. He told Charlie he would soon be relocating to Destin."

Leila's eyes got a glassy look and she lowered her head. "I so hate to hear that he is having any kind of difficulty, and what a bad time in his young life to lose his job," she said with a concerned expression.

There was a short pause in the conversation.

"Jane, I want you to know that I have real feelings for Mark," said Leila.

Jane felt a tightening in her chest. She resisted the jolt of anger that swelled inside of her, but hesitated to make certain she chose her next words carefully. "Mark has been through a lot in his life—he was practically raised as an orphan. If there is ever anyone on earth who deserves to have a traditional life, to get married and have children, and have the kind of normalcy he has never had—it is Mark Mabry," Jane replied with a cracking voice and a soulful tone.

"What an old fool I am to share my sentiments. Jane obviously has concerns for Mark too," Leila thought. She felt crushed by her own insensitivity and ignorance. She did not reply to Jane's comments. She really had no issue with anything that Jane had just said. Leila simply did not respond.

There was a long, uncomfortable silence as each woman reflected on the situation.

Leila finally broke the silence. "Jane, I want to thank you so very much for being there for me when I called for your help," Leila said with deep sincerity.

"I did not tell you," Leila continued, "but I was totally lost as to what to do. I walked back to my church in the woods and prayed to God Almighty, on my knees, for His guidance. Then, the Lord told me to call you."

Jane could see tears forming in Leila's eyes. "If it wasn't for you, Jane—I wouldn't even know for sure what happened to me. Oh God, thank you so much, Jane," Leila cried out softly.

Jane stood up, hugged Leila warmly, and walked out to her car. As she proceeded down Ebenezer Church Road, back to her distant world, she took a last glimpse in her rear view mirror. Leila had buried her face into her hands.

Jane just shook her head and thought, "It is hard for me to have any anger toward such a good, pure woman."

Chapter 36

Mark's long awaited drive to Destin was, for him, the beginning of an exciting chapter in his life's journal. The familiar little towns of northeast Alabama, with their boarded sidewalks and little cafés, were quaint beacons of days gone by. They sparked memories of Mark's own past. The unfulfilling successes of his advertising career were now being left behind him.

Mark's recent personal misfortunes ticked, like the miles on his odometer, through his thoughts as he drove southward. But he was able to neatly shelve the negative memories into the deep recesses of his mind. The prospect of new adventures gave Mark much welcome anticipation—and a pleasant challenge for the road ahead.

There was still one important piece of unfinished business that Mark wanted to reconcile. He had been able to manage his physical injury without undue difficulty. But when a person has an emotional pain, it doesn't easily go away. It cannot be covered with bandages, or repaired with borrowed skin. Silent wounds cut deep and will bleed a man dry, and Mark's dripping wound was Leila.

"I've tried, but cannot forget her," thought Mark. He had only occasionally been able to put thoughts of Leila out of his head. Even a brief recall of the sparkle in Leila's eyes, or of the softness of their intimate kisses, set him ablaze.

Leila captivated Mark like no one before. It was not just her innocent sensuality, but also the cleanliness of her heart and spirit, that provoked his insuppressible desire.

As the day lengthened and the distance to Ebenezer Church Road grew shorter, Mark fought the temptation to pay the lovely object of his obsession a surprise visit. Mark had no idea as to how Leila would receive him, or even if she were going to be at home. He wondered what he should say, and how she would respond to his yet unknown words.

Only reciprocal postage-stamped letters of regret had bridged the many painful days that had passed since the tragedy of the storm. "What has been transpiring in Leila's life, and what are her innermost feelings about our intimate moments together?" were Mark's two biggest unanswered questions for Leila. "Asking Leila either one, directly, would likely be a bad idea," Mark thought.

Mark's stomach began to tighten as he slowed his sports car through Red Bay. The temptation to see Leila again was too strong. "I must stop to see her!" he decided.

Mark hoped he would not run into Jake Delaughter on Ebenezer Church Road. He was relieved when Jake was nowhere in sight as he passed.

Mark looked longingly for the familiar doe in the curve, but she was nowhere to be seen.

The first view of Leila's old, blue Oldsmobile parked in her circular driveway gave Mark goose bumps of anxiety. He could feel the wetness in his palms as they sweated in anticipation.

He parked his car and ascended slowly up the squeaky steps onto the porch. Before he arrived at the front door, it opened.

Leila's eyes widened as she looked, for the first time in nearly ten weeks, at the gentle and loving expression on Mark's face. He was much more slender now, but as handsome as ever.

The deep and powerful emotions of all that had been shared by them surged through Leila's body.

"My dear, Mark," Leila gasped. She followed her heart toward him and fell into his waiting arms.

Leila hugged Mark around his still powerful shoulders with all of her might. She did not want to lose him again.

Mark held Leila tightly against his chest and softly stroked her hair as her head lay against him.

A long minute passed, and Leila looked up at Mark with tears in her eyes.

"Mark, I am so sorry that you were injured. We were headed to a place that my beliefs did not allow," she cried softly.

"Shh Shh, now, that is all in our past," Mark whispered. He wanted desperately to kiss Leila's lips, to taste her sweet breath, but he did not dare.

The sound of a blue pick-up truck grew louder as it approached Leila's house. Mark stepped back away from Leila, and she brushed the tears from her cheeks. They both recognized that the vehicle belonged to Jake Delaughter. Jake pulled off the road, opened the side door, and stepped one leg down to the ground.

"Is everything all right, Ms. Leila?" Jake asked in a deep concerned voice.

"Yes, Jake, everything is fine," replied Leila. "Thank you for checking on me." Apparently Jake had recognized Mark's car from an unobserved distance when it passed. He backed his truck around and returned toward his home.

"Come inside, Mark. I have missed you so much," said Leila,

pulling his arm.

Mark followed Leila into the living room. They sat down next to each other on the sofa. Leila reached over and took Mark's hands in hers. She reached up and gently touched Mark's forehead, then lifted her face closer to him. She kissed his wound softly.

"I was so drawn to you that day, Mark, and I have a commitment to God to save that special gift until marriage," Leila whispered. "I guess Jane told you about my rape?" She lowered her head.

"What?" Mark exclaimed. His mouth dropped sharply and his eyes exploded wide open.

It never occurred to Leila that Jane had not informed Mark of her victimization. She thought he knew.

"Jane hasn't told me anything!" Mark said almost hysterically. "What happened?"

Leila began to sob uncontrollably. "Oh, Mark, please hold me!" she cried.

Over the next twenty minutes, Leila painfully and tearfully told Mark everything—every agonizing detail of her rape. At times, she could barely catch her breath. She would have to stop, try to collect herself, and then wait to begin again.

At other times, Leila would just hang her head and cry. Mark listened intently to every disturbing word, and the horror of it all hit him like a powerful blow to his stomach. He became literally gut-wrenchingly ill. He felt Leila's anguish as though it was his own. Mark laid his head on Leila's shoulder and cried with her.

Leila thought no one else could ever share her pain – or be so sensitive to the excruciating suffering she had endured. She felt Mark's warm, salty tears as they poured from his caring eyes.

She felt them merge with her own droplets, then run together down both faces, like one stream through the forest. She realized that she was so very wrong—to have ever doubted her feelings for her Mark.

*****

The afternoon shadows grew longer over Ebenezer Church Road. The undeniable bond between the two near lovers strengthened—like the mighty arms of the large oaks that lined the winding roadway to Ebenezer Forest.

They were both totally drained by the intimate emotions of their reunion. Leila fell asleep with her head in Mark's lap.

Mark looked at Leila's lovely, sleeping face for a long while. He drifted into a half dream-half reality trance of warm thoughts.

"I am where I want to be, with the person I want to be with," Mark thought.

A sense of total completeness embraced him. He felt its powerful hold. He was in a light sleep—a state of pure fulfilment—and when he opened his eyes—he was in the arms of Leila.

*****

Leila later stirred and woke Mark. It was nearly dark outside, and the couple made their way back to the kitchen porch. They looked at the exact location where their passion had first sparked and exploded. Simply a spot on a porch, it nonetheless provoked painful memories.

Leila turned and looked into Mark's face. She smiled and walked slowly over to him. She threw her arms around Mark's neck, and they kissed each other deeply. The intensity of their kisses was there, magnetic as ever. They tasted each other's hot breath and inhaled each other's heat. Their embrace rekindled the fire and passion that each had so desperately missed.

Leila and Mark's prior sexual detonation was now replaced with a true, heartfelt, loving connection. Their mutual attraction had passed the greatest test of all – the test of time.

There was a commitment in these kisses, each would forever trust.

*****

Leila warmed some leftover soup, and they ate and talked. Afterwards, they walked back into the living room and sat down together on the couch. Leila leaned backwards into Mark's arms and turned to face him. He held her head above his lap. There was a small lamp in the corner and its flickering light danced in Leila's eyes as she looked up at Mark. Occasionally, Mark would lean over and slowly kiss her receptive lips. Fears and apprehensions of a lifetime slowly gave way to a wonderful feeling of oneness.

"What are your characteristics of an ideal relationship, Leila?" asked Mark sincerely.

Leila thought for a minute and then replied, "In a poetry class at Florida State, I read some writer's definition of a good poem. It said that a good poem should have wholeness, harmony, and radiance. I reflected on that for a while and concluded that the same criteria would describe the type of relationship I would love to have. With wholeness, the whole of the two united partners is a larger, greater force than what would be the sum of the individuals. You've heard the old saying, Mark – the whole is greater than the sum of its parts."

"Harmony is more common and probably the easiest of the three criteria to obtain, I imagine," Leila continued.

"But radiance, radiance is that special, elusive element," Leila said, now whispering, "where a couple walks into a room and everyone can see from their glow that they are truly in love. Those are the three elements that I have always sought in a relationship."

"Do you see the glow in my eyes?" asked Mark playfully.

"Yes, and I can feel your glowworm in my back," teased Leila, most uncharacteristically.

Mark laughed out loud. Soon, he began to kiss Leila deeply. Unlike times in the past, there was not a trace of sexual tension or fear.

Leila enjoyed Mark's strokes of her face, and his delicious lips, but she now knew that he would respect her covenants. His warm breath and manly scent tranquilized her into a mood of emotional, but not sexual, submission. There would be no sins against her body, as Reverend McGraw referred to it. "But maybe an occasional, minor episode of immoral desire," she thought to herself with a large, internal grin.

*****

Mark and Leila knew that Jake Delaughter would be waiting to see Mark's BMW exit Ebenezer Church Road. Leila walked him to the front porch, but neither of them wanted the special night to end.

They kissed each other good night with a passionate fury

that would have to last until their lips met again.

Words that are left unspoken are sometimes the most powerful. Little was said. They both knew that this was the beginning, the real beginning, and not the end.

"Please be careful driving to your villa, Mark, I do not want to ever be without you again," said Leila.

"You heal my wounds," replied Mark playfully. He kissed Leila goodnight, "I'll be back."

"You heal me, my dear," whispered Leila, before Mark drove on to Destin.

Chapter 37

A lifetime, or even two lifetimes, of caution and fear can be changed with a single kiss. Leila and Mark's late afternoon reunion had produced innumerable kisses.

Leila woke the next morning with thoughts of his hot, fleshy lips again pressing against her own. She was totally aware of her insatiable thirst for more of Mark. The enchanting afternoon of true intimacy immeasurably surpassed the unexpected moments of raw passion they had shared before. The closeness was entirely of her choosing—and a stirring fulfillment of her suppressed desires. She noticed her body tingling with the mere recall of their intimate connection. Her very soul had been kissed.

Leila always knew of her deep need to be held tightly in one special man's arms—forever. A penetrating and powerful sensation of internal warmth filled her as the sun rose on this beautiful morning in Ebenezer Forest. The thought that Mark Mabry was that special man consumed her every thought. She felt that her dreams and destiny were finally intersected—and she knew what she had to do.

She dressed hurriedly—but patiently waited two hours to finally dial Mark's number. He answered quickly.

"I was about to call you," Mark confessed. "Would you like

to come down to the villa today?"

"I have a church group arriving at 11a.m., another student group tomorrow. I know you had a long day yesterday, Mark, but I want to see you. I cannot wait to be with you again," Leila said in a soft, compelling tone.

"I'll be there shortly after noon," he replied. "If I sleep in a guest room, can I stay over?" he asked humbly.

"Yes, and don't eat lunch," Leila replied excitedly.

Leila placed the phone back on the receiver. Her heart was racing. She well knew the importance of what she was thinking.

Leila walked out on the porch and sat in her favorite chair. A pair of English sparrows flirted in a nearby tree as she prayed. She knew that only He had given her this opportunity.

A feeling of spiritual ecstasy was overtaking Leila's consciousness. She was proceeding beyond fear—beyond self-interest—even beyond self. She was being drawn into an unknown realm of total acceptance of another human being.

Leila's mind was flowing far beyond analysis, into the sacred place of faith and bliss. God was leading her into one of life's greatest gifts. "I am going to commit all of my love to Mark Mabry," she confessed to Him.

She remembered 1 John 4:8, "Whoever does not love, does not know God, because God is love."

Leila's will to share her love with God's approval enraptured her into a sublime and tranquil rainbow of thoughts.

Finally, she felt His confirmation.

She had His blessing.

Leila visualized herself crossing a river into a beautiful forest of unknown adventure. She felt the dying gasps of her own ego—and she rejoiced its departure with an open heart.

Her desire to give, and to give all, guided Leila toward sweet

surrender—to the commitment of love that she had always envisioned—and for which she had forever longed.

Chapter 38

Content and overjoyed with having received one of God's greatest blessings, Leila prepared a wonderful southern lunch for Mark. The aroma of pork chops and sweet potatoes aroused Mark's hunger. He ate heartily, and they talked into the afternoon. Mark felt the warmness of a home that he had never experienced. He knew it would be this way.

"I love to look at you," Mark told Leila on one occasion. On another occasion, when she was refilling his glass, he pulled her into his arms for a pleasant kiss.

They laughed when Leila realized that Mark was born two years after the death of her life's musical giant, Elvis Presley! When Mark mentioned he had attended his ten year high school reunion just a few years before, Leila decided not to mention that her 40th class reunion was rapidly approaching.

Later, as the church bus loaded up its hikers and disappeared from sight, Leila walked up and put her arms around Mark's waist. He took his hand and eased Leila's soft hair gently behind her ears. He looked lovingly at her whole face as she gazed at him with her sparkling blue eyes.

"I love you, Mark," Leila whispered. She reached up and stroked his face with her hand.

"I have only wanted to be with you, and no one else, since the first moment you opened your front door to me," Mark replied as he leaned down to kiss Leila deeply.

Leila pulled her lips back. "Do you think you could ever love me?" Leila asked with a trembling voice.

Mark smiled. "I have been in love with you from the very first moment I met you," he said.

"Oh, Mark!" Leila moaned as she pulled herself tightly against his body.

Mark took Leila's hand and led her to the living room couch. He turned backwards, propped his feet up, and laid his head in Leila's lap. She softly touched his angular face and then teased his full lips with her fingers.

"What about our age difference, Mark? Does that worry you, even a little?" asked Leila.

"I don't think you are too young for me," Mark replied with a big, broad grin.

"Seriously, Mark," she laughed. "You know it bothers our friends immensely. Do you think it is something we should sit down and seriously talk about?"

"I do not even know how old you are, and don't care. True love is ageless," said Mark.

Leila felt a gush of love and emotion that she could no longer contain. Tears formed in her eyes as she reached down naturally to rub Mark's rippled stomach and muscled chest. He cuddled his face against her breasts, and she pressed them even closer into him.

"Why, Mark? Why do you love me?" asked Leila.

Mark looked at Leila with the warmest and most sincere expression she had ever seen on his face. He spoke very slowly, "I do not believe anything happens by chance. I always believed that if I would follow my instincts, I would be led to you. I didn't know where I would find you, or what you would look like, but when I saw you—I knew you were the one for me."

Leila smiled. "Is that like predestination?" she asked.

"Yes and no, I had to be loyal to my instincts, or we would have never met," replied Mark.

"Did you consider that perhaps the will of God led us to each other?" asked Leila.

Before Mark could reply, they heard the roar of a familiar automobile engine. "Let's straighten up, Mark, that is Amanda's car. She oftentimes stops by without calling," Leila said as she hurried to her feet and straightened her dress. Mark stood up, tucking his shirt back into his pants.

Amanda recognized Mark's vehicle and took her time getting to the doorway. She knocked before entering.

"Hey, Amanda, come in dear," Leila said as she greeted Amanda at the door.

"Is everything all right?" Amanda whispered with a worried expression. "Do you want me to come back later?" she added.

"No! Please come in, Amanda," Leila repeated in a louder voice. She turned and walked toward the living room, motioning with her head for Amanda to follow. "You know Mark, of course," she said.

Mark stood up as they all entered the living room.

"Hello, Mark," said Amanda, sticking out her hand.

"Hello, Amanda," he said somewhat shyly.

"Well, that scar looks better than I thought it would look, Mark," said Amanda sarcastically. "The last time I saw you, you were lying naked near the chicken coop with a very nasty open wound." Neither Mark nor Leila responded.

"Are ya'll sure you don't want me to stop back later on my

way home?" asked Amanda.

"That is not necessary at all, Amanda, Mark will be staying over with me tonight, so have a seat," said Leila in a defiant tone. Amanda's mouth suddenly dropped wide open.

"Leila, what on God's green earth is going on here?" asked Amanda.

"What is going on here is that you are being very rude to us both," snapped Leila.

The tone of Leila's voice startled Amanda. The room was deadly quiet for a moment.

"Mark and I have officially decided to start publicly seeing each other. We hope that all of our friends will accept our decision," Leila announced.

Amanda was speechless. She finally spoke, "Both of you have been through quite a lot lately. I have seen the pain in you both. You can't live, or even rebuild, your life in a day – or a week – or a month! And besides, your age difference is actually embarrassing. You both need to really stop and think this over!"

Leila looked at Mark and he took her prompting.

"Amanda," Mark said softly, "I know that you may have difficulty in understanding this, many of my friends do also. But one of the most amazing miracles and phenomena in life, even though we meet thousands of people, is who we select and allow into our lives, who we want to hold, and who we want to love. Leila and I have both grown to realize that we are meant for each other, and that is all that matters. We are in love and committed to each other." Leila looked at Mark with a beam in her eye.

Amanda glared straight back into Mark's eyes and spoke directly to him with a strong resolve, "I don't doubt that you love Leila, Mark. Let me say it another way, I do not doubt that you both think you are in love with each other." Amanda turned and looked at Leila.

"As a person who has been married for over thirty years," Amanda continued, "let me tell you both something – you two don't even know each other. My goodness! You don't really get to know someone until you have lived with them for at least a year, sometimes much longer. I know my best friend very well, and I think what I am about to say fits you both. No other person can be anybody's magic cure for whatever ails them. Please, please, I beg both of you to not rush into this crazy, childlike folly!" Amanda shook her head in disgust and added, "The whole thing looks so hollow to me!"

Leila stood up abruptly. With an unfamiliarly stern voice, she said very loudly, "Amanda, you don't need to live your life in a day either! AND YOU CERTAINLY DO NOT NEED TO TRY AND LIVE MY AND MARK'S LIFE! I love you. Thanks for stopping by."

Amanda stared back at Leila with a blank expression. After a few moments, she slowly lowered and shook her head. She was obviously shaken by the finality of Leila's reply. Amanda turned and left in a hurry, without saying another word.

"Do you think she will calm down about our decision?" Mark asked as Amanda drove away.

"It may take a little time, but I think so," replied Leila. "We have had a number of spats over the years, and it has always eventually worked out," she added.

*****

When the shadows came, the two lovers returned to each other's arms. There was total comfort and happiness between them—and they were soon asleep.

The universe had, for now, brought absolute joy and fearless love to Ebenezer Church Road.

Chapter 39

Early Monday morning, Jane Anderson was sitting at her desk at the Atlanta Police Department when the operator buzzed her and said she had a call on line six.

"Hello, Ms. Anderson, my name is Agent Bob Kirk with the Federal Bureau of Investigation out of the Pensacola office. I am going to be in Atlanta through Wednesday and would like to schedule about a one hour interview with you relative to an investigation we are conducting in Destin, Florida," Kirk said very officiously. A meeting was arranged at Jane's office for three o'clock that same afternoon.

Jane was expecting to be contacted after FBI Agent Donald Baxter had asked her to leave the parking lot of the Bar Harbor Restaurant. Her plan to "hook up" with Doctor Ty Tyson had not gone as designed. Even though that evening was not a particularly nice memory for Jane, she did have a rather large curiosity about the scope of the federal investigation.

Bob Kirk arrived at his appointment at the precise time. He was a large, well-built man about Jane's age. He sported very short, but thick, brown hair and the look of a rugged, ex-college football player. Within minutes, it was revealed that he had previously, in fact, played football for the Ole Miss Rebels.

Like many other law enforcement authorities that had met Jane Anderson, Bob Kirk had an immediate and obvious interest in the stunningly beautiful sex crimes investigator. For the first few minutes of the appointment, the only questions Agent Kirk asked were about Jane. There was no wedding band on his ring finger, thus Jane was less agitated than usual – but she was still anxious to move on to official business.

When the conversation finally got around to Walton County, Florida, Jane's interest intensified.

After emphasizing the confidentiality of what Jane was about to hear, Agent Kirk said, "Ms. Anderson, the meeting you had in the office of Colonel Max Barnett, where you provided Barnett with a copy of your statement obtained from Leila Hewitt as well as her laboratory report, was intercepted by the Bureau under the Judicial authority of The United States Western District Court of Florida." That information surprised Jane, prompting her to sit up a little taller in her chair. She was genuinely shocked that there was a concealed tape recorder inside a law officer's office.

"The Walton County Sheriff's Office was one of the initial and primary targets of this investigation, but as is usually the case, other subjects have emerged. One of those subjects is Doctor Ty Tyson. Since the Hewitt incident, we are looking even more closely at Tyson," Agent Kirk said. He cleared his voice and continued, "We are particularly interested in the relationship of a small group of Destin residents with Sheriff Clark, Colonel Barnett, as well as a couple of deputies who are minor players."

"Are you at liberty to reveal the specifics of the suspected criminal activity?" asked Jane.

"Not really, except that it is continuing to enlarge at the present time," replied Agent Kirk. "I was directed here to officially request and receive any additional information you may have."

Jane was in possession of several copies of the complete incident report she had prepared for Leila Hewitt. She gave one copy to Agent Kirk as well as a copy of the lab report. He sat and read the lab report very carefully.

"I take it you have substantial experience with Rohypnol?" asked Agent Kirk.

"Yes," replied Jane.

"Because of the 'limited trace quantity', and there not being enough residual contraband to even support a re-testing, aren't there real challenges in these facts, regardless of what we suspect?" asked Agent Kirk.

"Not insurmountable challenges," Jane answered. "We have obtained a number of prosecutions here in Atlanta with similar evidence to go on," said Jane. "In fact, most victims are zonked out for nearly two days. When we do catch these drug traces within seventy-two hours, it is always in small quantities."

"What else do you have?" asked Agent Kirk.

"The supply of roofies does not normally come in small numbers," said Jane. "You usually will not even hear from more than five to ten per cent of the victims per year," she added.

"We are familiar with that," replied Agent Kirk.

"I believe that the prosecution of Doctor Tyson is fully supportable by the facts in this case," said Jane.

"Your position is duly noted, Ms. Anderson. What kind of witness would this lady, Leila Hewitt, make?" asked Agent Kirk.

"Excellent," said Jane. "In my opinion, she makes a good appearance, is well-spoken, and most credible."

"Good," commented Agent Kirk.

"I gather that your office has talked to Heather Hays, the

former employee of Doctor Tyson?" asked Jane.

"Yes, we have," replied Agent Kirk.

"Have you considered that Doctor Tyson's wife may be a murder victim?" prodded Jane.

Agent Kirk's eyes opened wider, "Actually, he is a relatively new subject, but he is being carefully and closely monitored. To answer your question, that specific inquiry of yours is something I will certainly include in my report of this meeting."

Jane gave a brief recount of everything she had learned from her limited vacation-time investigation. Agent Bob Kirk took notes, but shared very little information with Jane about the scope of the federal investigation.

Agent Kirk informed Jane that, "Your appearance before a grand jury any time soon will not be required. Indictments are on their way. Doctor Ty Tyson is not going to be included in the first round of the indictments. If and when he is ever targeted as a subject in the Hewitt case, I would expect that you will be a witness."

As the conversation began to wind down, Agent Kirk gave Jane another unappreciated admonishment of confidentiality.

"I hope Doctor Tyson does not get away with the rape of Leila Hewitt," responded Jane.

Agent Bob Kirk did not reply to Jane's comment, but he did say in a much more serious tone, "There is one other important thing you need to know, Ms. Anderson. The subjects of this investigation are considered to be very dangerous, so if you are in Destin, please don't do any more volunteer work and stay well away from Colonel Max Barnett and Doctor Ty Tyson."

"Yes sir," replied Jane as she gave a mock salute to Agent Kirk.

"If you do come back down, may I take you to dinner?" asked Agent Kirk with a sheepish grin.

"I guess that would be all right," replied Jane. "Be warned though, I can be dangerous too," she added with a wink.

Chapter 40

The two women had been looking into each other's eyes for as long as they could remember. Their lives, as is the case with so many other childhood friends, had gone in different directions. One married at a fairly young age – the other eloped, alone, into a wonderland of wildlife sounds, woodsy smells, and dreams. But the bond between the two had always been as substantial as the big oaks that shaded Leila's porch on Ebenezer Church Road. It was no different on this late summer morning when Amanda stopped by without calling.

"Leila, I want to apologize to you," said Amanda. "I have no business interfering with your feelings. I haven't been able to sleep very well since I left here the other day, and there are some things I need to get off of my chest."

"Would you like some tea?" responded Leila.

"In a while, dear, but I have a few things to say to you first," said Amanda. "I see the look of joy in your eyes when you look at Mark. I see the way he looks at you. I came over here this morning to tell you one thing – screw us all – go for it!"

Leila roared with laughter!

"No! I am serious!" replied Amanda. "SCREW US ALL! Look, you know I love my Hank, but there is something I think you may suspect that I have never really said out loud – I do not even know if I am still in love with Hank." Amanda's eyes looked down sheepishly toward the floor, and then back tearfully toward Leila.

"Our romance in the last decade seems to have just bleached out over the years," confessed Amanda. "Hank and I seem to be always just taking each other for granted."

"Please, you don't have to tell me all of this," replied Leila with an anguished look. "I think it is perfectly normal for the honeymoon bliss to wane a bit over time."

"I would give anything to still have the intense love and excitement in my heart that I have seen in yours since the first day Mark Mabry came into your life," replied Amanda.

"Look, Amanda," said Leila softly. "Please, it's not about what other people are experiencing. What Mark and I have found is just a feeling – I cannot even find the words to explain it—everything in my life is changing," Leila admitted.

"I have seen it in you, Leila," said Amanda sheepishly, "and I hate to confess this, but maybe I have just been a little jealous – and I am ashamed." Amanda lowered her head.

"Enough of all this," said Leila. "You know I love you, Amanda, and I know how much you really love Hank. Please stop all of this foolish talk."

"Mark is having a house full of friends down to his villa for a little party this weekend, why don't you and Hank just drive down to Sandestin and join us?" asked Leila.

"Hank is going fishing down in Apalachicola with some of his ole high school buddies this weekend. Would it be all right if I bring Cousin Jackie along?" asked Amanda.

"Of course! Come on, let's go get some tea," replied Leila.

*****

The party started Saturday at 4 o'clock in the afternoon. At that hour, a panhandle thunderstorm was pounding the Sandestin villa. Like many other summertime downpours, thirty minutes later "the devil was spanking his wife"—which is a Southern colloquialism conveying that the sun was shining while the rain fell.

The cool rain dropped the temperature considerably and did not last very long. The guests were able to quickly return to a more pleasant outdoors. Shortly afterwards, Leila, Amanda, and Jackie exited Leila's car and walked toward the lakeside party.

Many of the neighbors remembered Leila from her earlier visit to the villa. Her identity of being the one-time supposed "victim" of Mark's alleged act of rape was an unguarded secret in the small Sandestin community. The many surprised looks and suggestive whispers of the gathered guests could not be mistaken. They all took great notice when the three older ladies, and particularly Leila, arrived.

Jane Anderson saw the ladies' entrance, and the crowd staring—mostly at Leila Hewitt. She took the initiative to approach the ladies and greeted them politely. Becky and Lisa grudgingly joined the "welcoming" effort. Mark and Charlie were expected back shortly from a local seafood market with a tub of boiled shrimp. They didn't make it back in time before the air got very thick.

Caleb Hathcox, the new temporary CEO of Mackco Advertising Company, had arrived in Destin on Friday night. He had closed down one of the nightspots in Baytown the night before. Caleb spent the morning and early afternoon chasing his hangover at the beach with one cocktail after another. He ambled over to the three ladies in a mischievous mood. He immediately said to Leila in a half-slurred tone, "What are you doing here, Miss Leila? Mark told me a while back that you had died in an automobile accident."

"I am sure he told you no such thing," replied Leila in a serious tone. She turned and looked at Amanda and Jackie with a pinkish flush to her pretty face.

"Oh yeah, Mark most certainly did tell me that. I would not forget that news," Caleb said smiling as he took another sip of alcohol. "You have been duly warned. Don't ever let him purchase any life insurance on you, Miss Leila," he added.

"You must have me confused with someone else," replied Leila as her face turned a deeper shade of red.

"Young man, I think you are out of order with such dribble," interjected Amanda sternly.

Caleb turned his eyes toward Amanda and realized that his humor had not been appreciated at all. "Well, Mark did say it about Miss Leila here being dead and all, it was when we were kidding him about the attention he was giving her," he slurred. "But—hey, I'm bad—that was all before he starting seeing his ex-girlfriend, Mary Kate. I humbly apologize," he said shaking his head at Leila. "You sure ain't dead –yet," Caleb mumbled as he walked away.

Amanda looked at Leila, whose head had fallen downward

Becky seized the moment and asked no one in particular, "How long has Mark been seeing Mary Kate again?"

Lisa replied, "She is such a pretty girl, they are an attractive couple."

Jane looked at Leila whose eyes had squinted. She could see that the conversation was painful for her, but Jane could not resist the temptation. "Mark has a lot of girlfriends, we all love him," she said.

Leila was not up for the fight, but Amanda was.

"I think you young girls are way behind the news," said Amanda defiantly. "Mark has ONE girlfriend. He has been staying at Leila's place!" Leila looked up and into the eyes of Jane.

Jane's eyes widened and she could tell from the look on Leila's face that Amanda's words were true. It left her totally speechless. Becky and Lisa were equally stunned.

Jackie had not said a word through all of this banter, but was "Destin-tough" enough to chew the young girls up for supper and spit them out. "Come on, Leila and Amanda. Let's not get our wine from these nasty, little, sour, and *jealous* grapes!" Jackie said as she led her friends away from the hostility.

*****

Leila watched from a distance as Mark and Charlie carried the tub of steaming boiled shrimp out to the lakeside tables. The seafood was spread on sheets of white paper, and dozens of ears of hot corn were added. On his way back to the vehicle for a couple of bags of ice, Mark walked out of his way to give Leila a big hug and a kiss on her cheek. Not a person in attendance missed his significant show of affection. Mark continued on to fetch the ice.

As soon as the food supplements and refreshments were all in place, Mark walked back over to Leila. She introduced him to Jackie, and he shook hands with Amanda. Mark casually slipped his arm around Leila's waist. Leila gently pulled him to one side and whispered in her usual soft and gentle voice, "So, who is this girlfriend, 'Mary Kate'?"

Mark swallowed his Adam's apple, then cleared his throat.

Leila awaited his answer.

At that fortuitous moment, Charlie approached with an unfamiliar guest that conveniently diverted Mark's attention.

"Everyone, I would like you all to meet our new neighbor who has just moved into the house across the street," said Charlie. Mark took the opportunity and eased Leila away from the others.

Leila's brow was furrowed and tear drops were swelling in her eyes. Mark moved his hand from behind her waist and touched her arm. He leaned over and whispered into her ear, "There is no person on earth you need to be concerned with."

Leila looked up at Mark. Her blue eyes were now squinted and looked wet and full of anguish.

A painful knot gripped Leila's stomach. She felt a jealous craziness about herself that she had never experienced before. "Did you follow your instincts to find her, too?" she whispered.

Mark could see the intensity and anxiety on Leila's face. He said more loudly, "I love you. Meet me inside in three minutes." He then turned and walked briskly toward his villa.

Amanda had been standing just on the other side of Leila and, unbeknownst to Leila, heard the entire exchange. "I would keep that appointment, honey," she said with a wink and big grin.

*****

A half-hour later, Mark and Leila walked out of the villa holding hands as if nothing ever happened. They moved around the party in a fully public exhibition of sincere affection for each other. It was what they had always envisioned in their respective dreams. Everyone present could see the magical glow and genuine joy of the amorous couple.

Jane and Charlie were not smiling and they were not blind. They could see Mark and Leila's radiance, as well as their indifference to the thoughts and judgment of others.

It was clear that the lovers were in a fanciful spell from which no return was sought.

Chapter 41

Leila bolted upright in her bed. The loud roar of an automobile engine racing down Ebenezer Church Road toward her house had startled her from a deep sleep. She heard the brakes grab and the auto screech to an abrupt stop in her driveway. The car door slammed, and part of the mystery was revealed. "Wake up, Leila, you have got to see this!" Amanda bellowed.

Leila grabbed her robe and proceeded quickly to unlock the front door. Amanda was still wearing her pajamas and was breathing heavily. She had a newspaper in her hand and threw it down on the porch table, "My gracious, girl, you're not going to believe what's been going on in Walton County! READ THIS!"

CORRUPT WALTON COUNTY SHERIFF INDICTED ON DRUG and RACKETEERING CHARGES

Breaking News

The federal government has indicted Walton County Sheriff Wayne Clark and his chief assistant, Colonel Max Barnett, and declared them "Utterly Corrupt". The two officials, along with two other Destin men, were charged with dealing crack-cocaine, marijuana, ketamine and Rohypnol, the last two substances are commonly called "date rape drugs".

Clark has been the sheriff of Walton County for over seven years and previously served as Chief Deputy, the position now held by Colonel Max Barnett. The indictments culminate a one-year long Drug Enforcement Administration investigation into accusations of corruption. Officials said this is one of the most disturbing cases of police corruption they have ever seen and that other charges are expected to be added against Clark and Barnett.

Local businessmen and brothers Roy and Ray Ashton were included in the lengthy indictment. Roy Ashton is the owner of Bar Harbor Restaurant, Bar, and Marina in Destin. Ray Ashton is a local entrepreneur and has been previously reported to be a major financial and political backer of Clark. A key allegation is that the officers took confiscated drugs, issued fake destruction orders and sold the stolen contraband to the Ashton brothers.

The indictment alleges that Sheriff Clark and Barnett were aware of various illegal activities of the Ashton Brothers for over two years and failed to pursue potential investigations. It also alleges that the public officials were aware that the "date rape drugs" were being used by the Ashton brothers and others to victimize persons for unlawful purposes. No names of alleged victims were released pursuant to court order.

The Racketeer Influenced and Corrupt Organization Act was cited in numerous instances in the indictment including acts of public corruption, bribery of multiple public officials, obstruction of justice, money laundering, tax violations, and conspiring to arrange pay-offs from gangsters while protecting them from arrest. All four men were specifically charged with racketeering activity under the RICO statute which exposes each of them to potential life imprisonment. All four defendants have agreed to surrender themselves for a bail hearing within forty eight hours.

Roy and Ray Ashton had the additional counts of harboring illegal aliens included in their indictments.

FBI Agent Dusty Lucas issued this statement, "Those who betray their public positions of trust impugn the character and reputation of all public officials that daily risk their lives to protect the citizenry. The FBI, the DEA, the United States Border Patrol, the IRS, the United Postal Inspection Service and the Florida State Police hereby send a clear message that this type of disgraceful misconduct will not be tolerated."

The indictment alleges that Clark and Barnett failed to investigate illegal drug activity in Walton County even after a DEA agent called the Sheriff's office and reported that a shipment of drugs was being sent into Walton County.

According to FBI transcripts and surveillance of conversations between Clark and Barnett themselves, and their conversations with both Roy and Ray Ashton, all four men discussed their interactions and the potential for Federal investigations into their conduct. During a conversation on or about April 3, 2010, Roy Ashton asked Clark to "Let me know if you pick up any indication that the feds are snooping around". Tapes are alleged to show that Sheriff Clark replied, "Barnett has his ears to the ground—you'll be the first to know if we hear of anything like that."

United States Attorney for the Northern District of Florida, K.C. Jackman, declined to comment on the indictments other than to state that, "Indictments of other individuals are expected to follow as a result of this on-going investigation."

*****

Leila's phone was ringing as she motioned for Amanda to follow her inside. It was Jane Anderson on the line.

"Leila, there is a wire story in the morning paper in Atlanta about the indictments of Sheriff Clark in Walton County and Colonel Barnett, have you seen it?" Jane asked.

"Yes, I just read it," replied Leila.

"I am even more concerned about the fact that you live

alone now than I was before. The story indicates that there are other targets, and I expect that Doctor Ty Tyson may be one of them. An FBI agent informed me that this crowd of criminals is very dangerous. Is Mark actually staying out at your place every night?" asked Jane.

"Not last night, Jane, but Amanda is here with me now – she just brought the paper over," replied Leila. "I am shocked about the Sheriff and Max Barnett, I pray that Ty Tyson will be indicted in the very near future for what he did to me," she added.

"Just please don't take this matter lightly, Leila. With the type of sentences these guys are exposed to, I would be very cautious. Do you have a family attorney?" asked Jane.

"I've never needed one," replied Leila.

"Well, there is a possibility that you may be cold called by someone else's attorney at any time. I wouldn't talk to anyone except federal authorities if I were you. I particularly would not allow any stranger access to you at home, or anywhere else, under any circumstances," Jane advised.

"Do you think that Ty Tyson will actually get brought into all of this?" asked Leila.

"From what I have gathered, I think he is definitely a potential target. The federal authorities will likely need your help and testimony to make a case against him for what he did to you," replied Jane.

"Be careful, Leila," warned Jane before she hung up the phone.

*****

"I can't believe all of this is actually happening," exclaimed Amanda. "Colonel Barnett has been going to our church in Red Bay for thirty some odd years."

"That doesn't mean a thing," replied Leila. "Before Reverend McGraw arrived in Red Bay, old-timers said they had to have bouncers in that church every Sunday morning because there were so many scoundrels in the congregation...but that may have been pure malarkey."

The phone rang again. It was Mark on the line and he too had just read the morning paper. "Turn on your television to Channel 7 in Panama City," he said in an excited tone. "The morning news just reported that one of the men named in the indictment, Ray Ashton, was found murdered in his home an hour ago! The report said that more details will follow in the next broadcast."

"How did he die?" asked Leila.

"Who died?" demanded Amanda, trying to interrupt.

"They haven't said how yet. Look, Leila, I'm worried about you. I will call you again in a few minutes," said Mark in a concerned voice. "Please don't go anywhere without telling me, and let's call each other with any new developments," he added.

"OK, Mark," replied Leila. "You be careful, darling. Everything is going to be fine."

Moments afterwards, a late-model, solid black Ford Taurus with dark-tinted windows pulled into Leila's circular drive and parked behind Amanda's car.

"Who died?" demanded Amanda. Leila brought her up-to-date as they both walked toward the front of the house to turn on the television.

Amanda suddenly caught the profile of two large men in dark suits approaching the front of the house. She bolted toward the floor and pulled Leila with her.

"Get down! get down!" whispered Amanda in total fear as she jerked Leila downward. The screen door was closed, but unlatched. The large front door was wide open.

"There are two strange men on the porch," Amanda whispered in a horrified tone.

Leila and Amanda both quickly squatted to their knees behind the nearby sofa.

There was a loud knock at the door. After a pause, there were two more louder knocks.

Leila and Amanda crouched even lower in fear and remained totally silent.

Then a man said in a loud voice, "Ladies, there is a mirror hanging behind you, and we can see you clearly."

"Stay away! We have a gun!" shouted Amanda loudly.

"Ladies, we are with the United States Marshall's Office for the Northern District of Florida here to serve Miss Leila Hewitt with papers to appear before a grand jury next month. Whichever one of you is Miss Hewitt, will you please stand up and come receive these papers?" asked the gentleman laughingly.

Leila rose to her feet, straightened her robe and sheepishly walked over and opened the door. She accepted her service. "Please excuse our timidity," she said quite formally. "The suits scared us."

The two Marshalls handed Leila her subpoena with a chuckle, and hurriedly returned to their vehicle.

Leila shut the door behind herself and said smilingly to Amanda, "It's safe to unload your gun now, Amanda – I mean, Ms. Annie Oakley!"

Chapter 42

Later that afternoon, Mark drove to Ebenezer Forest. Worry over Leila's safety had dominated his day. "Hey, Leila, darling," he said as she walked outside to greet him on the front porch.

"Mark, I miss you so much when you are not right here with me," whispered Leila. She draped her arms around him and pulled him next to her. The sun was disappearing in the west below the trees.

Mark stepped back one step below Leila so they would be face to face. He slowly and gently wrapped his arms around her and kissed her soft lips. The afternoon shadows were dancing beneath the big gray oak as Leila passionately returned Mark's kiss deeply, with every ounce of her heart and soul.

Leila spoke first and very slowly, "We must thank the Lord every day for guiding us to each other, Mark. She tilted her head upward to the sky, then back at Mark."

Mark did not reply, but smiled broadly.

"I have always wondered what it would be like to have my husb—my uh—the man I love come home to me in the afternoon, to hold and kiss me the way you do," Leila added with a deep gleam in her eye.

Mark stared intently into her radiant eyes and said, "I do

believe that the Lord has been leading us down this path."

His eyes suddenly enlarged and his mouth opened a bit. He looked up in the sky for a few seconds, then back down at Leila. "Come on, Leila! LET'S GO BACK TO THE CHURCH RIGHT NOW, BEFORE DARK!" he said excitedly.

"What on Earth?" Leila responded in a surprised tone.

"YES," Mark urged, "it's the perfect time!" He grabbed Leila's hand.

"Let me change my shoes," Leila said laughingly as she rushed into the house. She returned in a brief minute, and they hurried over to the gate and briskly started down the lane. The wildlife inhabitants along Ebenezer Church Lane were not accustomed to such unexpected, late arrivals. The birds fluttered overhead as Mark and Leila held hands and laughed along their bustling journey into the forest.

There was more green grass in the plush church lane than in the open woods. It served as the dinner table for many rabbits. The bunnies scampered away as the lovers passed.

When the couple reached the narrow wooden bridge, two raccoons scurried from the far bank of the clear trickling stream. Squirrels were barking wildly along the whole pathway as if they knew this was a very special occasion.

Finally, the row of ligustrums gave way to the beauty of Ebenezer Church. The steeple atop the white church was its brightest feature. It gleamed brightly in the fading sunlight. When the couple arrived at the church steps, Leila asked, "Do you want to go inside?"

"No, right here is just fine," replied Mark.

Leila looked at Mark with a quizzical smile.

Mark felt the same kind of anxious tension he had experienced when he had been called on to give his weekly inspirational talk at Mackco Advertising, but much more so.

He stood tall and looked into Leila's beautiful blue eyes for a full minute. She returned his loving gaze with her own.

Mark then slowly pulled Leila nearer him and kissed her ever so softly on her lips.

The aura and sanctimony of the church before which she stood—together with the gorgeous man of her dreams—captivated Leila's every sense. She was in a paralytic state of utter helplessness and loving bliss.

Then, Mark began to slowly and carefully speak, "Life on earth is such a short and precarious journey." He paused and wet his lips.

"Time is so, so precious and is one of our earthly, most cherished possessions while it lasts," Mark continued so deliberately. "It cannot be slowed or stopped, and when it is gone, it is gone. We must use our time on earth wisely. We know that God leaves some decisions to us, for us to make, without doubt or fear, just faith," Mark paused, breaking into a warm smile. Leila smiled back at him.

Then, Mark fell to one knee.

While Leila was still absorbing the absolute shock and joy of the man she dearly loved suddenly kneeling before her, Mark continued, "Leila, will you please marry me?"

Leila was in a daze. All roads in her life led to right here, right now!

There would never be another Mark.

This was her forest.

This was her church.

This was the moment of her dreams and the moment of her life.

This was God's plan!

"YYYYYYEEEEEESSSSSSSSS!" she screamed, "YYYY-EEEEESSSSS!"

Chapter **43**

At the same hour that Leila and Mark were enjoying a loving and engaging trance in Ebenezer Forest, Walton County deputy sheriff Tommy Tucker stood at the edge of another forest in nearby Holmes County. A blue heavy duty Ford truck turned off the gravel road and pulled into an adjacent pasture. Roy Ashton stepped out of the vehicle and opened the gate to his farm. It was one of those predictable days of the week on which Ashton usually made the relatively short trip from Destin to feed his beloved Paso Fino horses.

Tommy Tucker raised his reliable 30:06 rifle and softly squeezed the trigger at his target. The 150 grain bullet traveled 162 steps in a flash. The deputy could see the frontal chest impact of the bullet through his high powered scope. Tucker figured that he had surely sent Ashton to a place from which he would never return. But just to make sure, he aimed at his target's head lying motionless on the ground. He pulled the trigger again, and watched Ashton's skull explode upon impact.

Tucker then hurriedly walked two hundred yards through the woods to his hunting jeep, then took a side road out of the woods. He had been well instructed to keep his cell phone off and not use it until he returned to Destin.

The traffic in front of the Golden Sands Mall was heavy. After Tucker had negotiated the delay, he called Colonel Barnett and said simply, "Good evening, boss, see you in a few minutes." That was the entire conversation.

Tommy Tucker pulled into the parking lot of the Bar Harbor Restaurant, Bar and Marina in less than ten minutes. Without a pang of remorse, he strolled nonchalantly into the popular establishment owned by the man he had just murdered.

Many of the very late afternoon patrons at the bar knew Deputy Tucker, and he worked his way through the crowd, shaking hands and smiling. Plain-clothed Colonel Max Barnett sat at a somewhat private table in a back corner.

Barnett, like Sheriff Clark, had not yet taken a voluntary leave of absence from the Sheriff's office in spite of his recent indictment. This was to the chagrin of most of the local community. An administrative hearing was scheduled in two weeks that would likely force him to do so. But in the meanwhile, Barnett and Clark were holding firm.

"Did you have a good day, Tommy?" asked Barnett.

"Yes sir, Colonel," replied Tucker, "things could not have gone any better."

Barnett took a drink of his bourbon and water. He stirred it again and took another sip. "That should make Sheriff Clark quite happy," he said.

A cocktail waitress made her way over and took Tucker's order, "A 'Bloody Mary', please."

When the server had departed, Tucker leaned closer to Barnett. He whispered, "I hope this is enough for 'Big Fuzz'."

Barnett scowled and twitched his jaw. He spoke in a lower tone than Tucker, "I know he is worried about his buddy Ty and doesn't want him indicted for a number of reasons." Barnett took another sip from his drink and continued, "We can count on Fuzz, no matter what. We will talk about this more tomorrow."

The two lawmen finished their drinks, paid the check, and left separately.

Chapter 44

Mark freely admitted to Leila that his proposal of marriage to her was not planned very far in advance. "My love for you is so powerful and real," he said with a beaming smile. "I simply could not contain it any longer."

When questioned by Mark about her quick acceptance, Leila said, "The second that it took for me to accept your proposal was more time than I needed."

The happily bonded couple could later barely remember the walk home from Ebenezer Church. Their powerful love for each other was as strong as oak and rock. The irreversible decision to soon marry was cast in the bluest steel.

They talked and laughed, and talked some more through supper, most of the night, and well into the next day.

They would marry, of course, in Ebenezer Church – and the ceremony would be conducted by Reverend McGraw.

"The guests will walk down Ebenezer Church Lane to our wedding, but we will leave in a horse drawn buggy," suggested Leila.

"Charlie will be my best man," said Mark.

"Amanda will be my maid of honor," declared Leila.

"I want to live on Ebenezer Church Road, with you, for the

rest of our lives," said Mark.

"Do you want to keep the villa in Destin?" asked Leila.

"No, not at all," replied Mark.

"Where would you like to go on a honeymoon?" asked Mark.

"After the wedding, when everyone has gone home," said Leila slowly, "I want us to go back to the church—and make love, for our—and my—first time—between the church and the spring—on a blanket, under the stars, where we can smell the forest."

"Where I fell even more madly in love with you," said Mark sweetly.

"There is where I want us to first join together as one – and to feel you inside of me, like I have imagined so many times before," whispered Leila.

The mere words spoken gave Leila a warm internal surge that she was gaining familiarity with since Mark had re-entered her life. She could feel herself breathing more rapidly and becoming quite desirous of her young lover.

"With the cemetery so near, won't you feel like your whole family is watching?" laughed Mark.

Still feeling quite sensuous, Leila whispered, "I hope that when the bells start ringing, it won't be from the church." A broad grin appeared on her lovely face, and they both laughed aloud.

As the night passed, Leila got sillier and sillier. "Are we going to take advantage of the many mail offerings that young newlyweds like us always receive?" she asked with a grin.

"Mark, you are not going to ever have to work—we can live on my Social Security checks," Leila said teasingly.

Leila later joked, "We need to stay out of antique stores, Mark, because they remind me of myself."

In each other's loving arms, the couple began to fall into overdue sleep. Leila's last words were pure and serious admission, "Mark, I have never been happier in my entire life. I am yours, forever."

Mark had already drifted into a deep and peaceful rest. He never got the chance to answer.

Chapter 45

Murders along the northwest Florida Emerald Coast are rarer than shark incidents. When a shark occasionally finds a tourist attractive, the story does not always even make the local news—much less the national wire. It would be undesirable press for the panhandle tourist industry!

When a sheriff, his top deputy, and a couple of business-men brothers are the beneficiaries of a federal indictment—and the latter pair are murdered shortly thereafter—an irrepressible story explodes!

Roy Ashton's body was discovered by rural neighbors twenty five minutes after his execution. Within hours, this gruesome enlargement of an already big case induced Rhonda Riveras to purchase a next day, early morning plane ticket. The flight from Atlanta to the new International Airport in Panama City Beach was short and sweet.

Rhonda Riveras was the new superstar of sensational news broadcasting. The University of Georgia beauty queen had an undergraduate degree in journalism and a law degree from Emory University. She carved out a specialty market in high profile cases where she would capture "the story" as an inde-pendent, then let the major networks bid on its purchase. The ongoing developments in Walton County, Florida, made it the hottest story in America.

Riveras rose to national stardom on the coattail of a prior high profile news story. It concerned a serial rapist in Atlanta. Unbeknownst to anyone else, her long-time friend, Jane Anderson, had been her "deep throat" in the case. Jane had already alerted Rhonda to the Destin indictments, and Roy Ashton's murder brought Rhonda quickly to "paradise".

It is a short forty minute drive from the airport in Panama City to Destin. Rhonda's first stop was Bar Harbor Restaurant, Bar and Marina. A large breakfast crowd was still in mid-feast, and she was instantly recognized by the patrons. She found it quite interesting that, even with the ink still wet on Roy Ashton's execution story, his restaurant was jammed with customers. Rhonda was seated at the last vacant table and ordered breakfast.

Rhonda's cameraman and other assistant would not arrive until noon, and she determined that this would be the ideal place to wait. It was a good choice.

One particular whiny-talking, loud-mouthed local at the breakfast bar caught Rhonda's attention. She was a hefty, but pretty, bleached blonde wearing an Auburn sweatshirt. She could be heard drawling to some guys, "Thaat's Rhonnnda, whhaaat's her naame oover theere! Grrreat jjjeessuus! Rooy suurre woouulda llliiiked to haave haad himseeellf some of thaat!"

The fact that the blonde knew Roy Ashton sent Riveras into action.

Jane Anderson had supplied Rhonda with a list of suggested names and talking points. Rhonda thought this Auburn fan would be an interesting character to quiz. Rhonda raised her hand and invited Ms. Auburn to her table via a summoning index finger. She came right over.

"You want to talk to me?" asked Ms. Auburn proudly.

"You look the friendliest," replied Rhonda smiling. "Please join me."

"My pllleasure!" said Ms. Auburn. "I'm Daisy Dodd—and I know who you are."

"You are a local resident, Daisy?" asked Rhonda.

"Aalll my lllife," she replied.

"Are you glad, with Roy Ashton dying, he is not going to have to go to jail for his drug dealing?" Rhonda asked in a whisper, throwing the bait right at her fish.

"Wweelll, wwee aaall wondered how he was goin to git out of it, bbut I kneeew when they kilt RRRAAAY that RROOOY was in sum biiiig trouble," said Daisy in a low voice.

"Who is they?" asked Rhonda.

Daisy swallowed the huge lump that had suddenly appeared in her throat. "I–I was just, uh, usin a figure of spppeeech," she said.

Rhonda smiled and said, "I already know who THEY are." She leaned forward and continued with a whisper, "So do the feds, and I think you do too! If you want to give me some info that nobody has, in total confidence, then you can pick up some real cash."

Daisy Dodd was hanging on every word.

However, Rhonda still had her foot on the accelerator.

"Did you ever sleep with Doctor Ty Tyson?" asked Rhonda, with a stern look in her eye.

Daisy looked shocked and took too long to answer.

"Do you have anything to tell me about him, off the record?" pressed Rhonda.

"I've prrroobly awl-ready said too much," replied Daisy.

"I will pay you a thousand dollars for the phone number

of every girl that has a real story to tell about Tyson, and I still want your story. The bigger the story, the more the cash. If you want to talk about Sheriff Clark, Colonel Barnett, or 'they', and have some real info, here is my card." Rhonda reached in her purse for a card and placed it in front of Daisy. "Think about it, all these guys are going down. I will be here for a few days. Call me."

Rhonda's phone rang as Daisy rejoined her friends. The call was from her assistant who had the full investigative report on the four indicted subjects. Rhonda told her to order another full investigative report on Daisy Dodd. A waitress brought her breakfast order to the table. When finished eating, Rhonda invited another local over to join her for a chat.

*****

Daisy Dodd left the restaurant and walked to her old Thunderbird. She immediately called Deputy Tommy Tucker and delivered only a part of her conversation with Rhonda Riveras. She told him that Riveras was asking questions at Bar Harbor Restaurant about Sheriff Clark, Colonel Barnett and Doctor Ty Tyson. She did not tell him that Riveras had asked about sex between herself and Doctor Tyson, or about the financial enticements she was just offered.

When the conversation ended Deputy Tucker called Doctor Tyson from his caller-blocked, personal phone and left a message on Tyson's cell phone, "Hey, doc, I need to get with you about the 'mouth of the south' ASAP, please gimme a call."

*****

Thirty minutes to the north, Leila and Mark were awakened by an excited phone call from Amanda, "Leila, Roy Ashton was murdered yesterday afternoon. You need to be very careful!"

Chapter 46

Colonel Max Barnett postponed the scheduled morning meeting with Deputy Tommy Tucker until 6 o'clock that evening at Barnett's house. A narrow, trash alley ran behind the large stucco home. Tucker was instructed to circle the area until he was absolutely certain that he was not being followed. He was to enter through the automated gate facing the alley at exactly 6 o'clock. Barnett had previously given him a beeper.

Tucker was to wait in the back parking area until he heard one short, horn toot. Then, he was to re-open the gate and let Big Fuzz enter.

When both men were inside the compound, they proceeded to the back door of the home and were greeted by Barnett. The three men continued to a security-swept room that Barnett used for such meetings.

Big Fuzz, a tall, broad shouldered man with a ruddy complexion, walked in smoking a cigar. His hair was thinning, but it was offset by a cheek-full of scraggly whiskers. His formal name is Clarence Bectom Rogers – but to everyone in Destin, he is known as Big Fuzz.

Big Fuzz rode into town on a Harley in the 1970's. Supposedly, everything he owned was on that cycle. In the years that followed, he somehow became the biggest landowner, developer, banker, and deal cutter in the area. He greased everybody he could on the way up. He made money every way possible, with illegal drugs being, by far, the most profitable. Of course, he has never personally touched a controlled dangerous substance in his life. He does not have to. In Destin, he is the king of the rats.

Big Fuzz spoke first, "Well boys, our problem is a long way from over, and we still have some work to do. Our friends in Washington are most concerned about the harboring of illegal aliens charge. They do not want that worm can opened. We had to do what they wanted with Roy and Ray. Of course, without them boys around to possibly flip, we are all way better off. The Pensacola crowd has no idea how much money we have handled and can only prove so much."

"I personally don't think Roy and Ray would have ever flipped," Max said, "and I know them boys in D.C. are scared shitless about all the wetbacks we have run through here and where they ended up. Yeah, it helped me and Sheriff Clark."

Big Fuzz took a drag off of his cigar and said, "As far as we have been able to find out, the FBI has no idea that the Sheriff is dying and won't make it six more weeks," Big Fuzz said and paused. "The boys in Washington are now really keyed in on there not being enough evidence to indict Doc. The stupid son of a bitch had to go and rape that ole Hewitt gal. Now, I have been told to take care of it. How are we going to do it?"

Barnett answered, "The government has two main pieces of evidence and they need them both. First, that sex crimes detective from Atlanta was in control of the chain of evidence, so we gotta take care of her, or the old lady—one or the other."

"To hell with killing a cop. I vote for waxing the old lady," said Deputy Tucker.

"Well, you are the waxman, Tuck, but I certainly agree with you," answered Barnett.

"It really chaps my ass that I have to do this for Tyson," snapped back Tucker. "Doc must have really put some world class sugar on the 'Big Man' in D.C.," he added.

"Don't forget you guys, the Justice Department is not supposed to allow any more indictments to get out of Pensacola, if we take care of our business," said Big Fuzz.

"Look, Big Fuzz," began Barnett, "Tommy and I will take care of the ole lady. But we have a new problem that came up this afternoon that you two are not aware of. You both know I've had a tap on Daisy Dodd's phone for a good while. Well, she called that hot crime reporter, Rhonda Riveras, two hours ago and made an appointment with her for ten o'clock in the morning. She has more dirt on Doc than anyone in town. More importantly, she was on the boat with the 'Big Man' ten years ago," He paused and took a sip of water, "The feds in Pensacola may find out about my phone tap. I am asking you to take care of this one, Fuzz, for me and Tucker."

"Be home with your wives tonight," replied Big Fuzz. "I'll have T-Mex take care of it."

Big Fuzz stood up and said, "One last thing, Max, you know you are going to eventually have to plead. But our boys in Washington have promised over and over that they will keep the lid on the deal you are offered. You know where you will be going –you are going to love it! Besides, your dollars, and Tucker's, will stay where they are right now – real safe."

"Thank you, Big Fuzz," replied Colonel Barnett.

"Thanks for everything," added Deputy Tucker.

Big Fuzz turned and headed out to his vehicle with Tucker right behind him. "Keep up the good work, fellers," were his parting words.

Chapter 47

"Tell me it is not true, Charlie! You have got to be kidding!" gasped Jane Anderson. She almost dropped her cell phone. "I don't think Mark has been mentally right since he got hit in the head!" she added.

"I'm sorry, Jane, but it is really happening. Not only will the wedding invitations go out in a few weeks, Mark wants me to buy him out of the villa," said Charlie McBride. "He plans on making Ebenezer Church Road his permanent address."

"He has gone bananas ever since he went down that friggin road," said Jane. "It's as if he is under some voodoo curse! We've got to help him out of this madness!" she added, clearly disturbed by the news.

"Too late, Jane, it is OVER! A done deal. As crazy as this is, he is really in love with Leila," replied Charlie.

"He has never had a family, Charlie, never had roots. He has never had anything, now he wants to marry his dang mother," replied Jane.

"No argument from me," answered Charlie. "Look, we have got to either accept this or...or nothing. We have no other choice."

"Hell, I even believed Leila had more sense than do a fool thing like this, much less rush into it!" said Jane.

"Her life is probably as empty as Mark's. Let's just give them some slack, it's their choice, their mistake, whatever," said Charlie dejectedly.

"I cannot figure Leila out—educated, seems sharp, but heaven forbid, this is insane," continued Jane.

"Look, are you going to help with the damn party or not?" asked Charlie.

"WHAT PARTY?" Jane asked.

"This coming Saturday, at the villa, I'm inviting a bunch of folks over. It will be like an announcement-engagement party for friends of Mark and Leila – so they will not pass out when they receive their wedding invitations," said Charlie, with sarcasm.

"As much as this displeases me, I will be there," said Jane disconsolately.

*****

When the conversation was over, Jane pressed her recliner back as far as it would go and rested her head. Her eyes were shut as she absorbed the shock of what she had heard. The thought of losing her very special friend – particularly under these circumstances—had finality to it that she thought would never come. "Mark has always meant so much to me," she confessed to herself.

*****

Not a muscle had moved in Jane's body for over thirty minutes when her phone rang again.

It was Rhonda Riveras. "Are you sitting down, Jane?"

"Hey, Rhonda, how's Destin?" replied Jane.

"You mean DESTIN—the city fast becoming the MURDER CAPITAL of the world? You are NOT going to believe this development!" started Rhonda. "I was floating balloons at the Bar Harbor Restaurant yesterday morning and gave my card to a tit-fly by the name of Daisy Dodd. I asked her to call me if she had any scoop. She called me later to set up an appointment, at noon today. When she didn't show up, I called her cell phone and a Fort Walton city cop answered. Daisy was robbed and killed this morning getting into her car at her apartment complex! But get this! The cop told me that a female eyewitness across the street saw the murder. The gun made NO NOISE! You know what that means!"

"Did she indicate what her scoop was?" asked Jane.

"Only that she had plenty of dirt on Doctor Ty Tyson," Rhonda answered. "Jane, you need to tell me more about this Tyson rape case. I need details, now, on everything. This whole case is getting huge!"

"WOW!" Jane started. "I'll be down in Destin by midweek. I've got permission from my boss for an official debriefing appointment with an FBI agent there Thursday. By the way, Rhonda, I have a date with this same agent Friday night. I should be able to really milk him out of the latest info on the whole investigation!"

Rhonda let out a big laugh and replied, "Be sure and bring your infamous *black anaconda* dress for this guy, so you can really de-brief him!"

"One last thing," said Jane, "I will take you to a party Saturday. I want you to meet the rape victim."

"Thanks, Jane." Rhonda said, laughing again even louder. "It sounds like a real upbeat shindig!"

Chapter 48

The early fall in Destin is every local resident's very favorite time of year. The seasonal tourists have mostly returned to their various states to their jobs and schools. The weather is perfect. Year-round Destinites who had vanished in the summer crowds suddenly reappear, as though they had been sifted with a sand shaker—and yep—there they are again.

When a well-known, beautiful, local lady is to marry a handsome young man slightly more than half her age—well, it might happen in Hollywood, but never around Destin. The interest was high and the turnout for this party at the villa was most impressive.

The first arrivals were the church folks from Red Bay. Reverend McGraw had driven a mid-sized, yellow church bus and it was fully loaded. Most of the old couples that made the forty minute drive might have shown up if even if the destination had been a casino in Biloxi, or a bingo hall in Panama City. All were very happy to be present, and more than a little curious to witness this somewhat unconventional occasion.

Amanda and Hank Harrison led a caravan of an even older group of guests that had once been members of the Ebenezer Church congregation. They had all known and genuinely

273

admired Leila Jane Hewitt her entire life. Even Jake Delaughter, the watchdog of Ebenezer Church Road, arrived in his only suit to attend this special affair.

Destin was not to be left out of the gray power tour de force. Cousin Jackie Andrishok arrived with a rather large contingency of older gals. Most had met Leila over the years, and like many astute Destinites, were very familiar with Ebenezer Forest. These salt-water women made a more tanned and weathered presentation than their country cousins. They moved around with more agility, thanks to their muscular tennis court legs.

Neighbors of the villa were also well represented. They meandered to the lake-side gathering in more flashy Sandestin attire. Mostly an affluent group, the wine bottles carried with them were duly noted by the Red Bay crowd for more reasons than one. Their number included several male "walkers". Jackie described these fellows as, "handsome gentlemen, but not quite rich enough to marry". Lisa and Becky were chatting with Caleb Hathcox, the now newly announced head of Mackco Corp in Atlanta. He was proudly describing his new vacation home in Seaside. Several of Caleb's weekend guests were with him as well.

A large group of younger Destin acquaintances all walked in together and sought out Charlie McBride. Charlie was exiting the villa, tall drink in hand. He had just phoned Mark to tell him it was time for him and Leila to start the three minute drive from Baytown to make their, now anxiously awaited, appearance.

At that same moment, Jane Anderson and national celebrity Rhonda Riveras were walking down the side driveway into the view of all the gathered guests. Jane wore a tight, chic outfit and looked as comely as ever. But the attention for the time being was on Rhonda.

Rhonda Riveras had been featured on NNN (National News Network) for three straight days and nights. The Destin indictments, and now triple homicides, had gripped the nation and beyond. Every thirty minutes, the stunning broadcaster was shown reporting the recent developments with a beautiful Destin beach as her backdrop. Her last lengthy televised report was a sensational diatribe that started as follows:

"HOW MANY MORE MURDERS IN DESTIN?

Lovely and courageous Daisy Dodd was EXECUTED in Destin, Florida, this week to become the third GRISLY victim in the ongoing DRUGS, SEX and IMMIGRATION SCANDAL that has this popular tourist destination GRIPPED IN HORROR and FEAR! While local authorities and the FBI are keeping busy charging minorities and old folks with ILLEGAL FISHING off local bridges, DRUG LORDS and KILLERS are not only RUNNING WILD – BUT KEEPING THEIR JOBS!"

As Jane and Rhonda neared the awaiting throng, the excitement was very high.

Jane had filled Rhonda in with all of the details of the Leila Hewitt and Ty Tyson story. For now, neither person had been mentioned in her broadcasts. Rhonda was searching hard for an angle to break a story on the doctor, but she had to be very careful.

Catching up with the two young beauties was a large burly man who was barely noticed. FBI Agent Bob Kirk's Friday night date with Jane had been postponed by her until today.

The festivity was not exactly what Bob Kirk had in mind, but Leila Hewitt's connection to the recent indictments was certainly very familiar to him – and he was most interested in this occasion.

*****

There was no high musical crescendo announcing the arrival of Leila and Mark. But the want of their arrival had ascended to high anticipation. They finally appeared.

Leila was stylishly dressed in one of her best colors, white. Her dress was elegant and stunningly vogue. It was tastefully accented with very light blue dots that seemed to mirror her dreamy, beautiful eyes of the same color. Stylishly swept to one side, Leila's thick blonde hair dazzled in the afternoon breeze. She had an arm locked tightly around Mark's waist. The other clutched her lover's gift of red roses. A blissful smile shined across her radiant face.

Mark was impeccably dressed in a dark blue suit. His eyes, smile, lips, – he never looked more handsome. He carefully escorted Leila across the lawn, advancing her very slowly and proudly toward their guests. Every woman at the party carefully admired, inch by inch, Mark's imposing and well-proportioned elegance.

"This has the feel of a trophy wedding," whispered Becky to Lisa.

"I am jealous," replied Lisa.

Ten feet away, Rhonda leaned over to Jane. "What an absolutely gorgeous couple," she said. Jane had a blank stare on her face.

"You never told me Mark is that damn good looking, Jane. If

he is your best friend, you really screwed up!" Rhonda continued.

"It wasn't because it didn't cross my mind," Jane conceded.

"This could seriously be the best looking couple, regardless of age, that I have ever laid my eyes upon. Their walking back here together looks like something out of a classic movie." Rhonda continued, obviously impressed, "Wow! Both of them are getting a great deal."

"Quite an interesting rape subject, huh?" asked Jane.

Rhonda shook her head in the affirmative. "I am telling you, both," said Rhonda to Jane and Agent Kirk, "just look at her! I was expecting some ordinary old gal. I have seen a lot of beautiful women, but I have never seen a more attractive, elegant lady, regardless of age! She has got some real star power!"

"Don't get any ideas," replied Jane.

"I'll have to agree with you though, Rhonda," said Agent Bob Kirk. "They make a very surprising and impressive couple."

*****

Leila had asked for Mark's approval if it was all right with him if Brother McGraw made the party's formal marriage announcement. There had been no disagreements between the couple since the day of the fateful storm.

Brother McGraw stepped atop a concrete bench in the villa yard and loudly cleared his throat a few times.

"Brothers and sisters," he began. "Brothers and sisters, please listen up," he repeated, and the crowd grew silent.

"We are gathered here, for a very special announcement. You, each of you, please rejoice with me over the announcement of an upcoming, most solemn and sacred event. It will be a union of marriage, one the good Lord has seen fit to allow in due time. This marriage will be consummated on the third Sunday from tomorrow at a very special, beloved chapel in the history of our Walton County. Of course, I am talking about our own, dear Ebenezer Church on Ebenezer Church Road. Praise the Lord!" Brother McGraw raised his arms high toward the sky.

Brother McGraw continued, "The doors of the historic chapel will be opened for the first time in the decades that have passed since our beloved Charles Hewitt was called to heaven and honored in that beautiful place. Ebenezer Church has waited patiently for its curator, who is also the curator of Ebenezer Forest and the daughter of Charles and Cathy Braud Hewitt, to have her special day in the sun. That day is coming soon. I proudly announce that our beloved sister, Miss Leila Jane Hewitt, has accepted the proposal of our host here this afternoon, Mr. Mark Mabry. This couple will soon enter, together, into the holy state of matrimony! PRAISE THE LORD!" he shouted as he began to applaud. The other guests quickly and enthusiastically followed his lead.

"Let us all bow our heads in prayer," Brother McGraw continued.

"Thank You o' Lord. Sister Leila has shared with me that You have given her Your blessing for this union. All of us here today know that Your will shall – and always will – be done. I ask that You bless Sister Leila and Brother Mark and guide them along Your path to eternal salvation and glory in Your name.

And we pray that all of us here today reach home safely, so we can continue to honor You. In God's name we pray, AMEN!"

*****

Only Jane, Becky, and Lisa remained at the villa with Charlie after the other guests departed. Charlie opened another bottle of wine and sat down next to his friends

"A year ago, we would have never seen this coming, would we girls?" Charlie asked.

"Do you all feel as empty as I do?" asked Jane.

"Well, at least Mark seems happy," responded Lisa.

"It's like he has just drifted into some crazy panacea," reflected Charlie.

"How many of us would like to be in his or Leila's shoes?" asked Becky.

Jane stood up from her chair. "If we were being totally honest, we all would, I know I would," she said, as she turned and walked away.

Chapter **49**

Deputy Tommy Tucker arrived at the back entrance of Colonel Max Barnett's Destin compound just after dark. The secured meeting room was the only location at which they engaged in topics like the one on their agenda.

Once seated in an over-sized leather chair, Barnett pulled a beer from a nearby refrigerator and offered one to Tommy.

Tommy shook his head no. "You know I don't have any vices," Tucker said with a chuckle.

Barnett grinned and took a large gulp of beer. "Well, I hope this is the last dispatch you and I ever have to discuss," he responded.

"Ty Tyson's name has never come up in the indictments, at all. I just don't think this is really necessary," said Tucker with a scowl now on his face.

Barnett answered quickly in a firmer voice, "Big Fuzz already explained why it's necessary, Tommy, and I agree. I sure as hell don't want my indictment charges expanded with some of Doc's crap! And besides, you heard Big Fuzz yourself, the boys in Washington say this will keep Doc totally out of all the Pensacola fire. There won't be a strong enough rape case left against him, and they won't approve any other Pensacola prosecution of him."

"That son of a bitch has been nothing but trouble for you and me!" replied Tommy.

"When this is behind us, you can ride off into the sunset, Tuck, and I'll be off to the pen in Dallas. So count your blessings," said Barnett as he reached over and tapped Tommy on the shoulder. "Now let's get down to business."

"Here is the plan," Barnett began. "I've got you some good news. Big Fuzz thought about it, and T-Mex is going to be the trigger."

"THANK YOU!" interrupted Tucker.

Barnett continued, "You've been assigned to the Red Bay district late shift all next week. There isn't but one way in and out of Ebenezer Church Road, and you know Jake Delaughter watches it like a hawk. He eats lunch every day at the Bruce Café. The hit will be on Wednesday. While Jake is at lunch, T-Mex will be dropped off on Ebenezer Church Road. About ¾ of the way to Miss Leila's place, there is an old, abandoned cow barn. He's going to hide there until dark, then walk down to Leila's and take care of business. If the Mabry boy is there, so be it. T-Mex is going to trash the house and make it look like a random home invasion and robbery. He's then gonna drive Leila's car out of there to Pier Park. He will stash the car there and be picked up. I want you on Highway 81 Wednesday night. And I want you to stay between Ebenezer Church Road and Bruce. If anything goes wrong, you will get the office call. I am counting on you to handle anything and everything that might happen. Whatever needs to be done, just do it!"

"Does that include taking care of T-Mex?" asked Tucker.

"Not unless you have to," replied Barnett.

"He probably has the same orders about me," said Tucker.

Barnett laughed. "You worry too much, Tommy, just make

sure no one is following T-Mex when he comes out of there," Barnett said and paused. "After T-Mex is gone, try to be seen by as many people as you can, write a few speeding tickets, you know what to do. Just stay off Ebenezer Church Road until it is all over."

Chapter 50

The belief that life is really all about choices should include a footnote that timing is also a vital factor.

Charlie McBride's father passed away after a lengthy illness, and he called Mark early Monday morning with the sad news. The funeral service would be held at noon, Wednesday, in Atlanta!

Mark did not hesitate to tell Charlie that he would attend the service. Charlie welcomed Mark to stay at his mid-city townhouse. Mark accepted the offer and told Charlie he would arrive in the city on Tuesday night. Leila could not accompany Mark as she was obligated to an incoming tour of visiting environmentalists.

The timing of Mark's absence meant that Leila would likely be alone until Thursday, she thought.

Wanting to spend some time together before Mark left for the funeral, Leila and Mark decided to spend Tuesday morning together. They agreed that a picnic would be fun. They both were very pleased that they shared the out-of-doors as a common interest.

Leila packed a picnic basket for her and Mark's day-trip to the beautiful Choctawhatchee River. It flows in a southwesterly direction through Holmes, Walton, and Bay counties until reaching its namesake bay. Very few people know that, if you take a short hike from the graveled cul de sac at Ebenezer Road's end, you will soon arrive at a high bluff overlooking the scenic river.

Leila spread a calico blanket beneath a large and familiar Florida maple tree. This private spot on the high bluff provided a wonderful vantage point to view the clean, beautiful and unspoiled waterway. Leila had been visiting this exact spot all of her life, but never before with a man – much less "her man".

She usually leaned her favorite pillow against the base of the maple tree. But today, Leila relaxed into the arms of the man she dearly loved.

"Oh, my dear, Mark," Leila whispered. "I cannot wait until we are married, and I can give my all to you."

"I want everything to be perfect when we marry, and it will be," replied Mark.

Mark wrapped his arms around Leila and pulled her more snugly next to him. She turned her face toward his, and he kissed her, ever so tenderly, on her lips. He lightly flicked the end of his tongue repeatedly against hers, then thrust it deeper into her mouth.

Leila could taste his hot saucy breath. Alone with Mark in this secluded spot, she slowly relaxed in his arms—more than ever.

Mark kissed her deeply and more deeply. Leila could not suppress the release of an ecstatic moan.

"Mark," Leila whispered, "this makes me feel...like we are one. I love you with all of my heart."

"I love you so very, very much." said Mark tenderly.

His romantic words set Leila's heart further ablaze. She felt a sensational warmth and unfamiliar wetness boiling beneath her dress. She was about to explode.

Mark squeezed Leila tightly, stirring her wistful desire.

Her hand was on Mark's thigh, and she subconsciously moved it to his bulge. The touch and shock of it startled Leila!

She pulled her hand away quickly – and after a few seconds, moved it slowly back.

She could feel his awesome stiffness only threads of cloth below.

"We have come so very, very far...and we are so very, very close," Leila thought, as she excused her own unprecedented liberty. She shut her eyes and held on tightly.

*****

"GET THE CAMERAS!" cried one. "OVER THERE!" screamed and pointed another. Mark and Leila's morning was interrupted by the shouts of a group of canoeists.

Six canoes, filled with college-aged passengers in swimsuits, were directly afloat in front of Mark and Leila. The youths were electrified with a school of *gulf sturgeon* that they were encountering. A hundred or more huge fish were in the school, swimming directly toward the canoes! The river was unusually low from a summer drought, and travel in both directions was restricted to mid-stream. Consequently, the sturgeon and the canoes commenced to pass each other almost at arms length! Every canoe, and the river itself, was heaving with violent waves. Some of the very large fish were rolling, and others were literally jumping out of the water.

When the passage was safely completed, the sturgeon

continued to their spawning grounds to the north, and the canoeists disappeared in the distant southern curve of the river.

"My gosh!" exclaimed Mark. "I had no idea!"

"This Choctawhatchee River is one of the best kept secrets in America," replied Leila, still smiling broadly at the adventure she and Mark had just witnessed.

"Ebenezer Forest is part of the Choctawhatchee River flood plain eco-system, and after we get married, you and I are going to help others preserve this whole basin!" Leila said as she lovingly gazed into Mark's eyes.

"I can't think of anything I would rather do than that—and be with you, Leila," said Mark very sincerely.

Leila and Mark talked a while longer about their coming marriage and their plans for the future. The wedding date was not that far off, and there were many details to complete. The excitement of their future together was a blessing in itself. They were grateful for, and cherishing, every single second of it.

*****

Off to the west, a storm was brewing and headed in their direction. They would soon feel the temperature drop markedly, and quickly realize that this day in the sun was almost over.

It had been a glorious day – one of dreams, love, and memories that would last forever.

Chapter 51

It was twelve o'clock noon, and had been raining off and on for over a day. The Bruce Café is a lunchtime favorite of area workers. It usually has more customers than seats, and this fateful Wednesday was no exception. Several hungry patrons waited patiently on the front porch. Jake Delaughter arrived early and his old blue truck was parked on the west side of the wooden building.

A middle-aged Latin woman slowed her red Ford Ranger down to a crawl and spotted Jake's truck. "Alli es eso!" she said in Spanish.

"Si," replied T-Mex, a dark skinned Mexican. "Vamanos," he added.

Eight minutes later, the couple turned east on Ebenezer Church Road and proceeded quickly to the location of a deserted cattle barn. T-Mex exited the Ranger and hurried through the rain to the dilapidated structure. Beneath his slicker-suit jacket was a black satchel carrying his weapon. Extra ammunition, and a few miscellaneous tools needed for an unlawful entry, were also in the satchel.

The senora turned the vehicle around at a nearby abandoned driveway and quickly drove away from the area.

T–Mex found a dry corner of the barn and settled in for the long wait until dark. The cold-blooded killer was only a quarter of a mile from Leila's home.

*****

Just down the road, Leila was enjoying a bowl of warm vegetable soup. Her morning had been spent finalizing the lengthy invitation list for her upcoming wedding ceremony. Mark was constantly in her thoughts, and she knew at that very moment he was attending Charlie's father's funeral in Atlanta. She did not know if Mark would be returning that night or the next morning. Although Leila missed her fiancé, she hoped that he wouldn't risk the long drive back in this bad weather. It was supposed to rain off and on all night. The forecast for Thursday called for blue skies.

Leila's phone rang, and the call was from Amanda. "The weather is supposed to get real ugly later this afternoon, honey. Since Mark is out of town, do you want me to come stay with you tonight?" asked Amanda.

"That is so sweet of you, Amanda, but I am about to start addressing the wedding invitations this afternoon. I will be just fine," Leila replied.

"Leila, if your electricity goes out tonight, please call me immediately. Hank and I will come right over to get you. You know how long it takes for the dad-gum utility company to get your power back on," said Amanda.

*****

At five o'clock that afternoon, Deputy Sheriff Tommy Tucker came on duty in the Red Bay district. He had not gotten a good night's sleep and was tired and apprehensive about his assignment. He knew that he was on his own if trouble developed, and he did not like the idea of being accountable if something went wrong with the plan.

The last blast of the bad weather front was reaching its highpoint as Tucker drove south from Ponce de Leon on Highway 81. A sheriff's radio transmission interrupted his plans and directed him to a location 3 miles south of Red Bay. There had been a head-on collision involving a beer truck and an automobile driven by a teenager. "Dang the luck," thought Tucker as he flipped on his siren and emergency lights. He knew this was going to be nasty and that it would take hours to wrap up. He pushed the accelerator to the floor and raced to the wreck.

*****

It was nearly dark and T-Mex was ready to earn his pay—and get the hell back to civilization. He was not experiencing one bit of tension. He had killed before, and he had killed women before. He had no idea who all he would find at the house and he did not really give a damn. His only concern was that he would not have any difficulty in locating the key to the blue Oldsmobile he was to drive back to Pier Park.

KA—BOOM! T-Mex was startled by the thundering impact of an ear-splitting lightning bolt. It had struck a nearby tree.

T-Mex reached for his satchel and pulled out a flashlight and his thirty eight special revolver. He grabbed all of his extra bullets and crammed them into his pockets. The slicker-suit jacket was retrieved off a nail where he had hung it. He put the garment back on over his head. The few remaining tools still in the satchel were transferred to his jacket pocket. He then reached over and shoved the empty satchel under a pile of rotten boards. He exited the barn into a steady rain.

T-Mex eased along quietly through the woods – always a safe distance from Ebenezer Road. He did not want to be spotted by an unexpected vehicle. When he reached the edge of the woods, he stopped to carefully assess his next move. Leila's house and car could barely be discerned in the distance. Rain was coming down more heavily now. T-Mex estimated that he was still about two hundred yards from his destination.

There was not one light on in the house that T-Mex could see. He surmised correctly that the storm had, at least temporarily, interrupted all electrical power. He waited a while longer. Soon, nightfall reduced Ebenezer Church Road to almost total darkness. He felt safe and was ready to move.

*****

Inside without light, Leila chose to lie down in her bed and enjoy the raindrops. This had always been her favorite way to pass a storm. Occasionally, lightning would brighten her room, and she imagined it was from God's lighthouse above—His beacon to help wayward or needy travelers.

Mark had called to say that he was on his way back to Ebenezer Forest. Leila was very pleased, but worried about the road conditions. Departing Atlanta at about 3 p.m. central time, Mark said he should arrive home in about 30 minutes. It made Leila feel so very much loved that he had chosen to make this

extra effort to come home as soon as possible. She rested peace-
fully, listening to God's musical serenade. Soon, she drifted into
a light sleep with dreams of herself with Mark.

*****

A guinea fowl is a plump domestic bird having dark-gray
feathers with small, white spots. They are native to Africa and
their eggs and meat are quite tasty. The Hewitt family had for
decades maintained these nervous birds—not for food, but
rather for their vigilant watchfulness.

When you put a few female guinea fowl in a bird pen, you
do not have to encage the males. They are so dedicated to the
females that they will remain protectively close. The top of the
cage, or nearby trees, become the males' permanent roosting
perches.

During daylight hours, the guinea flock can plainly see a
visitor. Consequently, they usually remain calm and fearless. But
when darkness comes and the intruder is unknown, the guineas
always expect the very worst. A frightened guinea will yelp out
shrill squeals and make other loud racket. It can be easily heard
from a great distance. Thus, when T-Mex unknowingly eased
into the birds' vicinity, and one bird broke the silence, all hell
broke loose.

Leila was awakened by the disturbance. She could tell from her
bed that some of the male guinea had flown from their roost. They
were now squealing from different trees! She knew from years of experience that when guinea did talk, they NEVER lied. Something
very unusual was going on in Leila's front yard.

*****

The vehicle in the circular driveway told T-Mex that Leila was likely at home. He also knew, that if anyone was in the house, the guinea commotion had probably alerted them.

He hurried across Ebenezer Road and stopped aside the front porch. The rain was starting to slow down, and T-Mex realized that the sound of his entering the dwelling would only be muffled for a few more minutes. Leila had a cell phone, he expected, which added to his urgency. Things were not going the way he had hoped – and he was not happy.

Only an exterior wall separated T-Mex from his target. He chose to wait a while, hoping things would settle down. If Leila was armed, he would give her time to, perhaps, set a weapon down.

*****

Inside her bedroom, Leila was frightened. She picked up her cell phone and dialed Mark's number. He answered on the first ring.

"It is probably nothing, honey, but I am a little afraid. Where are you?" Leila asked.

"I'm coming home, baby. I am well past Bonifay, almost to the Destin turnoff," replied Mark.

"The guinea fowl are spooked, and they haven't settled down. Something is happening outside. I don't have electric power and have locked myself in my bedroom," whispered Leila.

Mark could tell from her voice that she was really worried. "Listen, Leila," Mark began. "Here is what I want you to do, it will make you feel better. Do not leave your room. Will you promise me that?"

"Yes," Leila answered.

"Arrange the pillows under the covers as though you are sleeping in the bed," Mark continued. "Get the 410 gauge shotgun out of the closet and sit in that big brown chair. That will put you behind the door if it opens. You know the gun is loaded, and there are some extra bullets on the closet shelf—you will be very safe until I get home. Don't worry—everything will be just fine."

Leila followed Mark's instructions.

"I checked the gun, it is loaded. Please hurry, Mark," Leila replied. "I have a real bad feeling."

"I am, darling, do you want me to call someone? The sheriff's office? Or Hank Harrison? Or Jake?" Mark asked.

"No, all I really have now is this bad feeling," Leila said.

"Let's just stay on the line until I get home. We can talk very quietly, you mostly just listen," Mark suggested.

"Yes," Leila replied.

About a minute passed.

"Mark," Leila breathed.

"What?" asked Mark.

"Someone is on the porch," Leila barely whispered.

Mark replied in his lowest voice, "Don't make a sound!"

*****

T-Mex walked across the front porch and kicked the front door wide open.

Even Mark could hear the loud and horrifying smash.

T-Mex stomped loudly through the breakage and shined his

flashlight down the hall. He ran toward the back porch and then retraced his steps to the only door in the main hall that was shut. He kicked it with such force that even the hinges were knocked loose. It swung around and crashed against the left corner of a chair that he could not see.

His flashlight caught the form of a body asleep in the bed.

BAM, BAM, BAM, BAM! T-Mex fired four quick, booming shots as he approached Leila's decoy.

T-Mex then reached over, pulled the covers back and saw the pillows. His mouth dropped and he swung the flashlight around the room. At the moment the beam caught the brown chair, T-Mex raised his light into the wild eyes of Leila Hewitt.

BOOM!

The thunderous single blast of Leila's shotgun hit T-Mex squarely in his mid-section. Stray pellets of the bird shot also knocked the gun out of his hand. He was blown backward onto Leila's bed, severely wounded – but not nearly dead.

"LEILA! LEILA!" screamed Mark into his phone.

*****

Leila never heard him.

When the shotgun fired, Leila's cell phone fell from her lap and broke into three pieces. The battery bounced across the wooden floor and came to rest underneath a nearby bookcase. It would not be found until the next day.

Except for the beam of T-Mex's flashlight pointing toward Leila's closet, the room was still pitch black. She was in total shock, but aware enough to quickly and quietly load another shell into her shotgun.

T-Mex was moaning and cursing in Spanish. As dark as the room was, he could see absolutely nothing. He could not sit up and apparently had no idea at all that Leila was still sitting a mere ten feet away.

Leila made the quick decision that it was probably best for her to remain absolutely silent and motionless. She was fearful that an accomplice might be lurking outside—waiting to assist her would-be killer.

She chose to stay right where she was until help arrived.

Chapter 52

Mark's repeated scream of Leila's name went unanswered. The multiple gun shots that he heard threw him into a state of near hysteria. His beloved Leila, the love of his life and the very focus of his existence, needed him—and needed him NOW!

"I HAVE TO GET THERE AS FAST AS HUMANLY POSSIBLE!" Mark thought. Frantic and feeling totally powerless, he pushed the accelerator of his BMW completely to the floor.

His first conscious action was to call 911 and report the shooting. He could barely breathe as he shouted the location of the crisis to the emergency operator. "HURRY, PLEASE HURRY!" he literally yelled into the phone! Time seemed to be crawling on its knees as Mark's mind dashed through all of the possibilities of what might be unfolding at Leila's home.

How many people were there to kill her? Was his love even still alive? Would he ever hold her in his arms again? Would God help his dearest Leila get through this? All questions for which he had no answers.

Mark drifted into a daze of bewilderment and fury as he raced toward Leila. In a moment of lucidity, he called Amanda and Hank to alert them of the crisis.

"Oh, NO!" Amanda cried in horror. "I'm on my way!"

*****

Deputy Tommy Tucker was still working the major accident scene when he received the all-points bulletin of a shooting on Ebenezer Church Road. He knew something had gone terribly wrong with the plan.

Two younger deputies were assisting Tucker at the time of the call and they did not question him when he basically ordered them to stay put and finish what they were doing. He said he would call them for back-up, if they were needed. Tucker knew the bulletin that had been transmitted would quickly summon other officers to the shooting location. He also knew he needed to get to Leila's house fast! Tucker climbed into his police unit and bolted toward the shooting scene, just three miles away.

"There is very little time to clean up any trouble T-Mex might have run into," Deputy Tucker fully realized. He certainly did not want to turn on his siren. But not knowing exactly what he would find at the shooting scene, he reluctantly flipped it on to comply with the office regulation.

All of the tires of the deputy sheriff's automobile were squealing as he whipped it onto Ebenezer Church Road. The road was rain-soaked, but Tucker was traveling as fast as he possibly could. Wheeling into Leila's yard, the deputy quickly turned off the siren and the engine. The house appeared to be in total darkness. There were no cars present except the one he recognized as belonging to Leila. He pulled out his gun as he approached the house, and paused a few seconds at the steps. Hearing nothing, Tucker walked across the porch toward the front door.

*****

Jake Delaughter heard Tucker's police siren long before the vehicle raced past his old store. He could tell by the speed of the vehicle that something big had likely happened.

"Not again," he thought. He walked quickly back to his bedroom to throw on some britches and go offer his help to whoever might need it.

A short time later, Jake heard the loud roar of another vehicle as it whizzed by his house. There was no siren, just haste. He had no idea who was in the vehicle. He knew one thing for sure. The vehicle was travelling extremely, extremely fast!

*****

A dense, heavy fog was atop Ebenezer Church Road. The ul-tra-bright lights of Mark's sports car could cut into the haze and darkness only so much. Visibility was still very poor. His heart was throbbing and aching with concern for his beloved Leila. His high-speed race to his lover was near its end. He was almost there.

"Leila is my love, my life," he thought. "God, please let her be safe! Don't take her from me!" he prayed as he sped on.

Mark remembered the familiar curve in the road—but it was too late. He tore into it in excess of 60 miles an hour.

And then, appearing before him in the middle of the road was the golden doe!

In an instantaneous subconscious reverence and love of God and all of His creations, Mark whipped the steering wheel of his vehicle violently—to avoid the doe! He would never strike any creature of God!

The car started to slide. Mark was jamming his brakes as forcefully as he possibly could. The rain had reduced the white sand and gravel to an unstable muck. He saw the roadside ditch before his car plowed into it, sideways – there was nothing he could do.

The left frame of the vehicle burrowed into the dirt at high speed, causing the BMW to flip through the air. It landed upside down in deep vegetation, in Leila's Ebenezer Forest.

Crushed beneath the smoking wreckage, lay Mark Ryan Mabry—alive—but just barely!

Chapter 53

Leila remained motionless and mute as she listened to the law enforcement unit racing toward her home. When its emergency alarm was turned off, she could hear the vehicle's engine stop and one door slam shut.

Her distrust of Colonel Max Barnett and Deputy Tommy Tucker was forefront in her mind. Even in her shocked and distraught state, Leila was not ready to move from her chair just yet.

Leila's fright was heightened by sudden, eerie silence from outside. A sole guinea let out a brief, screechy cry. There was no other sound.

Inside, Leila's bedroom remained very black and ominous. She was able to detect T-Mex's occasional movement, but his gruesome moaning had gradually lessened. Leila suspected that he was near death.

"Whoever the law enforcement officer is outside, he is not rushing to my aid," Leila correctly suspicioned.

After a full minute's lapse, the utter stillness was broken by the creak of footsteps across her wooden porch. Leila could hear the front door squeak as it was pushed.

Then, a shocking yell came from T-Mex! "TOMMY—ES

USTED?" he asked in a scream. "ESTOY AQUI!" he added.

Leila was astounded by his outcry!

Her surprise was quickly interrupted by Deputy Tommy Tucker's clanking vibrations as he hurriedly walked to the door of her bedroom. He stopped at the entrance—with just a quarter inch of broken door between him and Leila.

Suddenly, Tucker turned on his flashlight and shined it across the room upon T-Mex, who was still lying paralyzed and face-up in Leila's bed.

"DE BEETCH SHOOT ME, TOMMY, GEEET ME OUDA HERE!" pleaded T-Mex loudly as he looked straight up at the ceiling.

Leila remained motionless and breathless, in shadowy darkness, behind the door.

"Where'd she go?" asked Tommy wildly as he approached the bed. He pointed his flashlight to the right, but was distracted by the reflection of T-Mex's pistol on the floor. T-Mex's quick reply led to further carelessness.

"SHE GONE! GGEEET ME OUDA HERE PLEEEEEZE, TOMMY!" cried T-Mex.

Tommy bent over and picked up T-Mex's pistol. He wiped off the handle and placed it in the bed aside T-Mex.

T-Mex could not lift his neck at all. He never saw Deputy Tommy Tucker raise his weapon.

BAM! Deputy Tucker shot T-Mex in the heart.

The deafening fire and thunder of the large caliber pistol's explosion rocked the house!

Leila's bedroom vibrated with the aftershock. She became stunned, nearly hypnotized, by the ear-piercing blast.

Tucker kept his light fixed upon the Mexican's body until death snatched his last quiver. Tucker turned to exit the room.

He took one step toward the door, but an unexpected object caught his eye.

Well hidden in the dark shadow of the door, Tucker saw what his negligence had missed.

He stopped and raised his flashlight in one hand and his pistol in the other. But the good Lord was not ready, just yet, to take Leila Jane Hewitt.

BOOM!

Leila fired her shotgun for the second time in twenty minutes. The house shook from her volley.

Deputy Tommy Tucker was knocked back into the bed-aside T-Mex.

This time there would be no moans or groans, Deputy Tommy Tucker was stone dead.

Chapter 54

Jake DeLaughter, in his old truck, was the first person to travel Ebenezer Church Road behind Mark Mabry. A flicker in the forest caught Jake's attention as he approached the fateful first curve. Jake stopped and angled his truck, allowing him to cast his bright front lights into the forest. The tail-lights of the BMW convertible were barely visible at its resting place, some thirty five steps beyond the roadside ditch.

Jake could see that the BMW was upside down! Smoke was rising out of the motor area.

At that moment, another vehicle came roaring up to the curve and stopped. Amanda and Hank Harrison were prevented from continuing as Jake's truck now blocked the entire roadway. The Harrisons did not have a good view into the woods. Both were out of their cars in a flash and raced up to Jake's truck.

"Who is in there, Jake?!" screamed Amanda.

"It is Mark's convertible, he just sped by my house," replied Jake.

"THERE HAS BEEN GUNFIRE AT LEILA'S HOUSE!" Amanda screamed even louder than before.

"A sheriff's unit is already back there," replied Jake quickly.

"Jake, pull up and let us pass. Leila is in trouble, then you check on Mark," said the usually quiet Hank Harrison. "Please! hurry!" he added.

Jake obliged the request, and Amanda and Hank continued on in high speed.

When the Harrisons disappeared from his view, Jake fetched an old light out of his rear tool chest and started working his way through the underbrush toward Mark. The engine was still running as he neared the sports car.

After circling around to the driver's side, Jake lowered himself to the ground. When he shined his light on the front seat, he first saw the occupant's badly crumpled body. As he moved the light to his left, it beamed directly upon the inverted and bloody face of Mark Mabry.

Mark's eyes were open.

"Can you hear me, Mark?" asked Jake.

Mark did not answer.

"Can you hear me, Mark?" Jake asked again.

Jake saw Mark trying to move his lips. He thought he heard a mumble.

"What, Mark?" Jake asked.

This time it was clear. There was only one word that came from Mark's lips....."Leila."

*****

Alone in her dark bedroom with two dead men, Leila was finally ready to vacate her house. She bolted toward the front porch – still clutching the shotgun. The steps came too fast. She lost her balance and tumbled head-first down the stairs. Her face struck the concrete birdbath, nearly knocking her unconscious. The shotgun broke into two pieces.

She scrambled to her feet, dazed and confused. She started running, half toppling, up Ebenezer Church Road toward the highway. She was oblivious to the blood streaming down her forehead. She was running for safety. She was running for her life. And she was running – in her mind – to Mark Mabry.

*****

Leila saw a vehicle rapidly approaching her. She did not know who was in the vehicle and stopped quickly in her tracks. Her eyes were wild and appeared huge on her face.

Amanda and Hank saw Leila racing toward them and then stop in the middle of Ebenezer Church Road. Hank had to apply the brakes firmly to keep from running her over. The auto came to a skidding halt just short of their terrified friend.

The bright lights of the Harrison's auto had blocked Leila's vision. But Amanda and Hank could plainly see Leila's bloodied head.

Amanda dove from the car and ran toward Leila, screaming her name!

Leila collapsed into Amanda's arms and began to uncontrollably sob.

"It's OK, baby, you are safe now," Amanda said.

"I must call Mark!" said Leila, still crying.

"What happened, honey?" asked Amanda.

"They were going to kill me!" Leila gasped.

"Who, baby? Who are they and where are they?" demanded Amanda in an urgent tone.

"They are gone," answered Leila, now softly.

"Gone where?" demanded Amanda.

"Not to heaven," Leila answered, then whispered. "I shot them—and they are both dead........"

Chapter 55

Within a few minutes, Ebenezer Church Road was swarming with local and state police. Utility lights had been restored, and Leila was in the Harrison's car in front of her own house. She had calmed down a good bit, but was still too shaken to press for information about Mark.

A tall state trooper pulled up and exited his unit. He was directed to Leila.

"Miss Hewitt, a wrecker is on its way to lift a vehicle off an injured male who is a friend of yours. According to Mr. De-Laughter, he is your fiancé. He is injured between here and the highway," said the trooper.

"OH NO!" screamed Leila. "OH NO! NOT MARK!" she gasped as she began to sob again.

"TAKE ME TO HIM!" she screamed.

The state trooper continued, "He has lost a lot of blood and the medical unit is on the scene. They are afraid that when his car is lifted off of him, he may bleed out."

"HE IS ALIVE! TAKE ME TO HIM NOW!" Leila demanded, struggling for breath.

"His eyes are open and he is semi-conscious for the time being," continued the trooper. "You must not upset him, he has lost a lot of blood already. His body is a little cold as he is in shock."

The trooper led Leila to his unit where she, Amanda, and Hank climbed into the back seat. They were at the scene of the accident within two minutes. Two other state troopers were standing near Jake's truck

"The woods are really wet from the rain. I am going to get you back there right now, the wrecker is almost here," the trooper said. He lifted Leila up in his arms and carried her through the underbrush to the BMW.

Three medics and Jake were standing in temporary lights that had been set up at the scene. An emergency crew worker had scaled a large nearby oak and attached a pulley to lift the light sports car off of Mark.

One of the medics had strewn a blanket on the ground next to the driver's window. He said to Leila, "Kneel down here very low and you will be able to see him—use this flashlight."

Leila knelt down, her forehead still partially splattered with blood. She shined the light into Mark's anguished face. Leila was shocked—not expecting Mark to be upside down. She fought off a breathtaking gasp.

Mark's eyes were wide open. They blinked when the light hit them.

"Jake, please shine your light on my face so Mark can see me," Leila requested without turning around. Jake dropped to his knees immediately and honored her request.

"Honey, do you know how much I love you?" Leila asked in a low tone. She thought she saw a weak smile try to form in the corners of Mark's mouth.

"Do you know how much I will always love you?" Leila wanted to know.

She saw him blink his eyes one time slowly. She thought it was an affirmation.

"God will see us through this, darling, I know He will," Leila said ever so assuring.

With the flashlight clearly upon him, Mark's top eyelids drifted slowly backwards. His upper lip fell in the same direction—back toward God's wet earth. His head dropped about an inch and his eyes glassed over.

Leila watched as her lover faded into eternal darkness.

And then she screamed, "HE IS DEAD!"

She tried to crawl into the car to kiss him one more time—to even touch him—just one more time.

She was sobbing and wailing.

The medics grabbed her by her ankles and pulled her from the wreckage.

That night, a large part of Leila Jane Hewitt died in Ebenezer Forest.

Chapter 56

Daylight eventually arrived, and yellow crime tape draped Leila's home. Four law enforcement vehicles were parked in her front yard. Officers could be seen milling about inside the house, while others were talking on the front porch.

Across Ebenezer Road, six news agency mobile units were in a roped off area adjacent to the guinea pen. Satellite dishes were rotating, and fixed cameras were set up to point at the activity on Leila's porch.

Off to one side, the attractive Rhonda Riveras began to record her morning report for National News Network.

"Good Morning, America! I am standing here in Ebenezer Forest in the Florida Panhandle. If you are driving to the Emerald Coast, Ebenezer Forest is almost to Destin, just 30 miles from the beach. Last night, at around 8 p.m., the beautiful architect of this natural wonderland and regional tourist attraction, 56 year old Leila Hewitt, was an intended murder victim of a yet unidentified male. The courageous and lovely Miss Hewitt was able to protect herself and slay her intended killer in her own bedroom.

Later last night, a Walton County Deputy Sheriff responding to the scene in uniform was also slain by Miss Hewitt! Details of this perhaps accidental shooting of the deputy are sketchy at this point. The BIG QUESTION remains, is this incident related to the three previous murders in this area which have followed the indictment of the local sheriff and three others?

I have received unconfirmed information that there IS a connection. There will be further details of this possible connection in future reports.

Also, in an unbelievably tragic and related story, the 32 year old handsome fiancé of Miss Hewitt died last night in an automobile accident reportedly racing to the aid of Leila Hewitt on THIS VERY SAME EBENEZER CHURCH ROAD! After killing two men, Miss Hewitt was apparently able to make it to the scene of a wreck where her young love, Mark Mabry, from Atlanta, reportedly died in her arms. Tonight, I will have a full report on this mysterious and fascinating woman, LEILA JANE HEWITT, and the tragedy that has unfolded right here in her Ebenezer Forest.

I want to direct your attention now – camera crew pick this up – here you can see two emergency vehicles that are arriving, just now, to remove the bodies of the two men slain by Leila Hewitt: one an unidentified male and the other a deputy sheriff. I am going to stay right here until the evening news. My name is Rhonda Riveras!"

*****

Five miles away, Leila was resting in the home of Amanda and Hank Harrison. A sheriff's unit was among the many cars parked in the front yard, as was a vehicle marked "United States Marshall". Inside, Jane Anderson and Reverend McGraw were the only visitors.

FBI agent Bob Kirk called Jane before midnight with the alarming news. She had driven all night from Atlanta. Kirk called her again at 7 a.m. to inform Jane that he and two other agents would be at the Harrison's residence at noon to take a statement from Leila.

Two television sets were turned on in the living room. The shootings, and Mark's fatal wreck, were the lead story throughout America. At 10 a.m., NNN reported that the Walton County Sheriff's Office had been recused from the investigation by the Attorney General's Office of Florida. Shortly, a Florida State Police car replaced the Sheriff's unit in the front yard. A state trooper soon called and informed Hank Harrison that the state police would also be present at the noon FBI meeting with Leila.

*****

At 11:30 a.m., Leila was awakened by Amanda, who helped her shower and ready herself for the lawmen. Leila was weary and understandably very quiet. When Amanda informed her that Reverend

McGraw was in the living room, Leila asked to speak to him.

Brother McGraw entered the room and walked over to Leila. He wrapped his arms around her and gave her a big hug. He had long been her closest connection to the Lord. She buried her face into his chest and began to weep afresh.

After a minute, he whispered, "Leila, you are not alone. The church, as always, is here for you."

Leila leaned backwards and looked up into her minister's face. Tears were running down her cheeks.

"Why? Oh, why?" she barely uttered.

"Everything comes from Him – both calamity and blessing," replied her pastor. "God always has His reasons. He will exalt you in good time."

The words seemed to soothe Leila. She thanked Reverend McGraw for coming, and Amanda asked him to stay a while.

*****

When the authorities arrived at noon, Leila asked if it was permissible for Jane to stay during the acquisition of her statement. The Florida State Troopers had no objection. Amanda and Hank were asked to leave the interview room in the event that details of the report were subpoenaed in the future.

The meeting lasted over an hour. Halfway through the meeting, one of the FBI agents made a hurried exit from the Harrison home. Within three hours, Colonel Max Barnett was shown on live television being led out of the Walton County Sheriff's office in handcuffs. It was reported that a Pensacola Federal Judge had rescinded his post-indictment bail privileges. He was remanded to jail, pending trial.

*****

At 5 o'clock central time, Rhonda Riveras, on a live feed from Ebenezer Church Road, gave the following report:

"Good evening, America. More shocking details have emerged and clarified this spectacular story from Ebenezer Church Road, down here in the Florida Panhandle! MISS LEILA JANE HEWITT, a 56 year old beauty and curator of her own paradise on earth, the historic Ebenezer Forest, was the target for MURDER last night. Not ONE – BUT TWO MEN tried to kill MISS HEWITT in her bedroom at separate times last night! BUT MISS LEILA WAS ABLE TO FEND THEM OFF with her shotgun AND BOTH ENDED UP DEAD, SIDE BY SIDE, IN LEILA HEWITT'S BED! Since our report this morning, the identity of the first man killed has been released by authorities and his name is Jorge Manuel Espinosa—also known as T-Mex. He is a Mexican green card holder.

Apparently LEILA HEWITT SHOT ESPINOSA in self-defense. The report now is that DEPUTY TOMMY TUCKER of the Walton County Sheriff's Office showed up at the Hewitt house across the street from where I am now standing and first killed Espinosa. He attempted to KILL LEILA HEWITT, but LEILA HEWITT FIRED FIRST and her shotgun blast, as I stated, left both men DEAD in Miss Hewitt's OWN BED.

Twenty minutes after killing Deputy Tucker,

Leila Hewitt arrived at the scene of an accident.
This man, you are now looking at a photo of 32
year old Mark Ryan Mabry from Atlanta, is Leila
Hewitt's fiancé. Miss Leila, as she is called in these
parts, had to be literally pulled by her feet out of
the wreckage of Mabry's overturned vehicle after
Mabry tragically died in the arms of Leila Hewitt!
What a horrific and sad night for this courageous
lady!

WHY would Deputy Tucker want to kill the
darling Miss Leila Hewitt? It appears there is
some connection of this bizarre series of events
here on Ebenezer Church Road to the indictment
of Sheriff Wayne Clark, Colonel Max Barnett,
and brothers Roy and Ray Ashton in various
racketeering charges recently filed here in the
Florida panhandle. This connection is still
unclear. Both Roy and Ray Ashton have been
recently murdered as well as another well-known
Destin resident Daisy Dodd. Colonel Max
Barnett of the Walton County Sherriff's office was
remanded to Federal custody less than one hour
ago. I will keep you updated as further details
emerge. From Ebenezer Forest, I am Rhonda
Riveras!"

*****

Before dark, television crews and dozens of journalists had
assembled in front of the Harrison property. There was a brief

scene where Amanda loudly told a man, who knocked on her door identifying himself as being associated with the London Times, "Get your skinny ass off my property!" and then slammed her door.

Leila was oblivious to the news reports and ongoing events—as well as to her emerging fame. She was inside the Harrison's home. Resting in a rear bedroom, she was dreaming of herself in the clear water pool aside Ebenezer Church – with Mark looking at her from a distance. It gave her an intense warmness inside. He approached her and took her into his arms. She could taste the scent of his sweet breath and his hot, fleshy lips and tongue.

Leila's dream progressed to a clear vision of Mark looking up at her while proposing on one knee. She mumbled "yes" in her sleep.

Leila could feel the sensuous stirring of her passion for Mark's love and for all of him. She imagined herself within the welcome throes of his ravishing and magnificent power. She floated into a deeper and deeper, titillating fantasy of love. While Leila slept, she temporarily forgot that Mark was dead.

Chapter 57

Those closest to a deceased loved one often do not have much opportunity to grieve before funeral services. It is usually never enough time.

Dealing with the catastrophic death of Mark was only part of Leila's recent and dreadful experiences, but it dwarfed all else that she had ever faced in her life. Mark had seized her heart. In a just a few short months, he had transcended all of her barriers. He had penetrated her innermost sanctum—her essence, her very existence. She had surrendered her soul and mind to him, without fear, with God's full blessing. And now, Mark was suddenly gone from this earth, forever....

*****

Things were happening so fast! Leila was expecting to live a quiet, peaceful life with Mark in Ebenezer Forest. But now, in the focus of global attention, Leila could not yet even return to her beloved home. The assembled news force camped on Leila's private property tripled in size. Spin off stories on the lives of Leila and Mark were being aired continuously around the world. The name "T-Mex" had surfaced, and his violet past had been revealed. Deputy Tommy Tucker was reported to be associated with the execution of the Ashton brothers. Leila's role in the death of these two killers had catapulted her to universal stardom. One network even referred to her as the "Grand Heroine of Ebenezer Forest".

The two killers who died before Leila on that fateful night were never really on her mind again. What happened in her bedroom had been tucked deeply away, where she had put every other unpleasant memory of her life. She tried to suppress her vivid recollection of where she last saw Mark, but it was difficult. Leila's last few words to Mark were so very important to her. She tried to separate them from her memory of his pained and anguished face. She prayed that Mark had heard her, and that he knew that her love for him was eternal.

******

Jane volunteered to handle all of the arrangements for Mark's funeral. Leila appreciated and accepted her offer. He would be buried Sunday afternoon in the small cemetery aside Ebenezer Church. It was rather short notice, but Mark had no family that would be inconvenienced. The service would be conducted by Reverend McGraw.

Amanda commissioned Jake DeLaughter to stand watch over Leila's home. He was actually staying there overnight until things settled down. It would be a while.

When the national press got wind that Mark's funeral service would be held at Ebenezer Church, the crowd grew even larger. There was a huge assemblage of media near Leila's guinea pen. It was just a hundred yards from there to the gate that opened up the grassy lane for access to the church. The burial ceremony of Mark Ryan Mabry was awaited by all.

The curiosity surrounding Leila Jane Hewitt was now epic. What was she really like? Was she tough as rope or just a gentle victim? Was she as clean and pure as reported—or simply just another North American cougar?

Recent pictures of Leila were non-existent! The world had been told she was a woman of rare beauty—but there were no pictures—yet.

Where was the mysterious and lovely Leila Jane Hewitt? There was only one thing everyone knew for sure—Leila would be at the funeral of Mark Ryan Mabry.

Chapter 58

A beautiful, palomino mare stood with raised head in the middle of Ebenezer Church Road. She had a slender and strong build. A collar harness was fitted snugly around her neck. Golden reins ran through the rings of her saddle, back to a polished black buggy. A gray-haired African American driver in a black tuxedo held the horse steady, as all in attendance waited. It was the same buggy team that Leila hoped would carry her and Mark back to this very spot after their marriage.

Most guests had already made their walk back to Ebenezer Church. Jane Anderson limited the news networks to only one pass each to Mark's funeral. Pictures were prohibited, except those taken of the attendants upon their arrival and exit from the church lane. There was one exception—a photo station was permitted next to the bridge over Hominy Creek, halfway back to the church.

Leila removed herself from most of the funeral details, except for a few that were sacrosanct to her wishes. Jane graciously provided the main support.

The press coverage had swelled to over 200 various reporters, cameramen, and attachés all gathered along Ebenezer Church Road. Dispersed among this crowd were over a dozen troopers and plain-clothed detectives, all wandering about as security. An officer in a United States Marshall uniform was walking amongst the crowd with a leashed German shepherd that appeared to be trained in crowd control.

Cameras had been rolling for some time as an extra-long black limousine slowly came into view. People standing in the roadway moved to one side or the other to let the vehicle pass. All eyes were on the limo. Only the sound of the cameras could be heard.

Amanda and Hank Harrison exited the vehicle first. The driver was next. He quickly hurried around to open the door for Leila Jane Hewitt.

Leila slowly and gracefully stepped outside of the limousine. She stood tall and erect.

The driver handed her a bouquet of red roses.

She then turned and gazed back down Ebenezer Church Road, her life's road, on which she had just traveled.

The snug black dress that she had chosen accentuated her attractive figure. Her thick blondish hair glistened in the afternoon sunlight. Atop her head was a formal black hat, with a short black veil. Yet her strong and beautiful face was not hidden. She held her head unassumingly high.

Leila's complexion had a radiant glow, smooth and flawless. Every single camera was upon her. Her sparkling, light-blue eyes could be seen around the world. People in living rooms, airports, county clubs, and jails – wherever they might get close to a television – watched a truly angelic, yet pensive face.

A black funeral hearse gradually came into view from the west. Cameras were alternating their focus between it and Leila, and the intensification of her emotion was obvious. Tears began to flow down each of her cheeks.

The hearse stopped in front of Leila, and two attendants quickly opened its rear door. Two other men joined them to help carry Mark's casket to the horse buggy. When it passed within arm's length of Leila, she reached out and touched it with her fingers.

Jane appeared from the crowd and led Leila to the open gate leading to Ebenezer Church. Amanda and Hank had been instructed to lead the walk back to the church. Jane took Leila by her arm, and they slowly followed the Harrisons.

The driver shook the palomino's reins, and the clippity-clop of the horse's hooves broke the silence of Ebenezer Forest.

Step by step, the procession slowly made its way down the shadowed lane. Leila had walked this pathway thousands of times before. Every inch of the trail was familiar to her. She knew the type, and even the life history, of every tree and bush. At spots where Mark had kissed her, she paused to reminisce. Ever so slowly, she continued on.

What was to follow at the church and gravesite was Leila's worst nightmare! She did not want to part with her beloved Mark—ever! She certainly did not want to place and leave him beneath the ground!

As the procession arrived at the bridge, Leila tried not to look at the cameras.

"This way, Leila!" one rude photographer summoned. Leila continued her gaze straight ahead.

Suddenly, there was a disturbance behind Leila. The combination of the bridge, running water and loud camera noises had spooked the palomino. The mare did not want to cross the bridge. The driver shook the reins, but the palomino would not budge. He hit the rump of the palomino with a switch stick. The mare refused to go forward!

The powerful palomino reared up on her back legs and let out a loud neigh! Cameras were rolling as the mare attempted to back up – she appeared to be ready to bolt!

Leila saw the dangerous development. She turned and walked straight back toward the agitated horse!

Leila reached up and began stroking the palomino's face. She leaned her own face against that of the mare and whispered to her softly. The enlarged nostrils of the horse slowly relaxed. After a short while, Leila took the reins in her hand and walked the now calm mare over the bridge.

*****

The church's steeple appeared in the distance, then the familiar row of ligustrums. Finally, Ebenezer Church, with all of its splendor, appeared in full view.

Thirty or more guests standing in front of the church had not yet joined the many others inside. They ended their conversations to turn and watch as the procession approached.

Fifty yards from her beloved church, Leila stopped. It was the exact spot where Mark stood just a few months before, watching her bathe naked in the spring. She had to force herself to take the next step, but she finally took it.

*****

The double wooden doors were opened as the horse and buggy arrived at the church. Mark's closed casket was carried down the center aisle and placed in front of Reverend McGraw. He was waiting patiently at the pulpit.

Leila, Jane, and the Harrisons followed closely behind Mark's boxed body. The four were seated in a side section, usually reserved for families. Every eye in the church was on Leila.

*****

"Friends, we are gathered here today in front of God and present company, to..." began Brother McGraw.

Leila knew the introduction well, too very well. She knew it was the same language used to commence a wedding.

"This could be, it should be, Mark's and my wedding," Leila thought as she began to rapidly lose control of her emotions.

Leila could not contain her grief any longer. At first, she simply started to cry. But then, she was swept into drowning decomposition, like a run-away boat, being smashed and lost in a tremendous, savage waterfall.

"MY MOTHER, MY FATHER, NOW, MY MARK," Leila muttered to herself, as her mind panicked! She commenced to weep aloud. Brother McGraw stopped. The whole church was dead silent as Leila continued to wail and bawl – now much more loudly.

Amanda quickly joined Jane's attempt to console Leila. But the tragedy of the whole week—the shootings, the calamitous and catastrophic loss of her MARK AND HER DREAMS—had Leila by her THROAT—and she totally broke down.

Leila began to scream and scream and scream!

The church froze in utter shock! LEILA'S SCREAMS WERE REVERBERATING OFF THE WALLS!

Mark's friends and former co-workers, Leila's friends, the Red Bay church crowd, Jackie and friends from Destin, men and women alike – every single one of them were ALL crying.

Journalists and reporters were equally dazed by Leila's spontaneous explosion into deep grief.

*****

It took a good while for Leila to calm down—particularly with Jane and Amanda also unabashedly weeping.

Reverend McGraw was clearly, personally affected by the stark, raw agony of the moment. Leila was the very strongest of his parishioners. Her total breakdown shook her lifelong pastor from collar to core! He was able to finally continue, but only with an emotionally improvised, impassioned service.

"Lord, I humbly pray that You let Your servant, Mark Mabry, go in peace. Mark came to this church a few short months ago through a gate. All of us here today came through the same entry. The Book of Matthew tells every one of us about God's gate.

He wants us to always come to Him and eternal life through a narrow gate. It physically may be of any size—but in your mind, I want you to see it as our Lord does—as a narrow gate. The gate that leads to destruction is wide and the way is easy, and those who go through a wide gate are many. But fellow Christians, let US keep OUR gate narrow and pure.

Mark's casket was brought to this holy place, this afternoon, in a buggy drawn by a brilliantly colored palomino horse. The Holy Bible tells us that the rider's name of a pale horse is always death!

Pale is synonymous with weakness and feebleness. Any

Christian that feels weak or feeble here today needs to remember that He died for us! One has died for all; therefore, all have died! Mark has died, but he and all Christians will rise again one day, together! We will all be seated together with Him, our Lord, in the heavenly place! On top of the mountain!

While we are still here on earth, I Corinthians 15:26 says that the last enemy that shall be destroyed is death!

ARE YOU LISTENING?

DO YOU HEAR ME?

THE LAST ENEMY THAT SHALL BE DESTROYED IS DEATH!"

Reverend McGraw lowered his voice slightly.

"Again, EVERYBODY HERE, are you listening? Do you hear me? Every ONE of you in EBENEZER CHURCH TODAY?" he asked.

Then, he bellowed in his highest voice, "THE VERY LAST ENEMY TO BE DESTROYED IS DEATH!"

After a few moments of silence, Reverend McGraw leaned forward and lowered his voice again. "I have repeated myself several times, for emphasis," he added.

Then he raised his right arm and -BAM—hit the pulpit! "AMEN!"

*****

After a rather long pause, Reverend McGraw continued, "Sister Leila has asked that Sally Whalen, our talented vocalist from Red Bay Church, sing this special tribute."

An older, well-dressed lady in her early seventies quietly made her way to the front of Ebenezer Church.

Sally cleared her throat and began to sing "The Old Rugged Cross", softly.

"On a hill far away stood an old rugged cross,
The emblem of suffering and shame;
And I love that old cross where the dearest and best,
For a world of lost sinners was slain.
So I'll cherish the old rugged cross,
Till my trophies at last I lay down,
I will cling to the old rugged cross,
And exchange it someday for a crown."

Leila drifted again into soft crying as the next three verses of the hymn were completed. This special song had not been sung in Leila's church since her parents' funerals.

As the singer returned to her seat, Reverend McGraw motioned for two rear side doors of the church to be opened. Leila proceeded outside to the small cemetery at the forest's edge.

The Reverend then invited all of the guests to join Leila. They quietly filed outside.

There was only room for about half of the onlookers inside the little cemetery itself. The others gathered as closely as they could—just beyond the short, white fence.

One empty burial space remained vacant next to Leila's parents—and she wanted Mark to have it. She would worry about her own resting place at a later time.

Reverend McGraw was the last to arrive at the gravesite. He approached slowly—with Bible in hand. He opened the Book and was preparing to read a few final verses.

Reverend McGraw was rudely interrupted by the deafening roar of an unmarked helicopter! It had arrived unexpectedly from the direction of Ebenezer Church Road.

A cameraman could be seen leaning out of the passenger side of the craft as he filmed the scene below. The chopper's blades were violently whipping the tops of the oak trees above the gravesite. Reverend McGraw's last, comforting words were muffled and barely audible as he spoke. The helicopter was not in any hurry to leave, and the Reverend was forced to continue.

As soon as the first helicopter pulled away from above Mark's final service, a second one took its place. This one had the letters NNN emblazoned on its side. On the ground below, Jane Anderson caught the eye of a sheepish Rhonda Riveras. It was obvious that someone amongst the guests had alerted the pilots that Mark's last rites had moved outdoors.

*****

When Reverend McGraw finished his last prayer, Leila retrieved her dozen roses from Jane and placed them on Mark's casket. She was not yet ready to leave Mark's side. Not one single mourner had walked away either.

Mark was about to be lowered into the soil.

At the very last emotional second, Leila suddenly lunged forward and spread her entire self over Mark's casket. She draped her arms lovingly around it as though it was Mark's own body.

She did not move a muscle—for over two minutes—as she lay upon his chest, albeit wooden, for the very last time. Amanda and Hank finally pulled her away.

Leila's final embrace was witnessed and recorded from above—her deep love for Mark forever memorialized in the hearts and minds of all who watched.

Chapter **59**

"When the heart weeps for what it has lost,
the soul laughs for what it has found."
Sufi aphorism-

*****

Leila's dear friends walked with her—ever so slowly—back down the familiar lane to her home. Her heart-wrenching farewell to Mark had exhausted most of her usually abundant strength and vitality.

But the virgin Ebenezer Forest was still alive with life—new and old. Leila could smell the fall acorns, ripe muscadines, and the lemon-like aroma of the magnolias. They all invigorated her. She deeply inhaled the heavy, rich woodland oxygen. It helped to cleanse her thoughts.

At Ebenezer Church Road, Leila marched right past the throngs of reporters—as though they were not there.

She continued straight to her front porch and opened the newly repaired front door. When Amanda and Hank followed her inside, Leila slammed it shut behind them.

Leila needed sleep—deep, long sleep—and it soon came.

*****

Back in Ebenezer Forest, Charlie McBride was watching Mark's casket be covered with soil. His head was turned downward as he grieved the loss of his dear friend. After the workers raked and smoothed the ground, Charlie stayed to arrange the flowers left by Leila and many others. He decided to wait there for Jane, who was locking up Ebenezer Church.

Jane finally walked over to join Charlie next to Mark's plot. All of the guests and workers had gone. They were the only two people left at Ebenezer Church.

Charlie spoke first, very slowly, "Before I left Atlanta yesterday, I received a call from Mary Kate Nelson. You surely remember her. She was calling from New York City. She had seen Mark's picture on the news there."

"That was nice of her to call," replied Jane—her eyes still red from her earlier tears.

"Mary Kate had something shocking to say," Charlie continued.

Jane's eyes widened as she awaited the revelation.

"She is pregnant—and get this—she thinks that Mark is the father!" said Charlie!

"WHAT!!!" Jane gasped aloud, as she raised her hand over her mouth—and nearly collapsed to the ground! She started to cry again.

"Leila would want to know this," Jane finally spoke in a bare whisper.

Charlie put his hand on Jane's shoulder. After a few moments, he said "Mary Kate has a while to go in this pregnancy–anything could happen. There is always the possibility... it may not even be Mark's child."

Jane's face was grimaced from the disturbing news. She slowly wiped fresh tears from her cheeks.

She turned her eyes down to the fresh dirt beside her, where Mark was forever lying.

Finally, Jane looked back at Charlie. Her lips were quivering and her face was flushed—as though she had seen a ghost.

After a few moments, she whispered softly in a trembling voice, "Maybe we should just leave this information here at Mark's grave."

"For now," Charlie replied, "I think that is best."

51822996R00192

Made in the USA
Columbia, SC
26 February 2019